D1112890

Moncrieff

Other Gothic suspense by the same author

KILGAREN
TRELAWNY

MONCRIEFF

A Novel By

Isabelle Holland

Weybright and Talley

NEW YORK

Weybright and Talley
750 Third Avenue
New York, New York 10017

Library of Congress Cataloging in Publication Data

Holland, Isabelle.
  Moncrieff.

  I.   Title.
PZ4.H735Mo [PS3558.03485]   813'.5'4   75-19262
ISBN 0-679-40129-6

Manufactured in the United States of America

Holland

For Jane Wilson
With affection and thanks.

Moncrieff

Chapter 1

At first it seemed merely strange, if somewhat calamitous, the way the lives of the three of us—Adam, Dauntry and I—were drawn together. We were such an unlikely trio: Dauntry from his prep school and Ivy League college; Adam, the barefoot boy from a Nova Scotia orphanage, Pulitzer Prize-winning writer, ex-convict; and me, surely the mousiest freshman ever to put timid foot into that small, undistinguished college sitting under the Rocky Mountains.

In a sense, that was where our story began. And yet, of course, in a more real sense, it began long before that in the tall, narrow house overlooking New York harbor and the spires of Manhattan, when an angry, rebellious girl slammed out of the house swearing never to return, and an angry, outraged woman allowed her to go. . . .

But that was a long time ago, before any of the three of us was born. And, as in many tales, it is easier to begin almost at the end, just before the terror started. But that early spring day when I picked up the phone in my New York office, I had no idea that the drama involving the three of us was about to begin its final act. And as I had thrust them out of my life, so I had kept them from my mind, except, of course, in dreams. And that day when the telephone rang, I was far too preoccupied trying to rush a manuscript into production. All I felt was irritation at the interruption.

I snatched up the receiver. "Antonia Moncrieff," I said, rather impatiently.

"Mrs. Moncrieff? This is Laurence Metcalf of Metcalf, Randall and Wells. I would like very much to see you and wonder if you could come along here to our office at your earliest convenience. We're at Forty Wall Street."

Somewhere in the back of my mind a bell sounded, but it was so faint I couldn't decide what had set it off. Was it one of those three names?

"What is it about?" I asked, my eyes still running down the page in front of me, checking my own editing and the copy-editor's symbols.

It was a reasonable question, yet the man's voice at the other end of the telephone hesitated. "It's about an inheritance, Mrs. Moncrieff."

That got my attention. I suppose everyone has fantasied such a moment—certainly anyone as pressed for money as I had been throughout my life: *If Miss X will get in touch with us, she will learn something to her advantage.*

"For me?" I asked, my heart beginning to lift in the way usually reserved for falling in love or spying the man in one's life across a crowded room. But with Ewen's school bills and our recent rent increase the mere hint of more money set off in me the lyric symptoms associated with poetry and passion.

"Yes," the cautious voice said.

"How absolutely super—" I started, and then reality intruded and brought me down with a thump. Not only did I not know anyone who could or would leave me money, I had forgotten Great-aunt Sarah Maclaughlin's chest of drawers. Not a year passed before she died but that she'd write telling me she'd left it to me in her will. "Oh," I said. "I suppose it's that chest of drawers."

"What chest of drawers?"

"The one my Great-aunt Sarah threatened to leave me."

"No." If a voice could be said to smile, this one did. "It's not a chest of drawers."

"Then what is it?" Despite all my native Scots pessimism I couldn't help asking with a total lack of delicacy, "Is it money? How much?"

At that the voice abandoned caution and laughed. "Mrs. Moncrieff, I'm afraid I'll really have to wait until you come here. It's too long and complicated and . . . er . . . private to discuss over the telephone. When can we meet?"

That sounded, I thought with a little bitterness, as though money were too good to be true. It usually was. "If it's not money," I said rather sadly, "what is it?" And added by way of explanation for my materialistic approach, "I'm afraid you've called at a time when I'm terribly busy." And I was, with three books to edit and start on their journeys through production for the late Fall list.

Another slight pause. "I'm really sorry to have to be so cagey," the voice said apologetically. "But it *is* complicated and takes some explaining. Perhaps it would be easier if I could come to see you some evening."

I sighed.

Mr. Metcalf laughed and then said almost teasingly, "I'm astonished that you don't show more . . . er . . . anticipation at the thought of inheriting something out of the blue—a windfall, so to speak."

"If you knew how poverty ran rampant throughout the length and breadth of my family, Mr. Metcalf, you wouldn't find it at all remarkable. About the only unexpected windfall I can imagine that any relative of mine would bequeath me would be some white elephant . . . And why would they take the trouble to ship it across the Atlantic, or—good heavens!—expect *me* to ship it across?"

"Ship?" Mr. Metcalf said questioningly. "Why do you think it would have to be shipped?"

"Because I don't have any relatives over here anymore. My parents are dead." After a second or two I added, "And Ian. And all the rest are in Scotland."

"Ian," he repeated. "That would be your brother."

"Would have been. As I said, he's dead." Even after all these years it hurt. My mother had died at Ian's birth when I was a child. I barely remembered her. The death of my father and my stepmother had left me almost untouched. I had fought too hard for my freedom from them to feel real grief when they died. But Ian—

"Yes. I know. I'm sorry."

"How do you know?" I asked, more sharply than I had intended.

"Well, in view of the inheritance it's natural. When we talk . . ."

"Yes, of course. Well . . . who exactly is it from?" I asked suddenly, trying another tack.

"That, too, I'll tell you when we meet."

By this time my curiosity was aroused. Nevertheless, a lifetime's training had tended me towards the skeptical approach. "Mr. Metcalf, do you know what the term 'white elephant' means?"

"I do," he said a little grimly.

"Would you say that the goodie you're about to bestow on me was a white elephant?"

"I don't remember saying it was a goodie. However, in answer to your question, yes. One could call it that. A very large one."

"And you want me to interrupt a busy schedule so that you can bestow on me something that you describe as a large white elephant, and that I will undoubtedly be sorry I have?"

"Where's your sporting sense? Anyway, I didn't say you'd be sorry. How about tomorrow morning around ten?"

"Can't. Editorial meeting all morning."

"Tomorrow afternoon?"

I flipped over the page of my desk calendar. Scrawled over the bottom half were M.B. + B.A., which, translated, meant Max Bainbridge and Big Author. Max, grandson of the original Bainbridge of Bainbridge & Laird, Publishers, was also editor in chief. For weeks he had been hinting at a large fish he was about to land and had set up this date for me to meet him.

"Sorry," I said to Mr. Metcalf. "Tomorrow afternoon is bad, too."

"Well . . . The trouble is, I am going out of town the day after that for a couple of days, and would like to see you before I leave. How about late this afternoon?"

That afternoon, I had planned to leave early to do some much-needed household shopping. Well, it would have to wait. By this time my curiosity was all that even Mr. Metcalf himself could wish. "All right," I said. "About five?"

"Fine. See you then."

After a moment's thought I picked up the telephone and dialed the extension of the publicity director, Melissa Corbett. "Melissa," I said when she answered, "could we postpone our lunch? I have to do the shopping at lunch that I was supposed to do this afternoon."

"Why can't you do it this afternoon?" asked Melissa, who never let tact stand in the way of her ravening curiosity about other people's affairs.

I hesitated a second. Melissa is a good friend and an excellent publicity director. She is also one of the world's great gossips. She means no harm and she can't help it. But for some reason I didn't stop to figure out, I didn't want to discuss the lawyer's telephone call. The trouble was, I thought, grimacing slightly, I should have remembered all of that before I picked up the receiver. In hesitating, I was lost. I heard the click as she put down the receiver, and waited for the rat-tat of her heels as she came along the hall. The sales, advertising and publicity departments were in a section by themselves, and I figured it would take Melissa at least one minute to come through the swinging doors from her wing out into the main lobby and through the door into the editorial section. I was wrong. She was there in just over thirty seconds. Under the sawed-off bangs, her dark eyes sparkled with interest.

"What's happening this afternoon? Anything new and interesting?"

I laughed. I couldn't help it. "Melissa, doesn't a certain restraint concerning other people's business ever inhibit you?"

"Never," she said emphatically, and propped her sturdy form on the edge of a table at right angles to the desk. "From your reserved expression I take it you're about to do something you don't wish to discuss."

"How did you guess?" I asked drily.

"I told you. From your expression. You get that *noli me tangere* look that would prevent anyone with the smallest sensitivity from pushing."

"But not you?"

"Of course not. Where would anyone in publicity be if they allowed sensitivity, restraint, breeding or good taste stand in their way?"

The silly part about all this was that if I had used my head I could have thought up something innocent and innocuous, like a dental appointment. But early rigid training in truthfulness had had its effect. Unless I took careful thought, I was compulsively truthful, and I had not taken careful thought. However, it might not be too late.

"I'm going to the dentist," I said suddenly.

"No, you're not."

"How do you know I'm not?"

"Because you would have said so immediately."

I sighed. "All right. I'm not going to the dentist. I am going to do something secret and private about which I wish no one to know."

"Then why didn't you say so right away? Instead of letting me come all the way over here?"

"Because—" Yes, I thought, why hadn't I? Melissa herself wouldn't have hesitated saying just that. "Because I'm a mouse," I said finally. "Just as everyone in school thought. Did you know I was once called Mouse Moncrieff?" I asked lightly, and the minute the words were out knew I had made a blunder.

"I thought Moncrieff was your married name?" Melissa said.

Oh, what a tangled web, I thought. For someone who had been brought up to tell the exact truth, the whole and nothing but, I had had to live more of a lie than the most enthusiastic imposter. I did my best to retrieve the situation. "It is. I married while I was in school."

"Oh. By school I thought you meant school—as in high or junior high."

That was exactly what I had meant. But I decided the best course would be to say nothing. Rather ostentatiously I turned back to my manuscript. It was, as far as Melissa was concerned, a wasted effort.

"Besides," she went on, ignoring my silence, "no one with your color hair could possibly, under any circumstances, be called Mouse. It would be against nature."

Involuntarily I glanced into the mirror on the wall beside the desk and poked a stray lock of hair back into place. In the morning light from the east window the red of my hair was even more fiery than usual. "It's entirely misleading. 'Mouse' is a much better indication of my nature than the color of my hair."

"I don't believe it. Quiet, perhaps. Definitely reserved. But not Mouse. No mother of Ewen could be called Mouse."

I laughed, knowing that the wily Melissa had used the one infallible method of getting my attention. "I agree. It's unworthy of Ewen. But Ewen or no, I have to get this manuscript finished and to the production department before I leave today, so be an angel and stop distracting me."

Melissa, who had been staring at my desk calendar, said, "I suppose M.B. is Max Bainbridge. But who is B.A.?"

"Big Author," I said. "But it's no use asking me who because I don't know."

"Is that the guy Max has been throwing hints out about all over the shop for weeks? You'd think he'd uncovered another Solzhenitsyn. I wonder why he wants to see you about him. I should have—"

"Melissa! PLEASE GO. I have to work!"

She got up. "In that case I won't bother casting any pearls. Don't blame *me* when you're the last to know who this mysterious author is. Far be it from me—"

Hastily she shut the door as my pencil sailed across the room.

I sat there, wondering if she really knew something about Max's author. Rumors and guesses had been humming along the office bush telegraph now, as she had said, for weeks. But as one big name after another popped up the cold light of reality killed it: this one had signed a new contract with his publisher; that one had been taken by somebody else; the long-awaited opus of a third had turned out to be a disaster, turned down all over town. Bainbridge & Laird was one of the oldest of the publishers. It had had its good days and bad. Forty years ago it published most of the top novelists. Twenty years ago it was way down the list to which agents sent important manuscripts. Five years ago, when Max III joined the staff, it had hit what we had all profoundly hoped was its bottom and since then had been climbing steadily up. It was still not among the top two or three, but it was high in the second rank and was again developing a reputation for well-written fiction. Max had no talent for picking out the James Joyces of the future, but he did have a gift for spotting comers among the more traditional manuscripts submitted. It was exciting. Max was not really an editor in the usual sense of the word. He was a hunter. He sighted the game and signed them up. Then he handed his prize over to someone else—usually me—for actual work on the manuscript, which suited me beautifully.

This *modus operandi* could produce some very acid comments from other editors, especially as Max, being the heir apparent, had fallen into the job. When he signed up a dud —and it occasionally happened—there was more than a touch of malicious pleasure in the groans. But as his successes mounted, he forced respect out of even the most cynical of his employees, especially those who had struggled up the hard way from prep school, Harvard and Yale and other publishing houses. It's difficult to think of witty put-downs about success, however commercial. Those who had come by the humbler route—for example, the sales department—were very happy with our middlebrow best-sellers.

Who could Max's author be? I sat there, resisting the temptation to stroll into Melissa's office and see what she knew. If there was any information to be had, she would have it. Partly because of her role in publicity, mostly out of inclination, Melissa haunted the cocktail parties and social circuits where such tidbits abounded and where Max himself was often to be found, along with other editors and leading agents.

One reason why I worked for Max's finds rather than

acquiring my own was that to be, in publishing parlance, an acquisitions editor, required a strong stomach, an ever stronger head and a boundless appetite for lunching and partying. I had traveled far from being the Mouse Moncrieff of my school yearbook. But I had never really overcome the paralysing shyness that had made my school years such a horror and that I covered with the reserve that Melissa called my *noli me tangere* manner. The prospect of taking agents and authors to lunch five days a week, to say nothing of cocktail parties afterwards, would have spelled to me not glamour but horror. Besides, and more important, there was Ewen. Right from the beginning I had been a working mother. There was no choice about that. If my son and I had a roof over our heads and regular meals, then I worked. My marriage to Dauntry had broken up before Ewen was actually born, and given the circumstances of that disastrous marriage, I made no effort to get from him any child support later. The subsequent financial struggle was horrendous, but as the price of putting Ewen and me out of Dauntry's reach, more than worth it. So year after year I had gone straight home from the office, taking with me what manuscripts had to be read, and reading them far into the night after Ewen had gone to bed. When he was younger there was always a baby-sitter for Ewen to come home to, but three and a half years ago, when he turned nine, he had strenuously objected to this.

"I don't need a baby-sitter, Mom. Besides, we can't afford it."

"I can afford the money better than I can worrying about you at home alone until I get there."

"Why worry? I'm not going to open the door unless I know who it is. It's only a couple of hours until you get home. Besides, I have Wilma."

"Yes, indeed, and what a protection *she* is."

Ewen grinned. "Yes, but anybody who'd want to get in wouldn't know she's all noise, aren't you, girl?" And Wilma, who was black and mostly Labrador, rolled over on her back ecstatically and barked. It was a ferocious noise, a legacy possibly from some mastiff ancestor, and had backed both deliverymen and guests almost to the elevator. What no one knew was that at even a sharp tone of voice, let alone a threatening stance, Wilma went immediately under the bed.

"Nemesis would be more protection," I said bitterly.

At the sound of his name Nemesis opened his green eyes and bent on me his unnerving glare.

"Nemesis'd dismember them," Ewen agreed, rubbing an inky finger between the cat's ears. At his touch, a loud purr filled the airwaves. Slowly Nemesis, all seventeen muscular pounds of him, got up and stretched. His coal-black fur glistened. I had seen that fur stand out on body and tail at least six inches when the cat's ire was aroused, and the snarl that emerged from his throat was pure jungle. He idolized Ewen. He tolerated Wilma and me and Ewen's other pets. Everyone else was an enemy.

I thought about this now as I pulled the telephone in my direction to call Ewen at his school. At twelve ("Going on thirteen, Mom") Ewen was mature and self-reliant. Even so, I liked him to know when to expect me, and with an appointment on Wall Street at five, I might not get home until nearly seven.

Ewen had a partial scholarship at St. Mark's School, a boys' school connected with the nearby Episcopal cathedral. It was a school orginally started for the choir, and until a few months before, Ewen had been one of the young choristers. But his voice had broken, and until it had settled, his singing, at least in the choir, was in abeyance.

"Could I leave a message for Ewen Moncrieff?" I asked the school secretary.

"Is that Mrs. Moncrieff?" Mrs. Abernathy said. "Do you want him to call you at work?"

"Yes. Please. Any time between two and three."

I thought about leaving the message, telling him I wouldn't be home until after six, and then didn't. I never quite liked making it public property that Ewen would be home alone for two or more hours.

"All right. Glad to."

I did my shopping, decided to have the sheets and towels sent, rather than lug them down to Wall Street, and was back for Ewen's call shortly after two.

"Hi," Ewen said. "You going to be late home?"

"Yes. Just wanted you to know. If you get hungry there's cheese and fruit and milk. But I don't expect to be much after six. There's a casserole in the refrigerator. Would you put it in a medium oven—around three hundred and fifty degrees —about a quarter past six? "

"Okay."

I hesitated. The reserve that kept people at a distance was a protection. But it could sometimes be a wall. Ewen was the one person in whom I confided.

"Guess what?" I said. "Somebody's left me something. A lawyer called today and wants me to see him this afternoon."

"Is it a horse?" Ewen asked hopefully.

"He said it was a white elephant."

"A *white* elephant? There's isn't such a thing. Unless it's an albino. I wonder if there are albino elephants. I'll just look—"

"Ewen," I all but yelled. "It's a joke. A white elephant is something you don't want. Like a chest of drawers you don't need. I didn't realize—I'm sorry it isn't a horse. Although I don't think the landlord would like our stabling it in his hall."

"The hall isn't *fit* for a horse," Ewen said indignantly. "I wouldn't stable Wilma there."

"True," I agreed.

The hall, which was poorly cleaned and dimly lit and not heated at all, had been the subject of many a tenants' petition—all of them unsuccessful. The ancient and decrepit West Side apartment house in which Ewen and I lived had only rent-controlled apartments. As a consequence, the landlord's less than benign neglect had achieved the status of high art. Of the three hall lights, two had been out for what seemed like months—but never the same two. The furnace broke down with depressing regularity, usually in the coldest weather. Every now and then all the upstairs lights would give out. But either the landlord had an informer among the tenants, or an infallible instinct for when the harried residents had borne enough to get together and withhold the rent. Miraculously, the furnace would give a clank and for one or two precious days a blast of warmth would greet the tenants as they opened the ancient and creaking front door. Then, when we had been lulled into a truce, everything would stop working, not, of course, at the same time, but artistically, in turn. We had no superintendent in residence. The houses on either side of us had been broken into. So far we had been lucky. But the tide of crime and vandalism was creeping towards us. The only thing that could stop it would be to renovate the old buildings on the street and make them into new apartments. But to do that meant getting rid of the present tenants. Which was why our landlord had achieved such finesse in tenant-torture.

"I don't suppose," Ewen said, with the kind of New York street smarts that always came to me with such a shock, "that it's money."

"He discouraged that idea, I'm afraid." Something made me add, "Ewen, quick off the top of your head. If it were money, what would you buy?"

"Depends how much it was," said my practical son.

"Well—a lot."

It was an exercise in masochism, because I was quite convinced that what Ewen would say would be, move to the country, or live on a ranch. He was a fanatic animal lover, and his current ambition was to be a vet. I was therefore almost stunned when he said, "I'd buy a house for us."

"Where?"

He really surprised me then. "In New York."

"Oh," I said.

"You sound surprised."

"I am. I thought, I was afraid, you'd say . . . somewhere in the country."

"Yeah, well, you wouldn't be able to work there, would you? Anyway, I've decided I'm going to be a city vet. If we had a house, we could convert it later into a vet's hospital. Look, I've got gym. I'll see you later." And he hung up.

I stared at the telephone, and then did what I often do when I've talked to him, although I'm always embarrassed when somebody catches me at it: I took the photograph of Ewen off the wall above my desk and looked at it.

When he was a baby, I worried about bringing up a boy without a father. A boy, I had always read, needed a father on whom to model himself: being reared solely by a female parent might fail to supply some necessary ingredient to the young male masculinity. Hoping to avoid this pitfall, I suppose I thought, or hoped, that my son might resemble the only other example of boyhood I had ever experienced—my freckle-faced roustabout of a brother, Ian. Perhaps it was because of that possible, or hoped for, resemblance that I named my son Ewen, which is simply another Celtic version of Ian (both being versions of that most universal name, John). When Ewen showed early signs of being very different from Ian, my early fears for his boyness reactivated.

I needn't have worried.

Ewen was one of the most thoroughly male creatures I have ever known. He exuded an unselfconscious, unworried confidence in his maleness from the time he was about four, and he did this while not adhering to any of the stereotypes. Long and thin, with a beaky, bony face, he was not particularly athletic and took only the dimmest interest in spectator sports. He had good coordination, but the only athletic activities in which he had any skill were swimming and riding. Competitive team sports bored him. At some point I had bought a secondhand television set, fully expecting to have to drag Ewen away from it to bed every night. Except for news programs and science features he almost never watched it. It was I who sat guiltily in front of some police or detective feature while Ewen would return to his studio-laboratory-zoo—all of which applied to his bedroom.

In the photograph his thick, light hair fell over most of his face. His eyes were narrowed into the sun. Over his shoulder, like a fur collar, was Nemesis. Beside him was Wilma. Sticking out of his blazer pocket was Einstein, his pet white rat. Between Nemesis and Einstein there was, magically, peace. For some reason Ewen's pets, however much they might spring from ancient enemies, never fought.

"How do you do it?" I asked him recently.

"I just explain the whole setup to them very carefully," he said, deadpan.

"Did you ever think of going to the UN?"

The smile that was so like his father's had quivered then across his face, tilting, lifting one side of his mouth, a smile of such charm and humor that it could draw people across a room. I should know. . . . It had drawn me across a far greater distance than that.

Ewen said, "Henry mightn't like it."

"Henry? Oh—Kissinger."

"And besides, animals understand better."

Since Ewen was rarely without some sort of livestock about him, I could believe he meant it.

"You're probably right."

Ewen, watching me, said, "Mom, why do you sometimes look at me like that? Like I was a ghost?"

Because you are, was what I wanted to say. But that would move the conversation onto dangerous territory. I, Miss Truthteller, had told my son nothing but lies about his father. So far, he had believed them, but I knew, had known for a while, that before too long now, he would know them for lies. When that moment arrived, he would have to know the truth, but the thought of telling him kept me awake more often than I liked.

"Do I, Ewen? I don't mean to. Maybe I'm thinking of something else."

It was a poor answer. Ewen didn't say anything. But he looked at me in the way he does sometimes, as though he were watching me from across a chasm—aware of how much truth I had not told him.

It was more than I could endure. I leaned over and kissed him, my hand over his thin boney one. "You look as though you were about to tell me, in the best English mystery tradition, that my evidence is a tissue of lies."

He didn't kiss me back. "Is it?"

"Have you done your homework?"

Which was not only a cop-out, it was stupid. Ewen had always done his homework. . . .

"You have to understand about the Standishes," the lawyer said, at five thirty that afternoon, sitting in his corner office with a view of two rivers meeting at the Battery. "This house was more than a house to them. It was a sort of symbol of the family itself."

"So that they would let it go to ruin, using it as a rooming house, letting the tenants make it into a slum rather than allow it to come to someone outside the family—me."

"Yes. I guess that's about it. If by 'they' you're talking about the Standish cousins who contested the will. Old Mrs. Standish, of course, *did* leave it to you—that is, she left it to your aunt—after, of course, the search for her grandson had been exhausted."

"From what you say I doubt if Judge Crater was looked for any harder." Restless, still unbelieving, I got up and walked over to the office window. The astonishing New York sunset was beginning its nightly performance. The great crimson ball was hovering over the distant New Jersey flats, mercifully smudged by distance. Great stripes of pink, orange and blue streaked the skies from north to south. To my left, above the East River and north Brooklyn, the flaming colors were muted with gray. Immediately around me the buildings were all lit. The twin towers of the World Trade Center looked like upturned cigar boxes scattered with gold sequins. Miss Liberty held up her portion of the sky. Across the harbor was Brooklyn. High above the Brooklyn Harbor, with its docks and warehouses, the elegant mansions of Brooklyn Heights looked back at me.

And one of those houses was mine.

I couldn't really take it in. All I could think of at the moment was Ewen's voice that afternoon on the telephone answering my question as to what he would do with money if he had it. *I'd buy a house . . .*

Something seemed to flicker over my skin and I shivered.

"What's the matter?" the lawyer's voice said from behind me. He came up and stood beside me by the window.

"Can I see it from here?" I asked.

"No. Not really. It's mostly hidden by trees."

After another minute of staring, I abandoned the view and went back to my chair in front of Laurence Metcalf's desk. Mr. Metcalf returned to his own chair behind the desk.

"Now," I said, "I didn't take in a third of what you told

me. Could you start from the beginning and tell me the whole thing again?"

The lawyer laughed. He was younger than I had expected. I had always envisioned members of top Wall Street firms as lean, gray-haired Brahmins who refreshed themselves from their labors with the hoi polloi by stirring games of chess in their gentlemanly clubs—a rather naïve view, I was fully aware, but one I couldn't quite shake off. Laurence Metcalf, a nice-looking young man in his late thirties, of medium height and build and with clear brown eyes, certainly had all the outward stigmata of the New York blue blood. His dark brown hair was longer than it would have been ten years before, but by popular and publishing standards it was still short. He had on a dark suit, a white shirt and subdued tie. On his walls were a photograph of a distinguished-looking elderly man, an 1850s print of New York Harbor and what looked like an engraving of a house of the same period, narrow, with the characteristic front stoop of the New York house. Underneath, in copperplate, ran the legend: *The Standish Place.*

"Yes, that's the one," he said, following the direction of my gaze. I shook my head, still trying to put together the pieces that he had told me when I had first sat down.

I had been shown in immediately and almost as soon as I had been greeted by the man who had risen behind the desk, said impulsively, "I can't stand it any longer. What is it? What is the white elephant?"

What did I expect? Grim disapproval? A Brahminly sniff? The pleasant-looking man just grinned. "You want to know right now? The end at the beginning?"

"Yes."

"It's a house." And when I stared, not taking it in, he laughed and came around the desk. "Look. I'll show you." He took me by the arm over to the window and said, "Do you see

that row of houses across the river there, above the Brooklyn
docks, above the highway?"

"Yes."

"Ever been there?"

I shook my head. Though I had lived ten years in New
York, I had managed never to go to Brooklyn.

"That's Brooklyn Heights. It may surprise you to know
that it is one of the most elegant sections, not only now but
also in the past, of the greater New York area. The rich
merchants of the eighteen thirties, forties and fifties, through
the end of the century, built their mansions above their own
ships and warehouses. Those houses are still there. One of
them is—" he looked at me, his eyes not much above mine
—"one of them is now yours. Does the name Standish mean
anything to you?"

Again a little bell seemed to ring far at the back of my
mind. I had heard the name somewhere, at some time.

Laurence Metcalf was watching me. "It's a well enough
known name, of course," he said.

"Yes," I agreed. I had heard the name. There had been
an article somewhere about . . . Suddenly a memory emerged.
"The Standish paintings," I said.

"That's right." He was still watching me. "They were
quite famous."

But even as I said it, I knew it wasn't that that had set off
the bell. I had read about the Standish paintings in the art
section of the *New York Times,* or perhaps in one of the news
magazines. The article had been interesting, but it was
something else, much further back, that was ringing the bell
and producing an emotion that I was astonished to discover
was fear.

I had the sense, as we were standing there, that I was
being very carefully watched.

Then the feeling had gone. "Nothing," I said. The

implausibility of the whole thing hit me in full force. "How on earth do I come to be inheriting a house owned by the Standishes?"

"Come and sit down. It's a long story."

It was, and in my state of shock, I had caught almost none of it. The words house . . . family . . . daughter . . . Germany . . . came at me unlinked by meaning. Then I heard, "Your aunt, Alice Moncrieff, housekeeper and companion to Mrs. Standish . . ." And that, at least, had meaning. Alice and Jennie Moncrieff, sisters, had grown up on a small farm in eastern Scotland and had come to the States, in the time-honored fashion, to better themselves. Jennie had married a cousin of the same name from Scotland, a young Presbyterian minister in Oregon. She was the mother I barely remembered. Alice, unmarried, and with no particular skill, became housekeeper to old Mrs. Standish, who had died and, it appeared now, had left her the family house if her grandson, that missing child of a missing daughter, could not be found; a daughter who had stormed out of her mother's house in a rage and had gone, unforgiven, out of her mother's life . . .

I tried to catch up with what the lawyer was saying—something about endless legal battles, a will filled with ambiguities, a quarrelsome family united only in their bulldog determination not to let the house go to a stranger, an outsider.

That was when I had got up, restless and uncomfortable, and gone to the window, and the patient lawyer had said, "You have to understand about the Standishes . . ." and had tried to make me see it as it appeared to them—a symbol of everything the family had stood for.

And then he had seen me look at the engraving. "It's quite a well-known engraving," he said. "You must have seen it before."

"Yes," I said doubtfully. "But I can't remember where.

Perhaps in the Morgan library. But, please, tell me again what you were explaining before. The psychic shock of inheriting a house threw a fog over my mind. I got about a third."

He smiled. "All right. Briefly, the Standishes, a wealthy New York family, made their big money in trade—import-export. And in 1847 they built themselves a house in the then highly fashionable Brooklyn Heights. Did you know that Brooklyn was then a separate city from New York, with its own mayor, town hall, police force, et cetera?"

I shook my head. "All I've ever known about Brooklyn was an accent and a tree that grew there."

He sighed. "As an old Brooklynite myself, I find that attitude both prevalent and painful. Did you know that Winston Churchill's mother, Jenny Jerome, came from there?"

"Yes, now that you mention it. What about the paintings?"

"The Standishes always fancied themselves as collectors. They had a couple of Sargents, a Bellows, a Stubbs and several lesser known but now quite valuable American nineteenth-century paintings. All of those went to famous collections in museums around the country. But, well . . . we now come to the last of the Standishes who left your aunt the house: Louise Anne Alexandra Standish, *grande dame* to her fingernails.

"She was born Louise Ransom. And the Ransoms, who came to New York well before the Revolution and had one or two signers of the Declaration among their ancestors plus a couple of governors and a senator or two, were even more *recherché* and stiff-rumped than the Standishes, whom they looked upon as mercantile parvenus with, it was hinted, a squalid little scandal in their past."

"How fascinating. What was it?"

The lawyer glanced quickly at me and then produced his engaging smile. "Who knows? Anyway, what was considered a scandal then would today be a yawn. Whatever it was, the Standishes had something the Ransoms needed—money. So in a more or less arranged marriage, Louise Ransom married Alton Standish II. In 1910 they had a daughter, Susan. In 1915 they had a son, Alton III, who, after passing with well-bred invisibleness through Groton and Princeton, was killed in the Battle of the Bulge. But Susan was, as they say today, something else.

"Everything that had been buttoned down and sat on on both sides of the family erupted in Susan, who was beautiful, bright and a holy terror. After being thrown out of two boarding schools for various frolics, she was also thrown out of her Swiss finishing school and ended up in Berlin, the free, swinging Berlin of the Weimar Republic. Alton Standish, who was dying, and knew it, went and got her and brought her back. Two weeks after they returned, he died. A month after his death Susan and her mother had a final quarrel. Susan slammed out of the house and returned immediately to Germany, where she became involved with a young German who, despite his Prussian Junker ancestry, was also a good painter and in the thick of the artistic movement of that day. Perhaps it was because his mother was not Junker. She was a Jewish concert pianist and had surrounded herself and her family with artists of all kinds. Anyway, Susan married Egon von Harbach." He paused, watching me.

Something flickered in the back of my memory. Only it was less a memory than a sensation that I associated with pain. This must have been reflected on my face because he said, "Heard the name?"

"Yes," I replied slowly.

"He became a pretty well known painter."

"No, it's not that. It's something else. I can't get it now. Go on."

"The family didn't even know about it until long after

the wedding. Then, when the Nazis took over, old Mrs. Standish, who, to do her justice, was one of the first to realize what was in store, started sending letters and cables and messages via the embassy and consulates to the general purpose of all is forgiven, come home while you can and bring your husband. But she heard nothing. All she got was a crate of three paintings. Then, finally, she got a letter from Susan forwarded through England saying that her husband was dead. No details. But that she and her son, Johannes, aged four, were coming home. That was the first Mrs. Standish had heard that there was a son. And she waited. But it was the last definite news she had. That was late in 1937.

"She started sending out inquiries, both official and private, but got no information until after the war when she learned that Susan had gotten through to Paris with every declared intention of catching some kind of ship from either France or England to the U.S. But the trail ends there—that is, all positive, documented information ends there. But there were a lot of rumors. One was that Susan got as far as England, was unable to continue her journey after the war broke out, and was bombed along with her son while living in London. There was another that she got as far as Lisbon. Another rumor claimed she had actually crossed the Atlantic. All of these were tracked down and produced nothing. If Susan actually got across the Atlantic, she disappeared the day she landed. Lawyers and detectives have combed passenger lists on every type of passenger and even cargo vessel of every possible year. Nothing."

Metcalf, caught up in the story, gazed moodily at his desk. "My father"—he nodded towards the photograph of the elderly man—"was old Mrs. Standish's attorney—the family has always handled the Standish estate. There's a whole file drawer out there"—he waved towards his outer office—"filled with nothing but results of that ten-year search. But in 1948

Mrs. Standish discovered she had cancer, and, I think, according to what my father said, that brought her up sharp and made her face the possibility of never finding her grandson. By then she was convinced her daughter was dead. This, I take it, was from some inner conviction rather than any evidence. But she now became convinced that her grandson was lost to her, too. And, of course, guilt had played its part in her search: if she had not quarreled with her daughter . . . if she had been more understanding . . . if she had tried to reach Susan before Hitler overran the rest of Europe—the usual remorse.

"When she knew she had only a few months to live she called my father in and made her will. She left money for the search to continue—she was a determined old woman; not even death was going to frustrate her search. But if at the end of another five years he had not been found, the house was to pass to her housekeeper, Alice Moncrieff, your mother's sister, who had been living with her since just before World War II. Louise Standish had never been exactly easy to live with. She had quarreled with most of her own relatives and those of her husband (she even started poking around in that old scandal, just to annoy the Standishes), and in the last years of her life Alice Moncrieff was about the only person with whom she communicated except, of course, my father, whom she summoned from time to time rather in the manner of Queen Victoria sending for her prime minister."

"But," I said, "given her starchiness, her whole reverence for tradition, wasn't it strange for Mrs. Standish to leave the house away from her family, however much she disapproved of them?"

"Well, of course, that was the line her relations took when they contested the will. They maintained that Miss Moncrieff had used undue influence on a dying woman and that the will should be set aside for that reason." He looked across at me. "You were about six when Alice Moncrieff died. Do you have any memory of her at all?"

It was like looking far back, across an infinite number of obstacles. "The trouble was," I said slowly, "Mother died a year later, and everything earlier than that is vague." I closed my eyes. "There's a sort of jumble in my head—faces, houses—but I can't remember whether they were real or something I dreamed."

"What kind of houses?" he asked, a little sharply, I thought.

I shrugged. "I don't know. Just houses. I seem to remember the fact of them rather than what they looked like."

"I see."

"Why?"

"No particular reason. Just curiosity. I wondered if Miss Moncrieff had—er—sent any pictures or snapshots of the Standish house, or perhaps a copy of the engraving on the wall over there."

It was an innocuous enough statement, yet in some odd way I had a feeling that he was making it up on the spur of the moment. But why would he?

"Not that I know of or have seen." There was a short pause. "What happened after that?"

He sighed and shifted in his chair. "Well, as I said, she died, and two sets of relatives—one set on the Standish and another on the Ransom side—immediately sued to have the will overthrown. Normally the Standish and Ransom clans did not have too much to do with one another, but they joined forces over the will, and the fight was on.

"Your aunt, Alice Moncrieff, stoutly maintained that she had brought no influence to bear whatsoever and recounted several episodes where Mrs. Standish had refused to have anything to do with her relatives, or quarreled so badly with

25

them that there was no communication between them. The relatives took very much the line that you did: that she was far too steeped in tradition and full of family pride to have left her home to anyone outside the family—let alone a housekeeper."

They slipped out, those four words, "let alone a house-keeper." I waited to see if he would catch himself. His cheeks flushed a little. "Sorry. I didn't mean it to sound quite like that."

"That's all right," I said. "I'm not ashamed of my aunt being a housekeeper. It's a perfectly honorable way to make a living, and on the whole I prefer people who have to make a living to those who are so rich they don't."

"Quite," he said quickly. "I agree with you."

"Do you? I bet a lot of your friends and associates work as a hobby rather than a necessity."

He still had that dull flush. "Some, perhaps. Anyway, to get back to your aunt. She fought the relatives as well as she could—considering that she was running out of money."

"Didn't Mrs. Standish leave enough to keep the house up? I thought she was rich."

"In her last years Mrs. Standish was not as mentally sharp as she had been. She'd always watched over her own investments and would not take advice. I know because a guy who worked with the broker the Standishes used—well, you're not interested in that. What I was getting at was that she thought she left enough money to keep the house up. But the first stipulation in her will was that no expense was to be spared looking for her grandson—and private investigators are extremely expensive. So, although it may be odd of me to say so, are lawyers, even if they don't charge high fees. There are simply the day-to-day expenses and the labor."

"Didn't my aunt retain your father, since he had been attorney to Mrs. Standish? Of course, though, she wasn't family."

"My father offered to represent her. But—she said she would prefer to choose her own attorney, which, of course, was her right."

"My aunt died in 1951. What happened then to the house?"

"Well, according to your aunt's will, it was to go to your mother, and failing that, if she were not alive, to your brother, Ian, and then to you."

"But that was twenty . . . twenty-four years ago. Of course, I was very young then, and Mother died a year later, when I was seven. But surely I would have heard about it from my father, and he didn't say anything at all."

"According to the records obtained from the lawyers your aunt used, they certainly informed your mother, and, when she died, your father. Because your brother was a minor, and, according to the will your aunt left, the house had to stay under the protection of the court until he, your brother, had achieved his majority. But then, of course, he died, along with your father in that accident."

That accident . . . Dauntry and I, only a few weeks into a marriage that was already for me a pain and a bewilderment, were visiting my father and stepmother. It had been a difficult visit, with my father outraged over our elopement, and Dauntry, who had insisted we come, exerting the charm that had cut such a swath across the campus and captivated me, but to no avail. Where his concept of morality and filial obedience was concerned, my father was made of granite. His resistance to Dauntry (and to me) was total. Then he and Ian got in his battered car and took the cliff road to the church for some kind of get-together or meeting. It was the sheriff, a member of my father's congregation, who told us about the faulty brake and the crash to the rocks below.

All that night I cried. People called to express sympathy. It was tragic, they obviously felt, about my brother. But their real empathy was how I must be feeling for my father. And I was both too timid and too distraught to correct that impression. My stern, distant father I mourned hardly at all. It was warm, rambunctious Ian, with his terrible jokes and loyal heart and inspired common sense, who had been the lodestar of my life, for all he was four years younger than I. After all, I had done most of his bringing up, and at that time I needed him more than I ever had before.

"I'm sorry," Laurence Metcalf said in a concerned voice, watching me. "I didn't mean to bring back painful memories."

"It's all right. It was a long time ago. Twelve years, in fact. What's happened to the house since?"

"The court battle has gone on—and on, complicated by the fact that periodically a stray hint that some agency might have located Mrs. Standish's grandson had to be run down."

I thought a moment. Never having been a householder, I have rarely given much thought to the details of maintaining a house, but the memories of conversations at the office, news items, drifted across my mind. "But who kept the house up —paid the taxes?"

He leaned back. "Various tenants—if you can call it being kept up. It's not in very pretty condition. I'm sorry about that. Of course, being where it is, the property itself is extremely valuable, particularly since The Heights has come back up in the world and is now as expensive as almost any area in Manhattan. We've already had several inquiries about buying which I'll be happy to pass on to you."

"So it *could* mean money," I said slowly. We could move out of that cramped apartment. Ewen's school fees and even some of his college expenses would be secure. My spirits rose. I forced my attention back to Mr. Metcalf, who was talking.

". . . we did try to locate you," he was saying. "But you had vanished—from the college, from your home, from everywhere we thought to look. Nobody seemed to have a remote idea of where you were."

"Yes," I said calmly. I had had a lot of practice in skimming over this period of my life. "I'd had it at the college." It suddenly occurred to me that if Laurence Metcalf knew so much about Ian, he must know a fair amount about me, more than I had ever allowed anyone—here in the east anyway—to know. My fears concerning the big lie I had told Ewen about his father seemed to rise up in the room there with me. I shivered a little.

"Are you cold?" Metcalf asked. "The building management has taken the energy crisis to its heart and happily turns everything off on the stroke of five. I can blast down at them and tell them to turn it on up here if you like?"

"No. I'm okay." There was no way out of this except the direct question. "I'm curious, Mr. Metcalf, while you were busy investigating my brother, you must have found out a lot about me. I'd like to know what you know about my marriage."

"Not as much as we tried to find out," he said cheerfully. "By the time we had got to the campus, both you and your husband had disappeared. We never did find you—at least not for a long time. It was easier, of course, to find your husband, Dauntry Leigh."

"Why was it easier to find him? I mean, you make it sound as though there were something else."

"There was. Didn't you know? Dauntry Leigh was, on his mother's side, a Standish."

Chapter 2

It was after seven when I got home. Wilma's deep baying bark and the smell of burning casserole greeted me as I unlocked the door.

"I'm home!" I called. And then, "For heaven's sake, Wilma . . ."

Standing on her hind legs, Wilma is as tall as I am, and her nightly greeting would have been more suitable if my absence had been one of years. I reared back, removing my cheek from her enthusiastic tongue and her paws from my shoulders. Then I plunged towards the kitchen. Plumes of smoke were coming from around the oven door. Turning off the heat, I opened the oven door and with the aid of several potholders managed to get the casserole out. It looked black, sticky and inedible.

"Ewen, why can't you . . ." But it was a wasted effort and I knew it. Ewen was in his room at the other end of the hall. I muttered to myself as I placed the dish on an asbestos pad and poked around in it with a fork. Then I tasted it, then I spat it out into the garbage can. Admittedly, the dish had contained an artistic arrangement of leftovers. Nevertheless . . . Ewen should have put on the egg timer or something. I poked the fork in again.

Doing a slow burn somewhat in the manner of the casserole, I went down the hall, with Wilma flopping after me, and thrust open Ewen's door.

Ewen's room, the larger of the two small bedrooms, was ordered chaos. At one end was a studio couch and desk. In the middle, set up on a table, was his lab, complete with racks holding test tubes, and at the other end were his animals: a family of white mice, another of gerbils, Einstein (the white rat) and Mr. Ears, a black-and-white Belgian rabbit. Actually, Mr. Ears was out of his cage and on top of a bookcase in a state of what looked like meditation. Below him, on a low table, was a large terrarium containing two turtles. Stretched out over half of the lab table, Nemesis lay with half-shut eyes, exuding a low, steady purr. Since all of this was contained in a room about twelve feet by sixteen, the density, to say nothing of the mixed animal and chemical odor, was overwhelming. I eyed my son, who was measuring something in a test tube, and said loudly, "It's too bad about your dinner, Ewen."

Ewen kept his eyes on what he was doing. "What's the matter? Did you burn it?"

"No. You did."

At that he turned. A look of consternation came over his face. "Oh—I forgot. I'm sorry. Is it ruined?"

"You may taste it for yourself." And I walked over, holding out a spoon bearing some blackened remains.

Ewen sniffed. "No, thanks. I guess I'm not hungry. Maybe I'll go out and pick up—"

"No, you will not. You will eat something else with me.

And I'm sorry you're not hungry—not that I believe it for a minute—because I wanted you to suffer just a little."

Ewen grinned. "Okay. I'm suffering. Anything I can do?"

"Such as. . . ?"

"Well," he said guardedly, "I can feed Wilma."

"All right. And you can talk to me. I have something to tell you."

"I'll be there as soon as I finish this."

I started to leave. Then I paused, hand on door. "Just as a matter of curiosity, did you have anything to eat on the way home from school?"

Pause. "Nothing much."

"What was nothing much?"

He looked up at me over the notebook in which he was entering something. "Oh, a Coke."

"And—?"

"A hamburger . . ."

"And—?"

He sighed. "Three candy bars. That's all."

"No wonder you could bear the thought of no dinner with such stoic calm."

"Well, I took a look at that casserole this morning. Mom, those were leftovers of leftovers."

"Not to be compared with the delights of a greasy hamburger containing heaven knows what."

"Don't be mad," he said, and smiled.

I smiled back. "All right."

I went back down the hall, taking off my coat on the way and putting it into a closet.

When Ewen appeared in a few moments, I was turning hamburgers over in the broiler. "I'm glad you're so fond of hamburgers. Because that's what you're getting."

"There's no such thing as too many hamburgers," said Ewen the gourmet. "Or hot dogs." He opened a can of dog food and, holding off Wilma, who was going into transports, put it into her dish. "There you are, old girl." He then started to open a can of cat food, and, on cue, Nemesis made a stately entrance.

"What was that you were going to tell me?" Ewen asked. "Hey—you said we'd inherited something. What was it?"

"A house," I said. "In Brooklyn Heights."

Ewen stared at me. "You're putting me on."

"No. I'm not." And as we sat down to eat I gave him the expurgated version of my conversation that I had prepared on the way home.

Ewen knew nothing of Dauntry, the failed marriage or my flight in shame and fear and humiliation. He didn't know that the name he bore was my maiden name. In fact, Ewen knew nothing except what I had told him: that his father, a soldier, had died in Vietnam. I had given myself a lot of good reasons for that lovely and fictitious myth: a fatherless boy needed something admirable to hang on to; the truth was much too ugly for him to hear until he was an adult; there was no use in muddying up his boyhood with stories about me that would simply confuse him. And the fact that New York was more than half a continent away from everyone I had known and everyone who had known me made it easier. Until about a year ago, Ewen had accepted everything—even the absence of pictures or snapshots of his father. ("We were married such a short time, darling, and were always meaning to take pictures, but never got around to them.")

But in the past few months, precipitated by his courses in school as much as anything else, Ewen had begun to ask some searching questions:

"How come my father wasn't against the war?" (Answer:

"He was one of the first over there. The war hadn't escalated in 1963 when you were born.")

"How come I've never heard of any relatives on my father's side?" ("He didn't have any family. He was an only child and his parents were dead." That part, at least, was true of Dauntry.)

One day, sooner or later, he would discover that Moncrieff was my maiden name, and when that happened, I would know that truth time had come. But not yet, I would sometimes pray. Not yet. Ewen had his father's uncomfortably penetrating eyes. I had seen—if not doubt—at least confusion creep into their expression when we were having one of the exchanges about his father. I didn't want to see true doubt there and certainly not disillusion and disgust.

I took a deep breath. "I know, Ewen, you said you wanted a house. But supposing I sold it, and with the money we bought a cooperative apartment?"

"No! I'd much rather live in a house. Who wants a co-op?"

"I do," I said, thinking of maintenance men, handymen, elevator operators—all managed by the house and conveniently in Manhattan. "Mr. Metcalf, the lawyer I was talking about, said the house was in terrible condition, that it had been used as a rooming house, that the occupants had put up partitions and that it would take money to get it back in shape."

"Well, then, maybe you wouldn't get so much money for it."

"No. I never heard of Brooklyn Heights being such a desirable location. But apparently it is."

"Sure. Jenny Jerome, Winston Churchill's mother, came from there."

"How do you know?"

"It came up one day in class."

"Well, why didn't you tell me?"

"I can't go around telling you every time I discover where some historic man's mother came from. I mean, Lincoln's mother came from—"

"All right, all right," I said hastily. "I get your point. In that case it will not be hard for you to understand that Mr. Metcalf says I can sell it for a handsome sum. Whereas, if we keep it, and move in there, where are we going to get the money to renovate it?"

"The bank," said my practical son. "And we can use the rent money to pay the bank loan. What's the matter? Why are you looking at me like that?"

"Because I don't know what I did to deserve a son who's ready to take his position as chief financial officer of the First National Bank."

"You're just lucky," Ewen said, and dodged my napkin.

"Look, darling, I'm sorry if this sounds like emotional blackmail, but I'm not sure I need renovating a house to add to my other activities. It's not as though I were in a state of uncertainty as to what to do with my spare time. I know."

"What do you want to do with your spare time?"

"If I had any," I said with emphasis, "I'd like to put my feet up."

Ewen didn't say anything. His long, thin fingers played with the crumbs on the table. I looked down at the shaggy fair hair. We both knew that I had used a powerful and slightly unfair weapon—my widowhood, or what Ewen supposed to be my widowhood. I had disarmed him with false pretenses, and one of these not too distant days he would remember this. My role as widow of a war hero (however wrong Ewen might consider the war), bringing my son up alone, was one thing. Would he see a divorcée who had run away from her husband

and, because of that, bringing up her son alone, in the same sympathetic light? Or would he feel he'd been had? A nice point.

"Can we at least look at it?" Ewen said, shaking back his hair and looking at me.

"Something tells me I'll be sorry. All right. I'll get the keys from the lawyer."

"Did *he* think you should sell it?"

"I guess so. Certainly told me I could get a good price for it."

"I wonder what's in it for him?"

"What do you mean, in it for him?"

"Why should he be so willing for you to sell it? I should think with all those years of it being in court, the way he said, he'd want to hand it over to the owner. Who's going to do the selling for you?"

"I asked him to."

"You're sure eager to get rid of it, aren't you?"

"Well, so would you be if you'd heard the kind of state it was in—with drug addicts and winos living there. Apparently it was the last eyesore in some good street and there've been petitions and everything else going the rounds about it."

"Who's been responsible for it?"

"I don't know. The whole thing was tied up in court."

"Somebody had to rent it to a bunch of deadbeats."

I looked at Ewen. "You know, you're absolutely right. I should have asked all these questions. But I was so taken up with inheriting the place, and so horrified with the way he described its current condition . . ." I hesitated. What was it he said? I could hear the well-modulated, cultivated voice saying, "I'm sorry to go into such grisly detail, but the place is infested with cockroaches and rats, the plumbing is old and my inspectors tell me that the whole place smells like a sewer. I could get a renovator in there to clean it up, but it would cost the earth to do it properly, so I thought, if you wanted to make a sale and get some ready cash, somebody else could have the pleasant job . . ."

And in view of what I had said about my chronic poverty and Ewen's school bills, Laurence Metcalf 's suggestion was not only logical, but kind. I took a breath to explain this to Ewen. But at that moment he looked up at me and I remembered that all he said was, let's look at it. It seemed little enough. "All right, Ewen. We'll go on Saturday."

When I called Metcalf the next morning and told him I wanted to at least see the place, I was surprised at his enthusiastic reaction. "Great. I wanted to suggest that you do that. But you seemed so definite about wanting to sell it."

"Did I? I guess I must have. But Ewen, my son, wants to look at it. He's an animal nut and I think he wants to set up a surgery for animals."

"Why not? They're starting younger and younger these days. Since you work, how about Saturday? I could pick you up in my car and we could drive over there."

"Fine," I said. "Thanks." Like most New Yorkers, riding in a car was a rare luxury for me.

But Ewen wasn't at all happy that evening when I told him. "I'd much rather we saw it alone, Mom. I mean, I don't even know him. Can't you tell him we'll go by ourselves?"

"It doesn't seem very polite, when he offered to drive us. Besides, you may not get tired of the subway, but I do."

A mulish look with which I was well acquainted settled on Ewen's face. "I'd rather we saw it alone. How can we make up our minds if some guy we don't know is bouncing around trying to make us do something we don't want to do? We can't even talk about it."

"And when has the presence of strangers inhibited you from speaking your mind? I can't recall any example."

"Lots. And just because you didn't know I was frustrated, didn't mean I wasn't. And besides, it's not fair. This guy thinks you ought to sell it, too. That's two to one. That's undue pressure."

I sighed. Ewen's conversation was getting increasingly political. But he was also disconcertingly discerning. "With you around, Ewen, I sometimes need an ally."

"Why?"

"Because you're stronger willed than I."

"Nuts."

"No, it's not nuts. You're just like—" I stopped, dismayed. I had never come so near that mistake before.

"I'm just like who? My father?"

"Whom," I said mechanically, and then tacked into the wind. "He was very stubborn, too."

"Sometimes I can't tell when you're telling me the truth or not," Ewen said. "You sound like you started to say something and then said something else. Who'm I supposed to be like?"

"I told you, your father."

"Well, why did you sound so funny? Why shouldn't I be like my father? Not that you ever say anything about him or tell me what he was like. What was the matter with him? Did he go to jail or something?"

"Of course not." I was appalled. Having done everything I could to avoid any circumstances where he should ask such questions, here they came at me blown out of the blue. A coward, I took refuge in agreeing to do what he wanted me to do. "Look, I'll call Mr. Metcalf and say we want to see the house by ourselves." And to make sure Ewen didn't get in any more questions, went down the hall and looked the lawyer up in the telephone book, since it was long after office hours. To my surprise, he didn't live too far away. I dialed the number and waited.

"Hello," he said on the fourth ring.

"This is Antonia Moncrieff. My son . . . he and I have decided that if you don't mind we'll see the house in Brooklyn by ourselves. Please don't take this personally. It's just that Ewen feels that we can be freer if we are alone."

"Of course not. I understand. And I think he's right. But be careful, won't you? The floorboards are rotten in places and some of the stair treads are loose."

My heart sank, but the sight of Ewen, loitering in the hall to make sure that I was doing my duty as he saw it prevented me from recanting. "We'll be careful. But I'd better come down and pick up the keys."

"No need. As you may have noticed when you looked up this number in the directory, I live not too far away. I'll come by if I may and drop them."

"Oh. That's very kind of you. All right. When would you like to come?"

"How about now? I was going to go out for a paper anyhow."

"Fine."

I could hardly be inhospitable, I felt, after turning down his kind invitation for Saturday. I put the receiver down.

"Is he coming over here?" Ewen said on a rising note of indignation.

"Listen, your majesty. I just got us out of a ride to Brooklyn on Saturday that I, personally, would have found much more restful than mass transit. I don't see how Mr. Metcalf's presence could have persuaded me into selling the house because I have made up my mind I want to do that anyway. I did the whole thing because you insisted. So the least I can do is to appear reasonably hospitable. Please try to be polite when he comes."

"He probably just wants to make time with you."

"He wants *what?*"

"Well, you're very pretty," Ewen growled.

Never before had my austere son said anything like that to me. I was overcome. "Do you think so?"

"Of course I think so. Doesn't everybody?"

"Well, you've been pretty reserved about it all these years."

"I don't see any reason to state the obvious."

"Oh, you don't? Do you have to become a male chauvinist pig this early?"

Ewen made a sound rather like a snort and disappeared into his room, followed by Nemesis.

I was in the living room trying to get the papers and magazines back into their rack when the doorbell rang, followed by Wilma's frenetic barking. Our buzzer system from downstairs had long since broken, which was another tenants' grievance, and the second front door, therefore, was kept unlocked. I was just going to open our door when I heard the panel in front of the peephole slide back and then the door being opened.

"Hi." I heard Ewen's cracked alto. "I'm Ewen Moncrieff. Come in."

They were chatting as Ewen brought him in. Wilma, having decided that the intruder presented no threat, was trotting along beside them and Nemesis brought up the rear. I thought Ewen would remove himself and his entourage immediately. But to my astonishment he stayed the brief while Laurence Metcalf was there.

"Here are the keys," the lawyer said, taking them out of his jacket pocket. He looked far less formal than he did at the office and—in some way that I couldn't really define—different. "I told you about the rotten boards—they're just to the right as you go into the living room at the back. And be careful on the stairs."

"That's part of all the repair that you said had to be done," I said, with my eye on Ewen.

"If that were all, there'd be no problem and I would be urging you to take over as soon as possible. However, I think Ewen was right. You should see for yourself. Let me know what you think. What a great cat that is. He looks like he knows he's an Egyptian god." Mr. Metcalf bent down, his hand out. "What's his name?"

"Nemesis," I said.

"How—er—symbolic. Here, Nemesis!"

The cat, who had been staring straight at the lawyer, turned, made his stately way to Ewen and then jumped on his shoulders.

Metcalf stood up. "So much for me! Snubbed!"

"He's not a friendly cat," I said, wishing Ewen would either leave or sit down. He was standing there with Nemesis draped around his shoulders, looking like the sternest of chaperones.

"Well, I've got to be getting along. Let me know how you make out."

I showed Metcalf to the door and then turned to confront Ewen as he came down the hall. "You weren't overflowing with civility. Why did you stay? I felt as though Mr. Barrett of Wimpole Street was in the room."

"Just wanted to make sure he didn't change your mind back."

"When you were not there to stiffen my resolve, I suppose."

Ewen just grinned and went back to his room.

"It's this way," Ewen said, as we emerged from the subway in Brooklyn Heights the following Saturday morning.

"How do you know?" I asked, impressed.

41

"Because I bought a map. I also went to the New York Historical Society and read up on Brooklyn Heights."

I knew that I was the subject of intense propaganda by my son. Nevertheless, I couldn't help it, maternal pride flowed through me. "And what did you find out?"

"Lots of things. That some of the best buildings in New York are here. That there are three basic kinds of architecture—federal, Greek Revival and Italianate Renaissance. Did you know that Brooklyn was another city until 1898 and that its population was nearly a million, the fourth largest city in the country after New York? That they're called brownstones because . . ."

"That's pretty good for somebody who wants to be a vet."

"If I weren't going to be a vet I'd be an architect."

"Why do you want us to live in a house so much?"

"Because it'd be ours. We wouldn't have to hassle with somebody all the time about the heat or the lights or locks on the door." He pushed back his hair. I wondered if a strong sense of property could be inherited.

We passed through street after street of tall row houses, reminding me a little of pictures I had seen of both London and Amsterdam. Some were brownstone-covered, others of mellowed brick. Many had outside stone steps leading up to a first, or parlor, floor, with the area way—the old service entrance, and now basement apartment—a little below street level. I had walked often through streets like this in Manhattan—in the Village, in Chelsea, in Murray Hill and Gramercy Park. But there was a different quality here, quieter and more detached.

Ten minutes later we turned into the street. Plane trees lined either side. The tall houses were well kept. It was a quiet little street, almost just a connecting way between two larger

ones. Children were playing. The street seemed like a print of
itself.

"This is cool," Ewen said.

Then we came to Number Forty-two, and it was as
though we had stepped into a different world.

"Greek Revival," Ewen said, but his voice had suddenly
lost its bounce. It was not so much that it was an obvious slum,
although neglect stared from the chipped and broken window
frames, the dirty panes, the once-painted door now covered
with graffiti, the dull, rusty railings on either side of the steps
going up to the front door. But there was an air of desolation
about it, as though it had lain empty for a long time.

It was a fresh spring morning, but I found myself
shivering. "Funny," I said. "From what Mr. Metcalf told me I
thought it had had tenants until recently. But it looks so
deserted."

"Squatters, maybe," Ewen said.

At that point there was an interruption. A boy of about
Ewen's age who had been loitering on his bike about ten feet
away took the popsicle out of his mouth and said, "You the
new owners?"

"Why do you ask?" I said, which is always a good reply
when you don't want to answer something.

He shrugged. "Everybody says it should be made over
inside from scratch. There've been squatters and drunks and
addicts and everything. And the garden at the back of it—
yuch! It stinks! Lots of parents won't let their kids play
anywhere near it. Not since that boy disappeared two years
ago."

"What boy?"

"Well, he didn't come from around here, but he was
playing with one of the kids on the block and somebody
invited them in. Only the kid that lives here didn't go because

his father said he'd lower the boom on him if he ever went inside, and he'd already had his allowance halved for a week. But the other boy did. And nobody ever saw him again."

"Come on," I said. "That sounds like a bad movie."

The boy's pink cheeks went bright red. His light red-brown fuzzy hair that seemed to stick straight out of his head almost quivered. "It's the truth. We've had the police and everything."

"Okay, so it's the truth," Ewen said. "Now it's ours so the hex is off."

I could have shaken Ewen for letting that cat out of the bag. I looked down at him. "Who's trying to pressure whom right now?"

He gave me a sidelong glance. "I just don't like his attitude. Why don't we go in?"

We went up the steps into a small porch. What had once been a mailbox sagged drunkenly on the wall from one nail. Where the other nail had been was now a hole. At one time the door had been painted a hideous chocolate brown. Now even that was mostly gone under the scratches, gouges and an infinite variety of scrawls, names, dates and pornographic sketches.

"Yikes!" Ewen said, but added hastily, "but a new paint job would do wonders, don't you think, Mom?"

There are times when my son startles me by looking and sounding almost like the man he is in the process of becoming. There are other times when he makes me think of the child he once was. This was one of the latter. At the moment he reminded me of the time when what he wanted more than anything in the world was a bicycle.

"Yes, darling. But if a lick of paint remains the solution to all of our problems, then I would be highly surprised."

For a moment he looked chastened, but his valiant resilience asserted itself. "Let's go in. Maybe it's better inside."

The door opened on what, a century and a quarter before, might have been a beautiful front hallway. But time, tenants and what looked like an irreversible downhill slide had obliterated everything except the graceful proportions. A cheap and filthy linoleum covered the floor. The dark papered walls were splotched and scrawled over and long strips of tattered paper were hanging down. A damp, unpleasant smell hung in the air. The door opening into the room on my right was partly off its hinges.

Ewen and I went through the door into a big square room that looked out over the street. Opposite the windows was an archway and closed double doors. There was no linoleum in here. Underneath the dark paint and varnish there might, I thought, be some beautiful wood. Ewen was walking towards the doors.

"Mom—" he started. Then underneath there was a loud creak and a crack. "Watch out!" I yelled. "The floor-boards."

Ewen leaped nimbly to one side. "I'm okay."

Pulling aside one of the doors, their wood as badly in need of polish as the floor, we went into another square room overlooking the garden.

"Ugh!" Ewen said. "It's like a morgue."

I looked around at the dark paper above and the sombre wooden panels beneath, rising a third of the way up the wall on all sides, broken only by the chimneypiece and windows. "It's all that dark wood," I said, and went over to inspect it. I ran my hand over the heavy and ornate carving that ran not only along the molding but down to the floor where the panels joined. "This must be a Victorian afterthought—and a calamitous one!"

Ewen was at the windows. I went over and stood beside

him and stared out on a wilderness—grass, weeds, nettles, some of it grown waist-high.

"That would take a tidy bit of work," I said.

"But look at the great trees at the end!"

We went from the bottom to the top of the house. On each floor there was a front room and a back room. The upstairs rooms, although sorely in need of repapering and having their floors scraped, were not in such dreadful condition as the first floor. At the very top was a huge attic with a skylight and two dormer windows at each end.

"What a super room," Ewen said. "I could use it as a lab. There's plenty of light and we wouldn't have to do any repapering. I could use it as it is."

Hanging on firmly to my refusal to commit myself, I didn't say anything. Ewen's comment hung in the air. It was so obvious that he wanted me to agree with him that it was difficult not to. But I locked my jaws together and said nothing.

On the way up we had simply glanced into the rooms, but on the way down we examined them. Each room had a fireplace, or what had once been a fireplace. At some point they seemed to have been bricked up. The grates on the top storey—undoubtedly, when the house was built, either the nursery or the servants' quarters—were tiny, too small for anything but small chips of coal. On the floor below, probably the master bedrooms, the ceilings were higher, the grates bigger and the mantels more elaborate. I walked over to the front windows, so thick with dirt that it was almost impossible to see out of them. Nevertheless I did notice that our friend with the fuzzy hair had acquired a few companions, all of whom were standing about and staring up at the house. There was also, I noticed, a man across the street who seemed to be loitering in a desultory fashion. Well, I thought, with a house in this condition, it's no wonder that the neighbors are deeply interested in what happens to it next. In a pleasant, scrubbed, middle-class neighborhood like this, it would be a thorn in the side.

"Mom!" Ewen's voice was a little more cracked than usual. "Could you come here a minute?"

I turned. He sounded odd. Ewen was standing by the back window and had probably been looking out there as I had been staring out the front. But even across this shadowy room his face looked strange, almost frightened.

I went hastily across. "Out there," Ewen said. "That sack. It's got something in it. I could swear it moved. You remember that boy outside said something about a kid disappearing."

In the middle of what might, at one point, have been a pathway, was something under or inside a burlap bag. "It couldn't be that kid," Ewen said almost defiantly. "If that boy outside was telling the truth, the cops must have been over this place with a magnifying glass."

"It's probably old clothes or papers or garbage, Ewen," I said. "And there's a pretty stiff wind. That's probably what made it look as though it moved."

We stared for a while at the desolate garden. High walls, unusual for New York, bounded it on all three sides. Ewen's "great" trees at the end completely concealed whatever was behind them—another garden belonging to the house on the next street, or the house itself.

"You know, it feels funny up here," Ewen said suddenly. And I knew then that I had been increasingly uncomfortable for the past several minutes.

"It's cold." I pulled my light raincoat closer around me.

"Yeah, but, Mom, it was *warm* outside this morning."

"Maybe it's suddenly gotten chilly."

"With the sun out like that?" He waved his hands towards the streaked and clouded pane. And it was quite true:

47

on the other side of all that ancient dirt the sun was throwing a golden light on the bright new green of the trees.

I smiled. "Are you trying to tell me that the place is haunted?" And the moment I said that I shivered.

"Of course not. But there's some draft from somewhere. Let's go down."

I was quite sure then that Ewen would be willing for me to put the place up for sale, and was shocked to discover in myself a sense of disappointment. We started down the curving staircase, the ground floor still hidden from view, when there was suddenly the slamming of a door below followed by rapid footsteps.

"Who's there?" I called out sharply.

Ewen, not one to waste time on questions, was plunging down the stairs two at a time.

"Hey—" he started. Then I heard him cry out and then the sound of something falling.

"Ewen!" I yelled, and ran down the stairs. As I rounded the last curve I saw the hole where a stair tread had come completely off, and, at the bottom, Ewen sort of folded up, holding his leg.

"Ouch!" he said, and started to straighten his leg in a gingerly fashion. I went down beside him. "Ewen, darling, are you all right?"

"Yes, of course I'm all right," he said irritably, hating to be fussed over.

"How's your leg?"

He held it out straight. "It's okay. I hit my shin and there's a bump. But nothing worse."

I stood up and looked around. The front door was slightly open. "We closed that," I said slowly. "And anyway, we both heard those footsteps. Somebody was here."

Ewen got to his feet. "What beats me is that we went up those stairs. Why didn't the top to that step come off then?"

He walked to the back of the hallway, limping slightly. "Here's the top or the tread or whatever you call it." He held up the piece of wood.

"I can't understand—" I started to say when he interrupted me.

"Look, Mom. I think I've figured it out. No big mystery. That lawyer, Mr. Metcalf, said to watch the treads. Maybe the one I fell on was just ready to come off and we loosened it when we went up, so when I came banging down it came off."

"And those footsteps? That door, slamming?"

Ewen grinned, walked over to near the door and picked up a crumpled piece of paper. "He was eating an ice cream bar, remember?" He smoothed out the paper and revealed the familiar cover of an ice cream manufacturer.

"Yes. He was," I said slowly, recalling the boy loitering outside, yet not completely satisfied. "You mean he followed us in?"

"Sure. I would."

That, I knew, was entirely true. Ewen's curiosity was rampant. "Well, how did he get in? I didn't leave the door open."

"There are probably other ways—especially if the house has been empty for a while. Let's go downstairs and see." He glanced at my face. "You just want to think it's something spooky and sinister."

"And you don't?"

"No. I don't. I like this place."

"You didn't like it upstairs. You said it felt funny."

"It was just cold. There was a draft." I was about to remind him of the warm day on which he had commented when, just as we rounded the stairs going down to the basement apartment, there was indeed a cold blast coming up towards us.

"See what I mean?" Ewen asked.

I decided not to concede defeat immediately and, instead, groped around the wall in the dark at the top of the stairs for the light switch. But when I found it and turned the little lever down, there was no light.

"The light doesn't work," I said.

"Doesn't matter," Ewen spoke, from halfway down the stairs. "I can see anyway."

"Maybe you can," I muttered, going slowly, "but it looks as black as pitch to me."

Like the apartments upstairs, the downstairs consisted of two rooms, front and back, plus a small bathroom and a modest but adequate kitchen. And, wonder of wonders, the rooms were in good condition, the woodwork and floors and the painted walls, though an uninspired institutional gray, unmarked. Straight in front of the stairs was the door obviously out into the area way. Ewen strode forward and opened it. Then he tried the outside knob. "This is open, " he said. "He got in here."

"Does it lock?"

"There's one of those buttons here—" and he pushed it. Then he tried the outside knob again. "That's locked it. But I don't think it's that strong. We'll have to have a good lock put on."

"All right, Mr. Fixit, but where do you suppose that cold blast of air came from?"

"I dunno. Maybe . . ."

"Maybe what?"

"Maybe we imagined it."

"Do you really think that?"

"No. I don't. It was there, but I don't think it means anything." He left the front door and went past me to the back. "Hey, look! There's another door."

He was standing in the shadows at the back of the hall. Then he seemed to disappear.

"Ewen!" I called out.

"Here." And he popped into view again. At this point I realized that there was a small L at the back of the hall.

"There's a door here. I'm going to open it."

I don't know what made me say, "Wait for me before you do." I'm really not an overprotective mother. But something very strong pushed those words out of me. I went towards the back. "Good heavens—it's black back here." And it was. When I reached the L my hand groped around the wall and found, again, the light switch. I pushed it down. "This doesn't work either," I said.

"Maybe it lights the other side of the door. I'm going to open it. I bet it leads to some stairs."

"Just a minute." Fumbling in my bag I found a book of matches. I don't smoke. But I pick them up whenever I'm in a restaurant for use around the house. "Okay," I said, striking the match, "you can open the door."

Muttering something about a big deal over nothing, Ewen turned the knob and pushed the door open. "I told you it was just stairs," he said, and I could tell he was about to step down.

The same impulse of a few minutes before made me grab him with my other hand. "Don't move." Standing there, gripping his arm, I looked down. At one time there undoubtedly were stairs. Right now there was nothing but black space, and, far below, barely visible in the match light, what looked like a stone floor.

Chapter 3

"At least let's get a flashlight and *see* what's down there," Ewen said. "I mean it's *dumb* not to. After all, it's our house."

We were back upstairs in the hallway of the parlor floor, arguing. Ewen, not in the least frightened, was fascinated by what lay below that black space. I was still wrestling with my own mental movie, featuring Ewen pitching forward —who knew how many feet—into nothingness to land on a stone floor below. And it was not as though he had not already had one fall today.

"Come on, Mom," Ewen said. "Sure it needs fixing, but I like this house."

"Fixing, you say! Like a whole new staircase."

"There's got to be a hardware store nearby."

I sighed. "All right." And then, because I didn't want to appear as much of a panty-waist as I was about him, I said, "You go. I'll wait here."

He hesitated, then grinned. "Well, don't go looking down any dark stairwells."

"Who do you think I am—you?"

With Ewen gone I walked through the rooms again, treading carefully up the stairs, bending down here and there to see how firmly the treads were nailed.

I had not told Ewen, but at some point when we were walking around the upper floors, I had been swept with strange feelings that I had seen this house before and I wanted to see if that feeling would return. Perhaps because I was looking for it to happen, it didn't. But I did discover that, as before, when I was away from the two lower floors, I was filled with an unexpected sense of contentment—as though this were indeed home.

"But we *are* going to sell this place," I said aloud to myself, standing in the middle of the back room on the second floor. I did not feel convinced. Strolling over, I went and looked through the windows out onto the garden. When I was a child I had grown vegetables back behind the manse and felt enormous pride when they were used by my stepmother at the table. She even—because she was a just woman—paid for them. If that two-foot-high jungle of weeds and nettles were cut and—

There was a loud rat-tatting at the door. I knew it was Ewen but I hesitated a moment. There was something about the garden that had caught my attention, something I noticed. What was it?

The knocking repeated itself, and this time it sounded like both fists. Patience was not Ewen's leading characteristic. But then, nor was it mine. I turned away from the window not having uncovered what it was about the garden that was nagging at me. But on my careful way downstairs, testing each tread as I stepped on it, I suddenly remembered: that lumpy sack lying in what was once a path was no longer there. I paused on the stairs, thinking about it. And then I decided that I must have been right about it being simply paper that had been blown there by the spring wind and had now been blown away.

"I thought for a minute you must have stepped down that hole," Ewen said cheerfully as I let him in.

"It didn't seem to fill you with undue mourning," I said.

"Well, when you opened the door, I knew it wasn't true."

"Logical."

He grinned. "I got a big flash, and the man said these batteries were extra long lasting. He was real pleased when I told him that we now owned this house. Said it had been a neighborhood headache for years. And there were a lot of kids my age fooling around there."

"Ewen," I forced myself to say, "I still want to sell this place."

He stood there, looking down at the flashlight which he was switching off and on. "It's your house," he said, shrugging. And somehow the change from ours to yours affected me far more than an argument or a direct assault on my decision.

"Let's go and look down that hole," I said.

Going down the first flight of stairs was a lot easier now. And when we shone Ewen's powerful light down the black space immediately at the cellar door, what was revealed was a rickety flight of wooden stairs shoved to one side. Bits of broken timber both on the stairs and the two-by-four columns that must have supported them showed that they had simply become unstuck and could be reinstated and reinforced.

"But why were they put over there?" I said. "A body who had been here before could fall down if he weren't watching his step."

"Maybe they moved them there for safety. If they were

broken but didn't show it, somebody could fall by stepping down onto them."

"Yes. That's true. Shine the light around so that we can see what else is down there."

The round white light passed over a dirt floor and rested on a furnace. Then veered to the wall to reveal old fuse boxes.

"Mr. Metcalf said the place was full of rats," Ewen said with a note of indignation. "I don't see any. And they'd be here if they were anywhere. I think he didn't want us to live here."

"Ewen, you're biased, although I can't think why. He was a perfectly nice man. Why don't you like him?"

"I didn't say I didn't like him. I just said I didn't think he wanted us to live here."

"Well, even you could hardly call this place in excellent condition for a widow with child."

"But it's not as bad as he said."

It was while we were on the way up that we heard the knock on the front door. "I'll see who it is," Ewen said.

I was not far behind when he opened the door. There stood a good-looking young couple. "Hi," the man said. "We heard through the grapevine that this place might be for sale. We're looking for a place. I guess you're looking at it too."

The woman said, "Can we come in?"

They were dressed in jeans and looked like a thousand other young couples both of whom work in the professions in New York. Ewen had turned towards me, and as clearly as though he were speaking, I heard him asking me to send them away, to tell them that they were mistaken, the house was not for sale. I looked over at my son. His blue-green eyes were watching me steadily.

"How did you hear?" I temporized, playing for time.

The young woman laughed. "This is a very close neighborhood. That's why we like it. I don't know which particular neighbor was the first to give us the good word, but we must have heard it from several in the course of a morning's walk."

By this time, without my actually having issued the words of invitation, they were both in the front hall. The man looked down at the linoleum. "That's a crime," he said, kicking it with his heel. "I mean, to cover floors like these with this garbage."

"You've been in here before?"

For a second he hesitated. Then his wife smiled. "All the houses on this side of the block are alike and the parlor floors have beautiful wood."

"I take it you already live in the neighborhood," I said. "My name is Antonia Moncrieff. This is my son, Ewen. We own the house."

"You're lucky," the man said. He glanced around. "That is, if you have money. It'd take a fair hunk of it to make this place livable. Fortunately," he said easily, "we have it." He smiled. It was the smile that did it. With it, I knew I had seen this young man before.

"You know, you look familiar," I said. "I must have seen your picture somewhere."

The wife smiled. "I guess you have—all over the place. My husband is one of the more successful male models."

That would account for the money that her husband was so relaxed about admitting he had.

"Can we go over it?" the man asked, going forward to the stairs. "It's just what we've been looking for."

"Of course," I said, keeping my eyes firmly away from Ewen's. "But watch the stairs. Ewen, here, had a tumble when one of the treads came off."

"Oh, we're used to looking at houses in broken-down states," the woman said pleasantly and with another smile. It

56

occurred to me that she, too, looked as though she were a model.

For no reason at all, I decided that I would go with them on their tour of the house. "I'll show you around," I said.

They both turned. "No need," he said, showing a lot of beautiful teeth. "We know just exactly what we want to look for."

"Yes," I responded sweetly, mounting the stairs, "but I'd like to be on hand if you have any questions." I glanced back and smiled.

He shrugged. "Suit yourself." I grinned to myself. All of a sudden his graciousness had developed a boorish edge.

The tour was not an exercise in neighborliness. The Beautiful People, as I called them to myself, asked no questions, and I offered no comments. As we went from room to room and floor to floor, they somehow seemed less and less like a house-hunting couple. They stalked through the rooms more like inspectors than purchasers.

Finally, as we were about to go up to the attic, the woman turned. "Do you mind awfully if we go on alone? It's so important for us to *feel* things together."

Ewen, of course, had objected to Mr. Metcalf on the same grounds. How could I refuse? Yet I found myself saying, "I'm terribly sorry. I do so sympathize. But, you see, I have been warned by our lawyer always to accompany any would-be buyer. There are unsafe places, and should you injure yourselves—particularly," I added, in a heaven-sent inspiration, "in view of your profession—I might be heavily liable. I'm sure you understand."

They did understand—fully—that I was not going to leave them, and they didn't like it one bit. But there was nothing they could do about it. After that, they threw themselves into their role of house-hunters, commenting on the front view, the back view, the closets, where their bed would be, the special furniture they had made, where it would fit, how they could widen the upstairs fireplaces and take the plaster off the wall to reveal the brick. It was a splendid performance, and I couldn't rid myself of the feeling that that was exactly what it was—a performance. They should, I thought, be getting Equity rates. Finally we returned to the parlor floor. The man turned.

"What is your asking price?"

It was, perhaps, unlucky for me that Ewen came out of the living room at that moment and stood there, looking up at me. The figure—an exorbitant one—was in my mouth. I cleared my throat.

"Of course," the man went on, "in its present condition, you couldn't expect to get a full price."

"No? Brooklyn Heights is a very desirable location, I'm told."

"Yeah, but it'd take fifty thou to put it in decent shape."

Whether it was because their physical arrogance aroused the angry mouse in me, or whether it was their casual mention of a figure that represented to me a fortune, I don't know, but I heard my own voice, as cool as his, saying,

"One hundred and fifty thousand."

"That's ridiculous," the woman said angrily.

"You've got to be kidding," the man said.

"I'm not," I replied, feeling, for some reason, deliciously revenged. "That is, if I decide to sell it. Why don't you leave me your telephone number and I'll call you?"

"That's not what the lawyer—" the man started.

"What lawyer?" I asked.

"Ours," the man said, heading for the door.

I followed them as they went through and started down the front steps. "Aren't you going to leave me your number?"

"Don't call us, we'll call you," he sneered.

"Mom," Ewen asked anxiously as I went back into the house, "what if they call and say they'll pay it?"

"They won't," I said with absolute conviction. "The woman was right. That was an absurd price."

"I didn't like them. There's something phony about them."

I turned to look at my perceptive son. "Yes. There was. But I thought it might have to do with the life-style they exuded, which seemed to be wall-to-wall everything."

Ewen grinned. He and I went over the house again. After a while, when we were coming downstairs, he said, "It wouldn't take fifty thou to put this in shape. That's a lot of garbage."

"Maybe if you wanted mink-lined walls it would."

"But we don't."

"No."

"Mom, maybe one hundred and fifty thou plus fifty thou—which equals two hundred thou—"

"If you say thou again I'm going to wash out your mouth with soap."

"Okay. Which equals two hundred thousand dollars, is not a big deal for them."

"Meaning?"

"Maybe he'll call you up and offer it. What would we do with all that money?"

I took a deep breath. "I'm glad you asked that. A few items that occur to me are, a better apartment, money for your school and college, a few clothes for me, a few bills paid, a few dollars in the bank, a decent vacation next year instead of day camp for you and a four-day bus trip to Montreal for us both. Maybe we could spend some time on a ranch. You always said you wanted to."

"Not that much. And anyway, I thought we had a cool time last year."

"Yes," I admitted. "So did I. I guess you're too young to understand the peace that passes all understanding that comes with a bank balance in five figures. But it's academic anyway. They're not about to call and say okay."

But I was wrong.

We locked up and went home. Two hours later, I was making a dress and watching a movie on television. Ewen was lying full length on the sofa with Einstein, his white rat, sitting on his midriff, when the phone rang.

"See who that is, would you, Ewen?"

I heard him go to the phone. In a few seconds he was back, "It's for you," he said in a funny voice.

I looked up. Ewen's face had that white, set look that I had seen on it once or twice—one time I remembered particularly was after Muffin, his previous dog, had been run over.

"What's the matter?" I asked.

"It's that man, the model. He wants to talk to you. He's just the kind of creep who'd have two hundred thousand." With that Ewen came in, picked up Einstein, pushed the unfortunate rat into his pocket and stalked back down the hall.

I went slowly to the telephone. Ewen's door, I noticed, was still open. I had always, I thought, wanted him to go to a good university and maybe before that, much as I'd hate to have him away, a good prep school, where he could be among men. That cost far more than I could ever hope to make. The money this man was about to offer would supply all of that with plenty left over. I did not think of myself as particularly materialistic, but I had never had enough money, and the prospect of being solvent for the first time in my life was powerful medicine. I picked up the receiver.

"This is Antonia Moncrieff."

"Hi," he said. "I was at the Brooklyn Heights house today." Vaguely I noticed that he did not give a name, then or now. "You quoted a price of one hundred and fifty thou . . ."

Ewen suddenly appeared in the hall, and for some reason, whether by design or not, most of his menagerie seemed to be in attendance. Wilma whuffed beside him, rubber bone in her mouth. Nemesis was on the other side. Out of his pocket peered Einstein. On his shoulder was Mr. Ears. I waited to see if the white mice and gerbils would turn up.

"Yes," I said.

"It's extortion, but we'll pay it."

Maybe it was Ewen and his zoo, maybe it was my aversion to fashionable jargon, maybe it was Mouse Moncrieff against the Beautiful People. Whatever it was, I heard myself say, "I'm sorry. I've changed my mind. The house is not for sale." And whatever reply the man might have made was drowned out in a whoop and a yell from Ewen. I hung up and was enveloped in a hug.

"All right, Ewen," I said. "Just don't go mad and get a goat. You smell like an animal yourself."

"I am an animal," he said indignantly. "A human animal. What's wrong with that? Oh, Mom, you're really cool! That's great!"

When I got to the office Monday morning I called Mr. Metcalf to tell him my decision.

"That's wonderful," he said.

Remembering Ewen's statement about the lawyer not wanting us to live in the house, I was a little surprised and decided to shame the devil by being honest. "Ewen, my son, said he thought you didn't want us to live there."

"In the sense that I don't think you know exactly what you've taken on, that's right. But I'm always delighted when an old house stays in the family."

"I'm not the family."

He paused. Then he said in an odd voice. "No, but you're the legitimate inheritor from the person picked by the last member of the family. The house was not put up for sale. That's what I meant." I had a strange feeling that that was not what he had started to say, and then decided I was imagining things.

"Speaking of being up for sale," I said, "we had quite an offer yesterday." And I told him about the couple.

"You really must want that house if you turned down an offer of a hundred and fifty thousand."

I was so pleased that he said thousand instead of the currently fashionable thou that I decided Ewen's suspicions of him must be unworthy. "You keep talking about this huge burden I'm taking on, and it's making me nervous. You sound like the model who said it would take fifty thou. The cellar stairs are broken, the parlor floors are covered in a hideous linoleum, the stair treads are loose and the whole place, including and especially the front door, needs painting. What else?"

"Did you have—er—occasion to try the plumbing while you were there?"

"No," I said, with a hollow feeling around my middle. "Is it that bad?"

"Wait until you try it, and then tell me the answer."

"You're nothing but a delight. Any other ominous warnings?"

"Not at the moment. Want me to try and find some kind of a contractor to get an estimate and do your repairs?"

"Would you? That would be marvelous. By the way, is there any cash left at all to take care of these?"

"Yes. Not much. A few thousand."

"And the rest of it went to looking for the vanished grandson and fighting off the rest of the family?"

"I'm afraid so." There was a constraint in his voice that wasn't there before.

A question that I had been vaguely aware of at the back

of my mind suddenly surfaced. "How much was there originally?"

"Does it matter? I told you: investigations, time, labor, fees—they all cost money."

"And lawyers," I found myself saying.

"And lawyers. We have to eat, too."

The sudden hostility had appeared out of nowhere. Characteristically, I was beginning to feel guilty, and then I caught myself: the question I had asked—How much money had been originally left with the estate?—was a legitimate one. "I know you have to eat, Mr. Metcalf. But why should you feel so defensive? It seems to me my question was in order."

"It was, of course. My apologies. I'm afraid you got the fallout from an unpleasant encounter I had with a client practically before I sat down this morning. He was lying in wait outside my door and fought me into my office. He seemed to think that lawyers specialize in fleecing the widow and orphan."

I was about to say that I was both when I decided that he might not see the humor of it. "I understand."

"Look," he said rather quickly, "why don't I dig out a contractor and an estimate and call you back. My secretary has been standing in my doorway for about five minutes with an expectant expression, and obviously wants me for something. Talk to you later."

A few minutes after I had hung up it occurred to me that he had not told me the size of the original Standish estate left to my aunt.

. It was about eleven when Melissa put her head around the door. "Would you like to hear the latest rumor as to who your Big Author is?"

"No," I lied. Melissa's visits were never known to last less than half an hour and I had a lot of work to finish before I attended the postponed meeting with Max and his author at three that afternoon. "Max has already put it off once, which means he'll probably put it off again. Anyway, I'd rather be surprised."

"You'll be surprised all right. However, if you don't want to know, far be it from me to force unwelcome information on you. I'll leave now—"

"All right, Melissa," I said, noticing that she had not moved from the door. "Who is it?"

With a fine sense of drama, Melissa took out a cigarette, tapped it against her finger, lit it and put away her lighter. Then she blew out a plume of smoke.

"Before you drop your bombshell, Melissa, tell me why you didn't go into the theatre. All of that build-up should precede, at least, a first-act curtain."

"As a matter of fact," Melissa said, "that's exactly what I originally came to New York to do—break into the theatre."

"Wasn't your talent instantly perceived? No wonder the theatre is declining if they failed to engage talents like yours."

"No need for sarcasm, dearie. I found I liked publishing better than I liked waitressing, which is what I did most of the time while I was waiting to be discovered. You realize, of course, that you've entirely spoiled the effect I was trying to achieve."

"Sorry. Who is it?" Afterwards I remembered that moment of indifference. It was to be my last.

"It's only a rumor, now. But—Adam Kingsley."

I stared at Melissa, my stunned attitude all she could have wished for. "*Adam Kingsley?*" I repeated stupidly.

"The same. The Great Man. The Pulitizer Prize-winner himself."

"But I thought he was . . ."

"Dead? No, as Mark Twain said, the notices of his death were grossly exaggerated. Probably wishful thinking on the part of all the people who hated him. Although, what with the accident and killing that child, there've been times when he undoubtedly wished he could oblige and be dead. Of course, the accident nearly killed him, too. Driving into a concrete embankment at God knows how many miles per hour could make an unholy mess. There was talk about his head or face or something."

"Are you sure, Melissa?" I faltered. "Nobody's heard of him for years."

"No, I'm not sure. I told you it was a rumor. But my gut feeling is that it's true." Melissa, now with the cork out, rattled on happily. "He's been out of jail now for some time; years, I think. But except for that interview practically at the gates of the penitentiary as he was going in, he dropped into a hole. I guess it was a case of how are the mighty fallen. You can't be a culture hero and then go on coast-to-coast benders and kill a child in a hit-and-run accident and remain a public idol. When the adoring fans turn, they turn. And that elaborate washing of the hands was led by his former publisher. God, that was ten or eleven years ago—more maybe! I remember when that letter from his publisher came out in the *Times,* to the general effect that no talent, however great, could make up for certain departures from human decency—I recall that phrase very well. Sort of like Profumo: it wasn't that he was cuddling down with whatever her name was, it was that he lied about it in the House of Commons. Well, Kingsley's publisher—Bob Hershey or Herschel or something—said it wasn't actually hitting the child in drunk driving, it was leaving the kid to bleed to death. There was medical evidence that the boy might have recovered if help had been gotten. Anyway, that was the last anybody heard from Kingsley . . . Now it seems he's been up in New Hampshire working on a farm . . . or something."

"Melissa—where did you get all this?"

Melissa assumed an expression of overwhelming virtue. "I never reveal my sources."

"Come *on!*"

"Well, if you must pry—some of it came from Julie."

"The typist? How on earth would she know?"

"When Sonia's pushed, which is a large part of the time, she sometimes borrows Julie to help out." Sonia Roth was Max's secretary.

Suddenly it all sounded as though it might be true, and the fear I had been pushing away now got a fang-like grip on my midriff. Somehow I found my voice. "But Bainbridge was never his publisher."

"True. Which is where our Max, superhunter, comes in. How he found out where Kingsley was and that he was working on a book, rumor doesn't relate. But that's who it is! At least, that's who they say it is."

Melissa, ending on a triumphant note, was walking around the office, hands in her jacket pocket. She turned then, facing me, her back to the window. I quickly turned away in my swivel chair, but not quickly enough.

"Antonia, are you all right? You look as though . . . You look terrible. I never realized you had so many freckles. They're standing out like you had measles. What on earth did I say?"

"Nothing," I said. And then I did what I have always done when my back is to the wall: I lied. "I had a bug over the weekend. The doctor told me I should stay home. I was feeling dizzy this morning . . ." I babbled on and on with my symptoms, my upheavals in the night, my Sunday in bed. Anything, anything to keep her from making any connection between the way I looked (and I was well aware that my freckles, almost invisible usually, stood out like gray pebbles when all color had vanished) and the news she had just handed me. For the moment, anyway, it looked as though I had succeeded.

"Well, why didn't you tell me, you silly ape, instead of letting me natter on like this? For heaven's sake, go home. I hope Ewen took good care of you when you were on your bed of pain. Why didn't you call me? It's not as though I lived on Staten Island."

"I guess I just didn't think. Melissa, would you be an angel . . . please don't be offended . . ."

"But you'd like me to get the hell out. Okay. But only if you promise to call me if you don't feel better."

When Melissa left, I got up and closed the door. I was well aware that the entire staff would know that I had had an attack of something before the morning was out, but there was nothing I could do about it. I was also aware that I had sewn the seeds of yet more trouble for myself by my lie about the weekend. My stepmother used to have a saying, "If you tell a lie, you'd better have seven more waiting to back it up." Melissa was very fond of Ewen, something about which I felt occasionally guilty, because I knew he wasn't that fond of her. Her probing questions and bossy manner put him off, and he had had no occasion to see the other side of her—her warmth, loyalty and support when the going got tough, which I had observed in a dozen different political struggles around the office. If she happened to call me on the telephone and got Ewen, she would be quite capable of engaging him in some heavy-handed humor about carrying chicken soup to his ailing mother. Well, I thought, putting my now genuinely aching head in my hands, that was, at the moment, the least of my worries. My major concern, a concern that was churning my insides to mush, was what I was going to do if the rumor were true and it was Adam Kingsley.

After a few minutes I got up and stared at myself in the mirror. Would he recognize me?

Thirteen years is a long time. And the difference between the eighteen-year-old frightened freshman I had been and the person I was now was even—I devoutly hoped—greater. The one thing that remained stubbornly identifiable was my hair. As Melissa had said, nobody with my copper-colored hair should ever have been called Mouse. Brighter than auburn, darker than Titian, it was, my father once said, the color of a copper beech, a tree common enough in the British Isles. The rest of me was totally undistinguished: gray-green eyes, pale skin and a thin face to match my thin body. Straight hair and a flat body had not yet become fashionable in my small Rocky Mountain college when I arrived there straight from a Presbyterian manse, frightened half out of my wits that everyone would instantly see me as the failure I knew myself to be. To put off that evil moment as long as possible and in the not very great hope that I could achieve the attractiveness I longed for, I wore my hair as curly as rollers and a home permanent could make it, and on the rare occasions when I was asked out, donned a stiff black organdy that even I would not have found becoming if my stepmother hadn't forbidden me to wear it on the ground that no nice unmarried girl wore black. To complete the impression I longed to convey, I ineptly filled it out on top with foam rubber and padding.

But after Ewen was born I abandoned such furbelows, as much for economic reasons as anything else. Hairdressers cost money. My hair, as straight as nature had made it, was pulled into a twist at the back. Once, an eon ago, a man had filled his hands with it and called me Copperhead . . . From reflex I pushed away the old memory that could still cause me so much pain. Instead of cheap organdy I now wore shirts and skirts and slacks and suits. Today it was a tawny-colored shirt and slacks. Except for my hair, my own father wouldn't recognize me. But it was a big "except."

I stood there staring. I could call Max and tell him I couldn't work on his author's manuscript, that I already had too much to do . . . that I was not senior enough or skilled enough, and he would treat such stupidity with the contempt it deserved. Max did not suffer fools gladly. I could do what Melissa suggested (although not for the reason she gave) and go home, sick. I could . . .

The telephone rang.

Still contemplating my options, I picked it up. "Yes?"

"Antonia? Max. Could you please come into my office right away. There's somebody here I want you to meet."

"Is it. . . ? " I stammered, as fright sent a chill up my body. "I thought it was this afternoon."

"Well, he came in this morning instead, which is even better because it gives you more time to settle how you're going to work this together."

I stood there after he hung up and stared at my desk as the minutes passed. Max, the son and grandson of what was called around the office The Founding Family, was a genial and informal man, called by everybody down to the mailroom boys by his first name. Which did not mean that from time to time he did not succumb to a fit of being the Bainbridge of Bainbridge. And he was obviously in the grip of such a fit now. Incredibly, and for a minute or two, I thought of simply walking out, giving notice over the phone and trying to find another job. But the sheer madness of such an act instantly presented itself. How would I explain such an inexcusably abrupt leave-taking to any prospective employer? And how much of a reference or recommendation could I expect from Max if I pulled that trick on him? I was hired to do just what he was summoning me to do now: work on the manuscript of a writer he had brought in. Reality was reality. Part of my problem, I sometimes thought, was that I had always known that.

The phone buzzed again.

Once or twice I had heard Max's bark when he was really

annoyed. I didn't want to hear it now. There was nothing to do but go down the hall to his office. I opened the door and walked out.

My first thought as I entered Max's office was that Adam was as big as I remembered him. He and Max, who had been occupying chairs in front of the desk, stood up when I entered the room. Preoccupied and nervous, I vaguely noticed a huge German shepherd behind Adam. With his back to the window, his face was partly in shadow and he was wearing dark glasses, but the hollows under his wide cheekbones were pronounced, and obviously Melissa had been right about the injury to his head, because his face was a network of scars. Something very like dizziness hit me, making the light in the room dance. Unable to greet him casually, I turned to Max. "I'm sorry I was delayed, Max."

Max gave a quick nod, then said, "Antonia, this is Adam Kingsley. Adam, this is Antonia Moncrieff, who will be working with you on your book." It was as he said that that something hit me with stunning impact: how could I have forgotten? In that incredible year at college I had been Mary Leigh. Leigh, because I was Dauntry's wife. Mary, because that was the name I had always been called by my family. It was my first baptismal name, Antonia, having been added as a gesture of gratitude to a fine Czech woman who became my mother's closest friend and my godmother. So that if by some happy chance Adam did not now recognize that hysterical frightened student in the assured woman who would help him with his manuscript, then my name would not give me away. Feeling reprieved, I turned towards Adam. His hand was out. A second before he spoke I registered there was something odd about the way he held it so still, about the way he held his head. Then he said abruptly. "I'm blind. I thought Max had told you."

"Sorry, Adam. I forgot," Max said. "Which you can take as a compliment if you like. Antonia, why don't you go and sit over there on the sofa."

It was terrible to be so relieved that someone was blind, but there was no question but that I was overwhelmed with relief. "That's a beautiful dog," I said, ashamed at my happiness.

Adam didn't say anything. We all sat down.

"Antonia," Max said, "Adam has brought in his new book. I've read it and like it enormously, but Adam and I both think it needs work, which is where you come in. I want you to read it as quickly as you can and then the two of you can get together. I can't see any problem there, but time *is* a problem. It's been fifteen years since Adam's last book, which, as we all know, was not received kindly, and nearly twenty years since his Pulitzer Prize. This book, in my opinion, has the potential of being even better than that and I'd like to bring it out on the anniversary of the Prize book, which will be next spring—April fifteenth. But aside from the usual static connected in trying to push a book through that fast, there are the mechanical difficulties connected with Adam's —er—blindness."

I saw Max glance quickly at Adam, who seemed without expression. "Maybe, Adam, if you could explain the process . . . ?"

"I dictated the book onto tapes. Then, also on tapes, I corrected it. Then I typed it."

The question was only in my mind, yet he answered it immediately, as though I had asked it. "Touch-typing is taught in the rehabilitation of the blind." He went on, "Normally you would suggest changes and I would simply make them into the manuscript or type new pages, and resubmit them and they might be changed again. It would speed things up a lot if we could discuss certain changes. I would tape the discussion, then dictate the changes either to a stenographer or onto another tape. They could be transcribed by a typist and fitted into the whole, and then you could read the finished chapter to me. If this cuts into your spare time I will be happy to pay you overtime." Before I could reply, he said quickly, "Max is going to give me a generous advance so I can afford to."

"It's not generous, Adam. I expect us to make plenty out of this book, so no need to get your pride up."

"I'm not. If I didn't agree with you that we'll both make money, I wouldn't accept such a large advance. But I would like this book to be published in April, and that will take a lot of doing. If Mrs. Moncrieff can afford the time, fine. If it would be difficult for her, I'd rather she wouldn't try. We can find someone else."

How devoutly I wished they would! I was scrambling in my mind to think of a tactful way of suggesting that they do just that when I heard Max say rather sharply, "No matter how much time it takes I want Antonia to do it. She's an excellent editor and she's always been skilled at working with authors, however difficult." There was a quick intake of breath as he caught himself. "I didn't mean—" His cheeks went bright red. "I'm sorry, Adam, I didn't mean to imply that you were difficult."

For the first time I saw Adam smile. "Why not? I am. We both agree that the book needs revision. I imagine that that is where the agreement ends. On what exactly is to be done is where we'll most likely diverge. I've always been stubborn, and being blind—by the way, it's not a dirty word: you can use it without embarrassment—hasn't made me less so. If there is an argument and I lose, it will only be after I have been convinced that I am wrong. And that's not easy."

"All right. Your point is taken. I'll make one of my own. Since I'm the publisher I'm going to exercise my right in deciding which of the editors here is going to work with you.

D'accord?" Max was sometimes given to expressions in French, which had been his mother's native language.

Adam laughed. *"D'accord."* His head turned in my direction. "Is that in accord with you, Mrs. Moncrieff?"

There was only a fraction of a second's pause before I answered, but, as I was to learn again and again, a hesitation, a pause, a pulling back that most sighted people would miss, the hearing concentration of a blind man will pick up.

"Perhaps Mrs. Moncrieff should have something to say about it, Max. You may be the publisher, but it's her time."

Max looked at me and opened his mouth. Then he closed it again. Then he said, "Well, Antonia?"

In that short space I had had time to think that there really was no choice. There was only one other editor who could do what he wanted me to do, and she was more than fully occupied with a biographical series that was being launched. If it were not I, then Max would have to hire an outside editor, freelance, which meant a lot more expense, and I would have to have a very sound reason indeed to suggest that he pay through the nose for somebody to do something for which I had been specifically hired and in which I was, however immodest it might sound for me to state it, particularly skilled. Besides, Adam was blind. He could not see me. I was safe.

"It's all right with me, Max. I'll be glad to work on Mr. Kingsley's book." No, not that safe, I reflected. I had almost said, "Adam's book," which would have been all right if I had been the kind of person who used first names immediately. But I was not, and Max knew it, and Adam would know it. I would have to be careful.

"All right. Here you are." Max handed over a heavy box. Its weight told me it was a large book. Max said, "Adam is staying at the Raleigh Hotel. I wanted him to stay with Betty and me but he's a nut about his independence, so when you get this read, you can reach him at the hotel."

I was leaving when Adam, who had stood up again, asked abruptly, "Mrs. Moncrieff, have we met before?"

Fear went through my body again like a spasm, paralysing, for a second or two, my tongue. Before I said anything, Adam added, "Your voice is familiar."

"No, Mr. Kingsley," I said, lying in a steady voice, "we haven't." It would have been all right if I had left it there. But, of course, like most liars, I couldn't leave it simple. "I've only been in publishing for the past nine years and . . . " my voice trailed off as, too late, I saw where that sentence was leading me.

"And I've been in jail for those years, you were about to say? No, only for two years, and that ended ten years ago. But you're right in a way. I've stayed very much out of sight. No, if I am right and I have heard your voice before, it must go back at least twelve years ago."

"Twelve years ago you were in England, weren't you, Antonia?" Max said.

"Yes," I said, knowing that that was what I had put in my résumé. "We haven't met, Mr. Kingsley. Perhaps my voice reminds you of someone else's." I didn't want to pursue that, either. If he ever ran that down he'd come up with the right answer. "I'll call you at the hotel as soon as I've read this."

It was after I had returned to my office and shut the door that I realized I was shaking. Well, I told myself, get used to it. This is just the beginning. . . .

I decided not to begin reading the manuscript until I got home where, after Ewen had gone to bed, I could be free from interruption. But in the meantime, I had better finish up with what was on my desk and turn over what couldn't be finished to somebody else.

I had been working about an hour when the door opened and Melissa poked her head in. Seeing I was there, she came all the way in. "I do hope I'm not interrupting," she said agreeably and quite insincerely, and wiggled onto the edge of the table next to my desk.

I toyed with the idea of telling her she was, but knew that nothing short of a frontal attack would have any effect. "Now tell me everything," she said. "I was right, wasn't I? I checked with the receptionist and she said it was Adam Kingsley. I think it's wildly exciting. Think of the publicity! I'd better speak to Max about a release."

I decided that I might as well make use of Melissa's hoard of publishing gossip without, if possible, showing too much interest. Not that, under the circumstances, curiosity would be unnatural. But Melissa's perceptions were uncommonly sharp. "What baffles me," I said casually, "is how totally he dropped out afterwards. You'd think that some enterprising reporter would have dug something up, or some editor would have sent a reporter to nose him out."

Melissa swallowed the bait. "I think they did when he got out of jail. But he did a sort of Salinger. I'm not sure how, but either he covered his tracks so completely that they didn't know where he was all this time, or he managed to evade their best bloodhounds."

"Speaking of dogs," I said.

"Were we? I thought we were talking about Adam Kingsley. I wonder what happened to the beautiful Sally?"

"His wife?"

"Yes, of course his wife. The radiantly lovely—the columnists' phrase, not mine—Sally Pembroke Kingsley. The girl who had everything, including the latest fashionable writer. Charter member of the Beautiful People . . . "

"You sound bitter."

"I suppose I do. I always resent it when one of those society babes throws her net over an honest member of the proletariat. God knows she and her set didn't do him any good. His second novel was a comedown, but nobody paid any attention to that because everybody's second novel is a comedown. But the third was a disaster. And I think the fact that he was geting drunk in all of the in places on both sides of the Atlantic had a great deal to do with that. Question: Can success spoil honest writer? Answer: Yes indeedy, with the speed of light. With his upbringing on some primitive New England farm . . ."

"Canadian."

"All right, Canadian, then . . . " She bent a questioning look on me. "How did you know that?"

"Didn't everybody? I thought the world knew. There were certainly enough articles about him. We had him in our Contemporary Lit course, anyway."

"Well, with his raisings, the fleshpots of the jet set were bound to rip him up. It was a long time ago, but I worked with his original publisher before coming here, and I gathered that the two years or so before the accident, he hardly ever drew a sober breath."

My memory was serving me with the kind of visual flashes that play so large a part in today's movies:

Adam on the dais in the lecture room, a tall, lanky, big-shouldered man who somehow seemed larger than life, the sun on his fair hair and in his face, making his eyes blaze with an aqua fire, energy pouring from him like heat from a furnace, holding that group of some fifty-odd boys and girls in some kind of trance. Did they all want to be writers? Of course not, but for an hour a day in that six weeks' summer school course, they believed they did, and that the magic that would enable them to become Fitzgeralds and Hemingways and Kingsleys—especially, in that class and at that time, Kingsleys—would flow from the compelling, driving creature in front of them.

"If he told me I could write War and Peace," *one enraptured boy said, "I'd write* War and Peace."

"Me too," sighed his girl. And meant it.

And I? I had started out the class in the back row and moved slowly forward as the weeks went on. Everyone else crowded around Adam. I didn't dare, for fear of the rebuff I was sure I would get. Others flocked to the rap sessions in the studio attached to the cottage that Adam and his wife were given and where Adam could usually be found, holding forth, glass in hand. Only at the very end, when the king-sized crush I had developed for the magnetic writer outweighed my timidity, did I squeeze myself into the studio along with the rest. . . .

"You aren't listening to me," Melissa said severely.

"Sorry, Melissa. My mind was wandering. What were you saying?"

"Pearls of wisdom. It's a shame you weren't paying attention."

Belatedly I wondered what useful information I had missed. "Was it about Kingsley?"

"No, I was practicing my upcoming lecture on political economy." Melissa did not like to be ignored.

"Don't be cross," I said coaxingly. "If I'm going to work with Adam Kingsley I need all the information I can get."

"I was just nattering on about his messy divorce, and all the unlovely details his adoring wife let fall while in the process of detaching herself." Melissa eased herself off the table. "But if you're going to sit there with that glazed expression, I'm going to trot along to Max's office and see if I can make some kind of an announcement. Maybe, even, a press conference. It's the first time in a long time we've had enough news to have one. By the way, what's he like?"

"Older than I"—I swallowed the near-fatal error—"than I had expected from the last pictures I had seen. And he's got a lot of facial scars. Also, he's blind."

" 'Also, he's blind,' she says casually. Good heavens, woman, why didn't you say that immediately? That *is* news! Wow! I can get him any interview he wants. The 'Today' show, the 'Tonight' show . . . " Her voice dwindled as she all but ran down the hall. Melissa would also have been an excellent police reporter or, as they now call them, investigative journalist. Her instinct for news and how to build a story was infallible, which was why she was good at her job.

I got up, shut the door, and went back to cleaning off my desk.

Chapter 4

But I was destined not to begin on Adam's manuscript that night.

It was late when I got off the bus. The moment I turned into the block and saw the police cars parked in front of our grimy, depressing apartment house I knew something was wrong. Every disaster to a child that I had heard about on the local television news show or read in the papers sprang to my mind. Ewen, I thought, terrified, and started to run, the heavy manuscript in my tote bag weighing me down like a body.

Both front doors were open. I saw blue uniforms in the hall.

"Mrs. Moncrieff?" asked one policeman. "I'm afraid I have to tell you—"

"Mom," shouted Ewen's voice from the top of the first flight of stairs. "Our apartment was burglarized. I got home and saw the door open and— Mom, what's the matter? You look awful!"

"Couldn't you tell her her kid was all right?" Mrs. Soboloff from downstairs was saying indignantly to New York's finest, who was looking guilty.

"Gee, ma'am, I'm sorry. I didn't think. I shoulda told you right away that your boy was okay."

I've never actually fainted and I didn't now. The voices that had been fading started sounding louder. I felt the cold iron of the banister under my hand.

"I'll get you some water," Mrs. Soboloff said, throwing an outraged glance towards the policeman.

"It's all right, Mrs. Soboloff, thank you. I'm fine." What I was struggling with now was a desire to kill not only the policeman who had given me such a shock, but Ewen, for not preparing me.

"Why didn't you call me at the office, Ewen? Instead of letting me come home and get scared out of my wits?"

"I only just got home and I did call the office and there wasn't any answer."

"Well, why were you so late?"

"We had an emergency meeting of the Naturalists Club."

"Lucky he wasn't home, Mrs. Moncrieff," the policeman said.

"Lucky's hardly the word." More like Divine Providence, I thought. I looked up the staircase at my son. "I'm sorry, darling. I should have thought before I reproached you."

"Yes, you should."

I started up the stairs towards him, feeling weak about the knees.

"Aren't you interested in what was taken?" The policeman asked behind me.

I glanced back. "I suppose I should be. Although we

certainly don't have any heirlooms or treasures. And our television doesn't work anyway. What did they take?"

The policeman was looking up at me from the bottom of the stairs.

"According to your son, nothing. That's the interesting part. Maybe you can discover something that's missing."

I turned to look at him and then glanced up to Ewen. "Is that true, Ewen? Nothing gone?"

"Nothing. I checked all the cages. Nemesis and Ears and Einstein and the gerbils and the mice are all there and they're okay. But what burns me up is that Ears and Einstein could have gotten out because this jerk had left the door open. I want the cops to catch him, Mom. You know, Nemesis could have run out in the hall and out on the fire escape or out the front door and I might never have gotten him back."

"I take it those are his pets," the man in blue said from behind me.

All of a sudden I wanted to laugh hysterically. I said over my shoulder, "I could have had a diamond tiara and necklace up there, to say nothing of gold bars and a hundred thousand dollars in a suitcase, and Ewen wouldn't waste a thought on them."

By this time I was up the stairs beside Ewen. Despite his known dislike of demonstration in public I put my arm around him and gave him a kiss which he accepted stoically. Ewen is one of the reasons I can't accept a lot of the basic tenets of behaviorism. I've always been demonstrative, and certainly with Ewen from the time he was born. But from the time he was born he has not been. Every now and then, as a rare gesture, he kisses me. I have no doubt about his affection for me, which is deep and reliable. But affectionate he is not. "How's Wilma?" I asked.

"Fine," he said in an offhand way.

"*Where* is Wilma?"

For a minute Ewen scowled. Then he grinned. "Under the bed. Where else?"

"Who's Wilma?" the policeman asked, drawing level with us.

"Our dog."

"Some dog."

Ewen fired up. "Wilma's okay. Not every dog's a guard dog. Besides, she had a shock when she was a puppy."

"What kind of a shock?" the policeman pursued.

"A bad one."

"Were you there?"

Silence. Then, "No. But I know that was what it was."

Having gotten over my fright about Ewen, I was ripe for the next one. The apartment was a shambles. I stood in the door and stared. Everything that could be turned over, had been. Chairs lay sideways on the floor, pictures had been knocked down, a plant had been turned over. I stared as Ewen went over and tenderly put it straight and started putting the earth back in. "I think it will be okay," he said.

All drawers had been yanked open, some were on the floor, and all were empty. Their contents strewn around.

"I can't believe it," I said finally, staring. But I understood now why Ewen had made such a point that his animals were all right. It was astonishing that any vandal who had perpetrated such destruction should have left them unharmed. But the television was there. So was our radio, so was the stereo. I went around putting things back in drawers and checking their contents.

"Anything missing?" the officer asked.

"Nothing. I think it's weird." In fact, I was having a very strange feeling, as though, in some way, Ewen and I had been violated. Idly I wondered if I would have felt better if something had been missing.

"Probably was scared off before he could remove anything," the officer said.

"By whom?"

"Anybody. Somebody in the hall downstairs coming in could have done it. There are some rip-off artists who'd walk down the stairs with a TV set or stereo, cool as you please, saying they're repair people. But others aren't that cool. You're lucky."

I felt a lot better when he said that, infinitely preferring an amateur or timid robber (with whom I could more easily identify) to some psychopath venting his fury without taking anything.

The policeman, plus a detective who arrived later, stayed a long time, asking a lot of questions: Did I have any enemies? Was the work I was doing connected with national security? Did I know any secrets that rival corporations might be interested in? When they learned that I was merely a desk editor at a publishing house they immediately wanted to know if I had edited any books recently that might threaten someone's reputation or contained any scientific and/or industrial information worth stealing.

"If you only knew how mundane my job is," I said wearily, after what seemed like hours. "Look, I'm grateful to you for coming so quickly and for your help and everything—"

"We haven't helped," the detective said. "I wish we could. Maybe, if we can find the person who did this"—he waved his arm around the chaotic apartment—"we'll accept your gratitude. But after talking to the people below I think it was almost certain to be an ordinary rip-off that got interrupted. Like I said, this mightn't stop cool veterans, but it would some guy who was afraid of being caught. You'll let us know if you come across anything that could give us a lead, won't you?"

I got up. "I promise. But I think I'd better start dinner for my son."

I could have killed Ewen, who was present during most of the questions and who now said, "Don't send them away on my account, Mom. I can always—"

"We're going anyway," the cop said with a grin as they turned towards the door.

After I closed and locked the front door I scowled at Ewen. "Lucky for you they didn't take you up on your generous invitation to stay forever," I said, making my way towards the kitchen.

"But I found their way of working fascinating. Just like a TV show."

I opened the refrigerator and got out some meat patties. "Well, I can do without knowing how the police go about their business," I replied snappily. "In fact, I could live a long happy life without ever finding out firsthand." After a minute, hearing Ewen moving around the kitchen behind me setting the kitchen table, I added, "I guess I'm nervous from what happened. I didn't mean to bite you."

"It's okay," Ewen said, and left after he finished his chore.

I sighed. Having the apartment ransacked like that had made me feel vulnerable and exposed. But behind that was a far greater dread: This time, by a lucky fluke—no, I thought, not a lucky fluke, more like a Grace from Providence—Ewen had not come home at his usual time. If he had, and the burglar had found him. . . . I was busy turning over hamburgers, but even with the broiler open and the heat on my face, I could feel a shiver of cold. All the things that had happened on the block that I had kept firmly away from the front of my mind rushed forward: old Mrs. Stein, recovering from a bout with flu, beaten by a burglar who had expected the house to be empty. . . . Mr. Watson, coming home early and surprising a thief, being taken to the hospital with a fractured skull. . . . Penny Andrews, taken at gunpoint up to her own apartment and raped. . . .

I took the warmed-over macaroni and cheese out of the oven and put the hamburgers on plates. Then I poured dressing over the salad and rapidly tossed it.

"Ewen, dinner's ready," I called.

I was vaguely surprised to hear his steps coming down the hall from the living room, instead of his own, as I had expected.

"Hamburgers," he said, rather as someone else might say "Caviar!" Pulling out a chair, he sat down, with Nemesis on one side and a rather chastened-looking Wilma on the other.

"What I like about you, Ewen," I commented, shaking out my napkin, "is your taste in food. It's reassuringly predictable."

"Would you like it better if I went ape over duck or steak?"

"No, because the way things are you'd live a life of deprivation. I hope you don't mind my saying so, but I think your friend Wilma should go to bed supperless. Her role in the burglary was not exactly in the heroic mold."

"How do you know she didn't bark?"

"From far under the bed, no doubt."

"Well, if you want Boris the Brave, why don't you get a German shepherd?"

And suddenly, before me, was Adam and the long, silvery German shepherd lying behind him. Without stopping to think, I said, "I met a German shepherd today. A blind author came in with one."

"Yeah? A guide dog? Cool! I've always wanted to know how they work. What did—"

I forestalled what was obviously going to turn into Ewen's favorite game, twenty questions. "I can't say anything about the dog at all, Ewen. The author and I talked and the dog never twitched so much as an ear—at least, if it did, I didn't notice."

"Oh. Who was the author?"

I hesitated, then said, "Adam Kingsley."

"No kidding! We're supposed to be studying his Pulitzer Prize book next term. I thought he was dead."

"No, just out of circulation for a long time. He had an . . . an accident that made him blind. I think he's been living in the country." Knowing Ewen's voracious curiosity, I was answering all the questions he would be sure to ask. Then I got up. "It's been a day, Ewen. I'm going to do the dishes, take a bath and go to bed. Why don't you go and take your bath now?"

"Okay."

What I really wanted, I knew as I heard Ewen going down the hall, was peace and time to think. So while I washed the dishes and then, because I found the activity soothing, dried them and put them away instead of leaving them to drain, I thought about robbery and the neighborhood and Ewen coming home alone and the house in Brooklyn Heights.

Squatters and vandals may have occupied it at one time, but there was no question about it now, the neighborhood was a lot better than this one. Against that would be the fact that when he got home from school Ewen would be alone in a house, instead of having neighbors under the same roof. Then there was his school. How would he get to that? The answer presented itself immediately: by subway; the school was one block away from the subway at one end and the house within easy walking distance at the other.

I weighed the answers and added them up. They always came out the same. I had decided, probably because of Ewen's brainwashing, to keep the house. Aside from everything else, the cheapest thing at this moment was to live in it. In its present condition, I couldn't rent it to anyone else, and if I sold it now, it would be at a considerable loss. I was no business tycoon, but even I knew that. So . . .

With the decision rapidly hardening in my mind, I went down the hall and called Lawrence Metcalf.

"It seems to me that's the most intelligent thing you could do right now," he said after listening to me. "I'm sorry about the burglary. It must have scared you out of your wits—not knowing about Ewen for a while."

"Did you inquire about the contractors?" I asked.

"I did, and I think we might have a pretty good deal. Furthermore, they'll do it in a hurry, because they're scheduled to begin another job very shortly—in about three weeks in fact. Congratulations! That's great!"

I suddenly found myself saying, "You know, the burglars didn't take anything. Do you think . . . ?"

"Do I think what?"

The trouble was, I didn't know. There was something, somewhere at the back of my mind that was bothering me. "It sounds insane to say I'd feel better if they'd walked off with the television set or the stereo, doesn't it?"

"No. You mean it feels spooky, as though the motive were something other than a criminal but otherwise unexceptional robbery?"

"Yes. I guess that's exactly what I mean. Does it sound crazy?"

"No, not really. A little paranoid, perhaps, but then, who isn't?"

"Thanks a lot."

He laughed. "I don't blame you. But I think the explanation is exactly what the cop gave you—whoever it was heard someone coming and ran."

"Probably." Why was it I was so reluctant to accept that explanation? I decided that that was the reason and not to make something ominous out of something I should be glad about.

"When can you meet the contractors? It'd better be at the house."

"Mr. Metcalf—"

"Why not call me Lance—which is what my friends call me, and I like to think we're friends."

"All right." I was surprised by the small glow of pleasure that gave me. "Lance. And I'm Antonia."

"Not Tony?"

"No. For some reason no one's ever used that nickname, which is just as well, because I don't like it, not for me, anyway!"

"Okay, Antonia. When can you meet the contractors at the house?"

"Tomorrow morning. If I'm going to move us into a new house and get it ready, the sooner the better. I'll meet them there at nine, if you can get hold of them before. If not, at ten or eleven. Please call them and let me know."

"All right. I think I have Angelo's home number. I'll call you back."

And he did, not five minutes later, as I was putting the garbage out for the super to collect in the morning. "Nine it is. And he emphasized that it was essential for him and his workers to act fast."

"Thanks, Lance. Will you be there?"

"Sure. There'll be things to sign. I'll bring them with me."

I was about to go and run the bath when I remembered that I had to clean up the living room and put everything back where it belonged. At that moment, when I was tired and a little depressed with the job in front of me, it seemed like more than I could manage. But to wake up in the morning and look on that chaos would be even worse. Muttering to myself, I went down the hall and stood stock still at the threshold, gripped in a misty-eyed wallow of proud motherhood. The room had been put straight. Everything was back in its place. Walking in, I opened a drawer in the low chest under an oval mirror and felt reassured that Ewen was not about to suffer translation into angelhood. The drawer was jammed with everything that had been on the floor, whether it had originally come from there or not.

"I didn't have time to make things tidy," a somewhat surly voice said from behind me.

I turned. Ewen, in pajamas and robe, was standing there scowling, his hair hanging in wet rattails around his neck.

"I think you did wonderfully. *Muchas gracias!*"

The scowl lightened. "It's okay," he said offhandedly, as though it didn't matter, and strolled forward.

"Ewen," I said, "the robbery or break-in or whatever was some kind of final straw. I've decided we're going to move into the Brooklyn house as soon as I can arrange to have the paint and floors and plumbing done. Would you like that?"

His funny, bony face lit up. "Hey, that's super! When can we move?"

"I don't know yet. I'm meeting Lance—Laurence Metcalf—tomorrow morning at nine over there to make the arrangements. I guess the answer is as soon as it is habitable. Do you hate it over here so much?"

"No. But I really liked it over there."

"It'll mean a long daily trip to school. Have you thought of that?"

"Sure. But some of the other kids travel on the subway. It's no big deal."

"Maybe over there you can make friends in the neighborhood. They look like they have other boys and girls your age." Judging by the invitations that came over the phone, Ewen was popular. But I worried a little over his tendency to be a loner, wondering how much, if any, was attributable to the general inconvenience and undesirability of our location, and how much to his being without a father.

Almost as though he read my mind he said, "It'd probably be easier to make friends in the neighborhood over there. I mean, here it's more of a hassle." And of course it was.

One of the things I liked about Ewen's school was that the boys were drawn from every walk of life and ethnic group. But, along with other parents, I was not enthusiastic about the area around the school itself. At times it approached the general ambiance of needle park, favorite hangout for pushers and users farther downtown. Common sense, as well as the newspapers, told me that there was no guarantee Brooklyn Heights would be any freer of that particular blight since it had invaded the most exclusive suburbs. But I had liked the look of the houses and the streets and the people I had seen and, having made up my mind to move, I was eager to believe that Ewen would have more of a neighborhood to play in than in our present location.

I didn't get to the office the next day until after lunch. Lance had not exaggerated when he said the contractors were eager to start work and get it finished. They had arrived with most of their tools and were hard at it, ripping up the linoleum before the ink of my signature on the contract had dried. The most expensive items would be new fixtures for the bathroom on each floor, plus new fixtures for the kitchen. All of this would be paid for by the remains of the estate, plus a bank loan. Even so, it would be a tight squeeze, so when Lance said casually, "Why don't you turn the basement floor into an apartment and rent it?" I snapped at the idea.

"And it's in better condition than the rest of the house," I said. "But, on the other hand, who'd want to live below street level? No matter what the advantages, the apartment's got to be dark."

"Oh, well, some bachelor or two working girls probably wouldn't be that particular. They wouldn't be in long enough to notice the lack of light."

"But then they probably wouldn't be able to pay the rent I intend to charge."

Lance grinned at me. "That's the fastest switch from outraged tenant to grasping landlord that I have ever seen."

I had the grace to feel slightly abashed. "Well, I intend to make it attractive, and having been a tenant, I know how to make one happy. But how soon do you think Ewen and I can move in?"

"Depending on how particular you are, almost immediately. Why?"

"Because I've been a statutory tenant in my own building for a long time now. I have no lease, and after the robbery—I know that front door was not properly locked—I rebel at the thought of paying another month's rent."

"Then I would say as soon as the walls, the floors and the bathrooms are fixed—say two to three weeks."

"Speaking of the walls," I said, walking over to one and pulling off a hanging strip, "how many layers of paper would you suppose are here?"

"God knows! Tenants have been slapping new layers on for years."

I thought a minute. "I like the idea of papered walls. I haven't seen them since I was a child."

"Well, the contractor brought some books of samples. You'd better go over them with him and give him your instructions."

That took another hour while I chose the patterns I wanted. "And you'd better take off some of those layers of paper," I said.

The man went over and with his metal spatula scraped at the walls. "It'll take longer. There must be an inch of paper here."

"Okay. Let's do it right at the beginning."

It was not until I got to the office that I even remembered Adam's manuscript. And any reminder I needed was supplied by the messages piled onto my phone. Aside from various other business calls, there was one from Max and another from Adam. I took a deep breath and called Max first.

"Did you get started on Adam's book, Antonia?" he asked immediately.

I waited for, and felt, my all-too-familiar guilt pangs. "I'm afraid not, Max. When I got home I found my apartment had been broken into and ransacked, and so"— I decided that now was as good a time as any to tell him about inheriting the house and the move that would, manuscript or no, take up a good part of my time— "so you see, Max," I ended, "I really didn't get too much of a chance to look at it."

There was a pause. As well as though I were reading his mind, I knew what was going on in it. Max is no more self-centered than any other publisher or editor or, for that matter, writer. I knew he was annoyed that, robbery or not, I should have failed to begin, at least, the most important manuscript that had entered the house since he himself had taken over from his father. But even Max was unable to express this in view of what I had told him.

"I'm sorry about the robbery, Antonia. That's unpleasant. It happened to our apartment once, although in our case they didn't turn everything upside down and did take about ten thousand dollars' worth of various items." He paused. "Do you think this move you're thinking about is going to take up a lot of your time? Maybe you should postpone it until after you've finished with the manuscript."

In a sense, he was right, and I knew it. If there were a lot wrong with the book now, it would need fast work to get it ready to be published in the spring, especially with the added technical problem of Adam's blindness. And that meant work at home and over the weekends. But a stubbornness took hold of me then, as it had done—sometimes disastrously—during other crises in my life.

"I'm sorry, Max. I'll try not to let it interfere more than absolutely necessary. But the fact is I can no longer feel safe in that apartment. If it were just me I wouldn't mind so much. But there's Ewen, who nearly always gets home before I do . . ."

I have always thought of an appeal to motherhood as foul play. It's the one excuse that no one has the moxie to rule out. Military generals with medals for wiping out whole regiments shuffle their feet and look abashed when some outrageous appeal is made in the name of motherhood.

Nevertheless, I used it.

"Yes, yes, I see," Max huffed. "All right, Antonia, do the best you can. But I can't emphasize how important . . ."

For what felt like five minutes Max told me what a publishing event this book would be.

I hung up, feeling guiltier than ever, which was no frame of mind in which to call Adam. But knowing that it would get more difficult, not easier, as I put it off, I dialed his hotel and asked for his room. As soon as I heard his "hello" I plunged in before he had time to ask if I had read his manuscript. "I'm sorry, Mr. Kingsley . . ."

He listened without comment, then said, "That was quite an experience. I'm sorry. Are you sure you want to tackle the book now at all?"

It was uncanny, the way he picked up the feelings I had not voiced. What would be even more uncanny—and must be avoided at all costs—was the reason for my reluctance. "Of course," I rattled on, "we're all very excited about it. I just wanted to explain why I hadn't got to reading it immediately."

There was a pause. I felt my nerves tighten. Then he said, "That wasn't the reason I called. I have some empty tapes with me which I will be happy to bring over along with a recorder. Normally, you'd make notes in the margin. Instead of that, could you dictate them into a tape, explaining what you want and why and indicating the place?"

"Of course," I said, realizing that I had been so preoccupied with the hazards concerning the person of Adam Kingsley, that I had not given much thought to the techniques of telling a blind writer how to revise his book. "But you don't have to bring them over. I can easily send a messenger for them."

"Thanks, but I'd like the exercise."

"It's no trouble—"

"Mrs. Moncrieff, I'm blind, but that doesn't mean I'm helpless and I don't like to be treated like a bed-ridden invalid. In the course of my relationship with most people I have to make this clear. And since we have to wortk together, it might as well be now."

I knew he was right, but I could feel my temper rising. There was an edge to his voice that was like a slap.

"All right, Mr. Kingsley. I'm sorry I seemed to act that way. But it's a new trip for me, too."

To my surprise I heard him laugh. "That's better. I'd rather deal with your anger than cope with your guilt and pity. I don't need either of those."

"I'll try to remember. Yes, I'd like to have the tapes, but I think I'll buy my own recorder, because you're going to need yours to play the tapes on, aren't you?"

"Yes. But I was prepared to buy a second, since I need one anyhow. However, if this is an office expense, I'll let you buy your own."

"I don't wish to do you out of your exercise, but I can also buy the tapes."

"True. However, last night I was thinking about the book and suddenly had an idea about some revision which I dictated into a tape and I will bring that over."

"All right. What time will be convenient for you?"

"How about lunch? I can give it to you then."

Every instinct I had was to refuse. But as I was about to speak the words I knew it would, one, be merely a postponement, and two, it might be easier to have lunch with him, from which I could leave if I had to, on a pretext, than to receive him in my office, from which I would have no escape.

"Or," he said, exactly as though I had spoken, "if you're busy I could leave the tape with the receptionist."

"I'd like to have lunch," I said. "I was just checking my calendar." As I spoke I made a face at the desk calendar's blank page, knowing I had accepted not because lunch would be easier but because he had offered me a way out. "Where would you like to meet?"

"Where and when you say, with the only proviso that the restaurant accept a dog."

"Would any refuse?"

"Oh, yes. Although they'll give some other excuse, such as they're all booked."

"Good heavens! Do you like Italian food? There's a place called Ernesto's on West Fifty-fifth Street."

"Yes, I do like Italian food and I don't get much of it in wildest New Hampshire. Tell me exactly where it is."

"It's about midway between Fifth and Sixth Avenues on the north side of the street . . . " I hesitated.

"And?"

"Nothing. I was about to ask if there was anything else I could do or tell you. But I thought you might bite my head off again."

"No. Not unless you start trying to protect me."

"Have no fear! I won't! But I will call and find out how they feel about dogs. If you don't hear from me within half an hour I'll see you there."

Mr. Lee, the Chinese owner of Ernesto's, was indignant that I should even ask, although he supported Adam's statement about some restaurants becoming suddenly fully booked when someone who was blind and with a guide dog appeared. "It's not so much the dog," he said. "It's a funny mixture of guilt and fear."

One thing I did make sure of: I arrived early and was there when Adam with his German shepherd made their entrance. Whether it was the tall, rather gaunt man, with the dark glasses and scarred face, or the magnificent black and silver dog that attracted the attention, I don't know. Probably both. But for a moment there was a silence. Eugenio, the headwaiter, rushed forward. Mr. Lee himself suddenly appeared and spoke to Adam. Then everyone started talking again.

Lee had given us a corner table, and I realized he must have had experience with guide dogs when Adam, who had threaded his way perfectly between the tables behind the dog said, "The waiter said this table's in the corner. Do you mind if I sit next to the wall? I can put Tania there so she'll be out of the way of people's feet."

"Not at all." I moved out, and Adam, feeling his way, went in. When he had reached the wall he sat down, then he bent and drew Tania under the table to the wall beside him. "Sit," he said. The big shepherd sat and then lay on the floor.

"That's a good girl," Adam said in a warmer voice than I had heard him yet use, and he ran his hand down her head.

"She's a beautiful dog," I said.

"She is that."

And then, without thinking, I said, "Ewen would love her."

"Who's Ewen?"

"My son."

"Oh. I didn't know you had a son, although there's no reason I should. How old is he?"

I kicked myself mentally. There were several reasons why I had not intended to introduce the subject of Ewen, one of which was that I find professional women who chatter about their children tedious.

"Twelve," I said. And then made a deliberate effort to change the subject by asking, "Would you like a drink?"

"No, thanks. I don't drink. But you go ahead if you would like one. I can have a soft drink or some coffee while you're having yours."

"No. On the whole I prefer not to drink at lunch."

"Don't abstain on my account."

"I'm not." And then I added, because I couldn't resist it, "I, too, can be independent."

He grinned. "All right."

Eugenio suddenly materialized at our table. Having satisfied himself that neither of us wanted a drink, he rattled off a list of the specialties of the house.

"Mrs. Moncrieff?" Adam said when Eugenio was through.

My appetite, always erratic, had vanished. I settled for a chef's salad.

"I'll have the lasagna," Adam said.

"Wine?" the waiter asked hopefully.

"Not for me," I said hastily.

"No, thanks," Adam said. "No wine." He had, I noticed, taken command of the lunch.

The waiter went away. And there we were, I thought, my nerves tightening, with no book or waiter or menu between us to act as a conversational tool. Then Adam spoke, and what he said did nothing to ease my tension.

"Why are you so nervous?"

I made myself take a slice of Italian bread and butter it before I answered. "You know, it's spooky, you saying that. You can't see me, so it must be my voice. Is this the noted acute hearing of the blind?"

"It's not acute hearing, just concentration. If you find it spooky, we can change the subject."

"Yes. Let's. I have other . . . there are other causes for my nervousness at the moment."

"Other than what? Me?"

Out of the frying pan into the fire, I thought, with a sense of despair. All my life I had been an incredibly inept dissembler. Like a hunted animal, made stupid with fright, I had tried to lead my pursuer away from the one thing I was trying to hide only to find that I had led him directly to it.

I pulled myself up and made one final effort. "I think it's perfectly normal that I would be nervous and tense with the prospect of working on the novel of such a legendary author as yourself."

"Nuts!" Adam said with brutal directness. "I have written nothing for more than fifteen years. Before that I won a Pulitzer Prize. One is handed out almost every year, so that hardly makes me unique. The two books after were bad. Everyone else knew it, and after I was able to think about it, so did I. Besides, you've worked with other authors. Max mentioned one or two when he was singing your praises as a skilled editor. I would say it's the robbery you told me about this morning, except I heard the same note in your voice when I met you in Max's office two days ago, and it hadn't happened then." He paused.

I had abandoned all pretense of nibbling the bread I had buttered. How on earth did I think I could carry off, in the long weeks that lay ahead, my pretense of not having known him? Given, of course, his uncanny perception—what did he call it? Concentration—and my inability to disguise my feelings.

At that moment Eugenio arrived with my chef's salad, which he had tossed, and a dish for Adam for which he apologized profusely. The lasagna had, alas, run out. He had taken the liberty of bringing canelloni instead. If the gentleman did not care for canelloni, he would take it away instantly and bring anything the gentleman wanted.

"Canelloni is fine," Adam said abruptly.

Perhaps it was the brusqueness of his tone, for Eugenio, with a hurt expression, started in on his apology all over again. Made even more tense by poor Eugenio's nervousness, I produced, without thinking, one of my Scottish mother's soothing expressions. "It's all right, Eugenio, dinna fash yourself. It's okay. Truly."

After Eugenio set down the canelloni and walked away, Adam said, "What did you say?"

Knowing I had betrayed myself in some way, I was silent. Then I said, "I was just trying to soothe poor Eugenio—"

"I'm not talking about that. What was that expression?"

I finally said, "It's an old Scottish saying. Dinna fash yourself. It just means, 'Don't get upset.' "

I heard his fork clatter to the floor.

"Yes," he said. "I remember now. I remember when you said that before."

Too late, so did I.

I had been crawling forward row by row as the weeks of summer school passed until, by the time our first paper was due, I was sitting right under the podium where the magnetic writer walked back and forth, lecturing, talking, questioning, laughing, reciting and in some magic way building a warm, powerful, emotional bridge between him and the packed classroom. It was the kind of power I had seen only once before, in my father, between whom and his congregation was the same shared passion that Adam had established between him and the young people who lined up an hour ahead of his class to make sure they could find seats. Actors, I learned later, had it; preachers had it; Adam had it. As long as I live I shall never forget the way he looked, the sun pouring in on his Viking fair head, his astonishing eyes, almost an aquamarine blue, blazing with vitality and the same nervous energy that kept him moving and gesturing.

It was when he was handing back our papers, scribbling an occasional additional comment on one or two of them as he talked to the students they belonged to, that I first confronted him.

"Mary Leigh," he called out, looking around.

I went up. Knowing that he would be handing back the papers, I had spent an hour in front of the mirror that morning, teasing and crimping my hair so that it stood out like a red bush, ignoring, as far as I could, Dauntry's vicious jabs as he watched me.

"What are you primping for, Mary? The subcounty Four H buttermilk beauty contest? Or—" His gray eyes widened. "Don't tell me, let me guess. Is it on behalf of The Great Man himself, the Nova Scotia troubadour? Now, that's an inspiring thought. . . ."

Our marriage, a disaster from the start, was barely six months old. I had never become accustomed to Dauntry's verbal facility in attack, but I had acquired a technique of appearing not to notice. Nevertheless, my hands, trying to work with my stubbornly straight hair, were shaking. Which accounted for my rather untamed coiffure and the smudged mascara. Nevertheless I was rather pleased with myself when I stepped up to Adam Kingsley's desk on the podium.

"You write well, but your style is stiff," he said abruptly.

Those remarkable eyes of his moved swiftly up and down my body. Something electric went through me and seemed to be crackling between the two of us, quite unrelated to the rather childish crush I had had on Dauntry when he was courting me and which I had calamitously interpreted as love.

"You need more freedom in your writing," he said. And somehow, he was not just talking about writing.

"Yes, I know," I agreed, as mesmerized as a bird in front of a snake. And the fact that his breath smelled of liquor at eleven in the morning, just added to my excited sense of brushing against another world.

He smiled faintly, and ignorant, foolish and unsophisticated as I was, I knew he knew what effect he was having on me.

"I'll write it on your paper," he said, and he wrote, "More freedom." Only in the middle of the last word his pen went dry and he shook it. At that, a large dollop of ink appeared on the front of my essay.

"I'm sorry," he said. "Maybe there's some kind of ink remover I can use. I certainly didn't mean to mess up your paper. It's good. Let me try—"

That was when I had said, almost ecstatic with confusion and delight, "Dinna fash yourself," as I had heard both my Scottish mother and father say numberless times.

He laughed. "What does that mean?"

And I had said, as I now just again explained, "It means, 'Don't get upset.'"

We sat there in the restaurant, the silence lengthening.

"But you must have known," Adam said finally, "from the time Max told you he had taken my book, that we would be seeing one another. Why did you act as though we were strangers? And your name . . . It was different then, wasn't it?"

"Yes. It was Mary Leigh." I took a breath. "Leigh was

my married name and after . . . after I was divorced I decided to take back my maiden name."

"Isn't that unusual?"

In one sense it was a relief that I no longer had to try and hide the fact that we had known one another. In another sense it made things even more difficult to keep hidden that which had to remain hidden. "I suppose so," I said carefully. "But the divorce was . . . not friendly, to put it mildly. And I wanted to forget the whole thing."

"I see." Adam put his hand up and pushed his glasses back up his high-bridged nose. I remember his eyes, the most outstanding feature of an arresting face, and wondered if the reason he wore glasses was that they had been destroyed.

"But where does Antonia come in?"

"My second name, after a godmother. I never liked Mary," I said lightly. "So when I finally got out of school and came to New York I decided I might as well start fresh with Antonia, which I preferred."

"I see," he said again, and I thought, how strange that he still used that common expression that must mean so little to him. And then I jumped because he said, "I do, you know. See, I mean. It's the brain that sees, not the eyes. The eyes are simply a filter or window that lets in images, but it is the brain that sees and interprets."

"I see," I said. And then we both laughed, and for a rare moment I was at ease with him.

Then the unease returned as he said, "But if I hadn't recognized your voice you would have gone on with the fiction that we had never met, wouldn't you?"

"Yes. I guess so."

"Why?"

"Because that was a very unhappy time for me. I don't know," I said slowly, feeling my way, "how much I may have told you about it at the time . . . "

The dark brows, striking against the graying fair hair, drew together. "Did you tell me any? I don't remember . . . yes, we met at a party at the end of the summer session, didn't we, and talked there?"

"Yes." My heart was pounding. "It was the English Department's farewell party for you."

"I remember the beginning of it, but, as usual, I was drunk pretty much all the time then, before, during and after, and I don't remember the end of it. What happened?"

The relief I felt was so great it almost made me dizzy. I made my voice as even as possible. "Nothing much. You talked to me and other adoring fans, then my husband came and took me away."

"Yes. I'm sorry I was in a blackout. But then that was happening pretty frequently. You must have been very young for such a disastrous marriage experience. But then I suppose very young marriages often are disastrous."

"Yes," I said carefully. "Dauntry and I were not at all suited. He seemed very glamorous to me . . . I can't think why he married me, because I was certainly about the least glamorous person on that rather rustic campus . . . " As usual, I was talking too much, babbling on in my amateur efforts to lead Adam away from the danger zone.

"Don't you have red hair?" he asked abruptly.

"Yes," I said

"Umm—" he said. "I seem to remember you as having frizzy red hair and large kind of gray-green eyes and a terrified expression. What terrified you? Your husband?"

"And life in general," I said drily.

"Why?"

"Mr. Kingsley—"

His brows went up. "I thought we were old friends."

"All right. Adam. I would love to give you the story of my life, but I have to get back to the office."

Isabelle Holland

"And, besides, you don't feel like giving me a psychiatric rundown of your problems."

"Something like that."

"Well, why don't you say so? Tell me to mind my own business?"

"In publishing we walk delicately around leading authors who are liable to bring us prestige and money."

"I think we will get on better if you don't walk delicately around me. And if I'm treading clumsily, either physically or any other way, then tell me so."

"All right."

"I mean that."

"What makes you think I don't?"

"Your voice. You'd be surprised how much more clearly a voice comes through when you're blind and not distracted by appearance. You sound as though you had a mountain of reservations as regards our contract of candor. I didn't say tell me everything. I said tell me if I am treading on ground I should stay off of."

So much about him had changed that it was almost shocking to see what hadn't: notably a directness that at times could be merciless. There was no way to meet it except head on, and I had never been good at that. But I could see that I had to make some effort at it.

"Then, as part of our contract, as you put it, if you feel reservations in me . . . in my voice, instead of trying to hammer me open to see what's wrong, why don't you just stop and get on another subject, or just stop?"

"Fair enough." To my surprise, he held out his hand. That was one of the times when I was aware of his blindness; the moment he started talking I forgot. But, of course, if he wanted to shake hands, he had to hold his hand out and let the other person make the contact. I reached across the table and put my hand against his. The long, strong fingers closed around mine. To my great shock, my heart gave an unwelcome and remembered hop.

"Okay," he said, "if you're ready, let's go." Leaning down, he found Tania's harness with his left hand. "Under the table," he said. "Forward." She came under the table and stopped when she got to the other side. He patted her. "That's a good girl." Then he rose, felt with his hand to the edge of the table and leaned down and took Tania's harness with his left hand.

"After you," he said.

Chapter 5

That evening, after I had washed the dinner dishes, I went into the living room, hauled Adam's huge manuscript from the shopping bag in which I had brought it home, and sat down with it at the end of the sofa with my feet up on the coffee table. Before I opened the box containing the book, I glanced around the living room, mentally calculating the hours of packing that lay in front of me. Two walls were filled with books. That, of course, was not counting the books in my bedroom, those in the hall shelves and in Ewen's room. Then there was the silver, inherited from my mother, the china, the glassware . . . I yanked my mind away. If there were twice as much packing to do, I still had to read the manuscript.

I had meant to read about half, but five hours later I was into the final third. Many years' experience had made me a lightning reader, but I found that I had slowed down, a sure sign that I was enjoying myself. Though rough and in need of both revision and cutting, Adam's novel entitled, simply,

Journey, had all the ingredients of another prize-winner and best-seller and was a far more mature piece of work than any of his previous books. But that was not the only reason I found it absorbing. The book was on several levels: the first and most obvious was the semi-autobiographical aspect. Poor boy grows up, achieves success, marries rich blue blood, goes to pot, and has to begin a second and more difficult journey back. On another level it was the story of the Prodigal Son, and on yet another the myth of the self-fulfilling prophecy. The themes, both psychological and mythic, wove in and out. What fascinated me was the portrait of the wife, and I couldn't decide whether it was a straightforward treatment of Sally. Pembroke, of the Pembrokes of Virginia, or some semimythical figure projected from the mind of the narrator of the book, because one of the faults of the book was that the reader could never be sure whether the narrator—it was a first-person chronicle—wrote of the objective reality outside himself, or only of reality as he subjectively saw it—or both. I also felt fairly sure that the confusion existed because of Adam's unfamiliarity with the technique of dictating to a tape.

I finished *Journey* at about a quarter to three in the morning, and was sitting there in the rapidly chilling room, thinking about it, when Ewen's voice spoke from the doorway.

"Why are you still up, Mom? Is something wrong?"

I nearly jumped out of my skin. "Good heavens, Ewen, you scared me! What do you mean, why am I up? I'm up because I had to read a manuscript. I've done that before."

"Yeah, but not till nearly three."

I got up, and realized how stiff I was after sitting all those hours. "Aren't our roles getting a little confused? Are you telling me I should be in bed?"

"Yeah. That's what you're always saying to me. What's so special about the book?"

"Just that I should have read it last night. But what with

the place being turned upside down and the police in and out for hours, I somehow didn't get to it. And Max wasn't pleased. Neither, for that matter, was the author, although I suppose, to do him credit, he didn't actually complain."

"Who is he?"

"The one I told you about. Adam Kingsley."

"The one with the dog—the guide dog?"

"Yes."

"Gosh, Mom, I wish I could meet him. I'd like to do a paper for the Naturalists Club on guide dogs."

"Well, you don't have to meet him for that. There must be some agency or outfit you could call."

"Well, sure. But it's not the same as talking to somebody who actually *does* it."

"Well, I'm sorry, Ewen, but you know that I like to keep my professional and personal lives as far apart as possible."

"Yeah, I know."

"You sound as though you don't have much sympathy with that idea."

"Well, I think it's kind of dopey. What difference does it make? I mean, what's knowing some author going to do to me and what's me knowing the authors going to do to them?"

"Nothing. It's just that I like to have a life apart from my work. And I don't see why people who come to my office with their books, hoping to get editorial advice, have somehow to encounter me also as wife and mother."

"Whose wife are you?"

There was such an odd note in his voice that I looked up. "Nobody's—at the moment. Why? Do you wish I were?"

Ewen mumbled something and went out of the room. A few seconds later I heard his door close.

Okay, Sigmund, I muttered crossly to myself as I got up to go to bed. Answer that one.

The next day at the office I spent a half hour listening to

the tape that Adam had brought me. As I had suspected, a lot of the trouble with the novel was caused by his unfamiliarity with the oral method he now had to use. A book listened to can turn out very differently from a book read—especially if it's a method used for the first time. And this was his first attempt following his blindness.

"I know," his voice over the tape finished up, "that the revisions I listed have to be made. Normally, I would do that before I submitted the manuscript, but I thought I'd get your views now and try to incorporate them, or the whole process could take an endless amount of time."

I snapped off the recorder, reflecting that it was going to take an endless amount of time anyway. Then I turned to my typewriter and started writing a lengthy and detailed editorial report which would have to go to Max first, and then be read to Adam. It was an itemized account of what I thought should be done and had to be checked frequently with reference to chapter and page number and I didn't finish it until around four in the afternoon. Then I clipped the pages together and took it down to Max's office.

"Sit over there while I read it," Max said.

"Don't you just want me to leave it with you?"

"No, I want to talk to you about it when I've read it, and about Adam. *Asseyez-vous.*"

Watching him read what I had written would make me nervous, so I strolled over to the window and looked down Fifth Avenue. To the south were the library lions and to the north rose the towers of Radio City. I stared at them for reassurance.

When I had come to New York ten years before, I had come without knowing anyone, which was the way I wanted it. After two years of running from one small town to another, first waiting for Ewen to be born, then trying to support him, and all the while fending off questions I didn't want to answer,

I embraced enthusiastically the huge anonymity of the city. I had managed to save enough money to keep Ewen and me for a while and to pay for baby-sitting services while I was looking for a job. The day after I arrived I went job hunting and in the course of the day arrived at Rockefeller Plaza. I had read about the famous Plaza, seen photographs, watched it in the movies. Yet the reality stopped me in my tracks. Disregarding my next appointment, I spent the following hour looking up at the buildings and down at the skating rink, and since then those angular towers have symbolized for me not only the city itself but what it had given me—the blessed freedom of being unknown . . .

Max's voice turned me around. "I think you're absolutely right, Antonia. This is an excellent report. I can see you and Adam are going to turn that good novel into an even better one. There is a problem, though."

"What's that?"

"Money. By the sound of this"— he flicked a finger against the report—"it's going to be a long haul."

"Yes. I'm afraid it is. And I don't see how it can be shortened. Does it have to be brought out on the anniversary of his Prize novel?"

"Yes. It's too good an opportunity to miss. Think of the publicity!"

"I suppose it's the hotel bill you're worrying about. I thought he said you'd given him a good advance."

"I did. But I hate to see the whole thing eaten up by a prolonged stay in one of New York's more expensive hostelries. Besides that, he's been living on just about nothing while he wrote this book."

"I thought he said he was farming."

"He was. That is, he has been living and working on a farm owned by a farmer who was once, in Adam's high-flying days, a tenant of his."

I leaned back against the sill. "But what could he do on a farm?"

"Almost anything to do with animals. The farmer has some stock, a few cattle, chickens. Of course, Tania leads him around. And he walks the three or four miles into the village every day to negotiate any business that has to be done and order supplies and exercise himself and his dog. And that's another thing. Living in a hotel is not the best possible thing for him. Being in an apartment would be better. He could then get out and buy stuff for himself. He still walks his three or four miles a day, of course. Has to."

In a curious way, I knew what was coming. Yet I asked, "Well, what do you have in mind, Max?"

Max, who had been swiveling back and forth in his chair, turned towards me. "Didn't you say you were about to move into a whole house in Brooklyn Heights? I was irritated that you chose this moment to do it, what with this book. And there's no getting around it, it's going to take up a lot of your time, getting settled there. But then I started to think. Maybe it's a stroke of luck after all. How about letting Adam rent a floor or something from you? He could pay you some because he wouldn't do it otherwise. He's almost compulsively independent, as you've probably discovered, and you could work with him directly onto paper."

I was absolutely appalled. "Max—No!"

"Why not? What's the matter? Don't you like him? I grant you he can be ornery and difficult, particularly if he's in one of his 'leave me alone I'll do it myself' kicks, but it will cut out the money problem for him and the transportation problem for you. Otherwise either you'll be living in his hotel room or he'll be living in your office. Or the book won't get done."

My heart was acting in a very odd fashion, and a queer panic seemed to seize me. "Max, that's an invasion of my personal life, and I don't think you have any right at all to suggest such a thing—let alone make it sound like an order."

"Who's ordering you? I just thought that in view of the fact that moving at this time is your idea, and even you can't claim it's not going to take a big bite out of your time, it might be a way to do what you want and get your job done at the same time. Not, of course," he added, with pointed sarcasm, "that getting your job done should be a major consideration."

"That's hardly fair."

"All right, Antonia, forget it." He threw my report across the desk.

I stood there for a moment. Then I picked up the report and walked out. When half an hour later I had arrived at no solution to the problem, or even at any calmer state of mind, I called Adam and was rather surprised to discover he wasn't in his room, nor in the lobby. Feeling reprieved, I left a message and hung up.

Five minutes later the telephone rang. I picked up the receiver. "Adam?"

"No, sorry. This is Lance."

"Oh." I felt a little foolish. "I had left a message for one of our authors to call me."

"Not Adam Kingsley, by any chance?"

"Yes. How did you know?"

There was the slightest pause. "I guess because he's the only Adam who is also an author that I've heard of."

"But he hasn't been writing for fifteen years."

"Well, Ernest Hemingway hasn't written for even longer than that, particularly considering he's dead. But he's still the first Ernest I'd think of."

"That puts Adam in high company."

"Don't you think he deserves it?"

"I've never compared the two. Anyway, Lance, what did you call me about?"

"Sorry to be the bearer of sad tidings, but the first of what will probably be a lot of mess-ups and snafus has happened. The plumber thinks he's found a break in the pipe in the wall, which probably accounts for the stains on the ceiling in the downstairs living room. Anyway, he wants you to come and look at it and tell him what you want him to do. It will make his whole estimate a lot more expensive."

"Oh, God!"

"Cheer up. There's a long way to go."

"Thanks. What is he doing at the moment?"

"At this very red-hot moment, or at least five minutes ago when I left the house to find this phone booth, he was sitting on the floor of the upstairs bedroom, smoking his umpteenth cigarette, which he sometimes manages to get onto a plate which he is using as an ashtray."

"And where does he put it the rest of the time?"

"Need you ask? On the floor."

"What do you suggest, Lance?"

"I suggest you come over here as soon as you can. You won't get to see the plumber, because he's about to put down his tools and leave. But you can see what he wants to know and you can leave instructions for him. Or, if you prefer, you can come over here tomorrow morning at eight when he comes to work again."

"If I came right now, would he stay?"

"If you paid him overtime."

"All right. Tell him I'll get there as fast as the subway can get me."

As I hung up, I realized this was exactly what Max was talking about. Why did everything have to happen at once?

I was about to put everything on my desk into a more or less neat pile when I reflected that everyone would know then that I had left for the day. This whole thing certainly hasn't improved my honesty, I thought morosely, deciding to leave the top of the desk looking as near as possible as though I had just stepped into the ladies' room. Slipping into my raincoat, I picked up my bag and was about to sneak out the door when the telephone rang. The thought of the plumber collecting time and a half for sitting on his backside and making cigarette burns in the floor was a powerful inducement just to let the telephone ring. But it might be Max. I picked up the receiver.

"Hello?"

"You called me?" Adam's voice said. And then, "This is Adam Kingsley."

"Yes. I did. I've written out a report on *Journey* and what I think should be revised, and I was going to ask you to come over so I could read it to you and we could discuss it. Unfortunately, I find I have to leave the office right now . . . " I hesitated. "I'm sorry. Could you come over tomorrow morning? We could work in the conference room."

"All right. What time?"

"How about nine thirty?"

"Okay. I'll see you then."

I was on the subway under the river before it occurred to me that I had not said a word about the book itself, and I had worked with writers long enough to know how urgently they waited for an opinion from their editors. But Max must have told him how good he thought it was originally, I consoled myself. But then, Max wasn't an editor. If he were, he wouldn't have me to do his editing for him, and Adam was certainly intelligent enough to know that. It was the kind of mistake that if it hadn't been for the plumber and other like complications, I would never have made. It seemed terrible to think that Max might be right about my divided loyalty and attention.

For some reason the house looked considerably worse than when I had visited it that first Saturday morning. Perhaps it was because of the afternoon light and the way it faced, perhaps it was because the sky had grown overcast. Whatever the reason, the hall looked bleak when I came in. The linoleum had been torn off, but the floor underneath made me almost wish it hadn't been. Stained, blotched and splintered here and there, it was a mess. Sure enough, a long stain, which I had not noticed before, seemed to pour down from a darker stain in the ceiling of the wall next to the upstairs bathroom. A window had been broken in front, and all kinds of paper and refuse—matches, cigarette stubs, even dried crusts of bread—were spread around the hall.

"Surely," I said to Lance, who was waiting for me, "the plumber didn't do all of this."

"You've forgotten the men who pulled up the linoleum. Also, I think the neighborhood kids have discovered the place."

"But if it's been empty all this time, why have they only just discovered it?"

"Who knows? The plumber's still up there."

"What's he doing?"

"By the look on his face, working out his overtime in geometric progressions."

"I thought you said he was nonunion labor? An old-fashioned scab. What right does he have to demand union benefits?"

"None. But if you present that point of view to him too strongly, he might just pick up his snake and go home. And then you'd have to hire union labor at twice the cost."

Avoiding the stair that still lacked a tread, Lance and I went upstairs.

The plumber was staring vacantly into space. A pile of cigarette stubs littered the dirty white saucer beside him. Others, crushed flat, were on the floor. So were some charred scars.

Lance said, "Would you explain to Mrs. Moncrieff what you told me?"

Slowly the man got to his feet. "It's like this," he started.

Ten minutes later the one fact I had fully grasped was that it was going to cost me about two hundred and fifty dollars.

"Well, what made you go down into the wall in the first place?" I asked, staring at the huge hole that gaped in the bathroom wall and spread into the bedroom in which we were standing.

"He told me to," the plumber said, pointing a dirty thumb at Lance.

I turned. "What made you think it necessary?"

"The stain in the ceiling downstairs. It wasn't here when I was last in the house. Did you see it before?"

I had to admit I hadn't. "But wouldn't that mean somebody had been in using the waterpipes?"

"Possibly. I told you, kids had probably been here. You saw the refuse downstairs."

"But I can't understand why suddenly people are starting to break in? How long has the place been empty?"

"Not that long. Maybe six months."

"And in those six months nobody broke in? They've just started now? Why?"

"Antonia—I have no idea. One day the right combination of an empty street, a rainy day and a vagrant came together, or a bunch of kids with nothing to do. Who knows?"

I stood there, fighting a rising frustration. "I wish I knew what to do. If this kind of thing happens often, I simply won't be able to afford having the place fixed."

"May I make a suggestion?"

"Please do. Anything up to and perhaps even including setting fire to the wretched place would be acceptable."

"In that case you won't resist it as much as you might have. How about having the painters and paperhangers in as soon as we can book them and then your moving in immediately?"

"I don't think I'd enjoy coming home to find huge holes in the walls any more if I were in residence than not. In fact, on the whole, I'd rather not be here."

"You could arrange to have the fix-it men come on the weekend . . . "

"At time and a half?"

"Or even arrange to take a day off in return for your own working on Saturday. At least you wouldn't also be paying rent."

Of all his suggestions and ideas, that found me the most receptive. "I guess . . . " I started to say.

"And don't forget my idea of renting out the basement floor. You could practically pay for your repairs that way."

"And if the tenants objected to having the pipes taken out and the appliances removed, I could simply say it added to the Bohemian charm, I suppose."

He smiled. "Why not give it a whirl?"

Occupying the front and center of my mind was Max's suggestion that Adam rent a floor. "I'll think about it," I said finally. "In the meantime, could you find out how soon the absolutely essential repairs plus painting and papering could be done?"

Adam and Tania arrived at the office promptly at nine thirty the next morning and I took them into the conference room.

"Now tell me the layout of the room and where we're to sit," Adam said. I noticed he was carrying a briefcase in his right hand.

After describing the table, the chairs, their relationship to the walls and other pieces of furniture, I was interested to see that he made his way there without too much fumbling.

"Would you like me to help you?" I asked at one point.

"No, thank you. I can manage." And he could, arriving

at a chair at the other end of the conference table. "Okay, Tania. Sit." And the big dog lay back of his chair. "That's a good girl," he said, and stroked her head.

"Do you always say that to her?" I asked, taking the chair opposite.

"Always, when she has led me aright, or refused to lead me into an obstacle even though I have given her the command 'forward,' or simply done her job well. Don't you like to be praised when you've done a good job?"

"Yes," I said. "But I don't think humans behave to humans with the same courtesy. Isn't it a pity?"

He smiled faintly. "Yes. It is."

He took a tape recorder out of his briefcase and put it on the table and switched it on. "I hope this doesn't bother you," he said.

I shook my head and then realized he couldn't see me. "No," I said. Then, "Speaking of courtesy, or lack of, I failed to tell you how much I liked your book. I think it's better than anything you've done."

"That's good to hear. Why don't you tell me now what you think should be revised?"

His tone was perfectly polite. Yet there was something in it that pushed me back into myself, as though I had been intruding.

"All right." I picked up my report. "I'll read you the report I gave Max." And I proceeded to read it aloud, not omitting some of the more pointed criticisms I had intended to leave out or soften.

When I was finished he sat there without saying anything, his head still, his hands folded in front of him. Then he said, "Yes. I think I agree with you. The revisions are more extensive than I had thought, but they would put the book in better focus." He put his fingers up and rubbed his temples for a moment. "But that's going to take a hell of a lot of time, working solely with the tapes. I'd better go back to New Hampshire or my hotel bill will look like the national debt."

He snapped off the recorder and put it back in his briefcase. Then he leaned down. "Tania." His hands found the dog's head. "Come along, girl. Back to work."

I stood as he did. "Do you think you'll be able to get the book finished in time to have it published on the anniversary of your Prize novel?" I asked. "That's what Max wants."

"When would you have to have it to meet that deadline?"
I did some hasty calculations. "In about a month."

"No. What with traveling and mailing tapes back and forth, I can't make that. I'm afraid Max is going to have to resign himself to missing the anniversary. What does it matter, anyway?"

"He says it's good publicity."

"That sounds just like him. If it's a good book, and I intend, with your assistance, to make it just that, who's going to care whether it's on the anniversary or not?"

"Max does," I said, with absolute conviction.

"Isn't that pretty trivial?" He put his hand on Tania's harness.

"As far as the actual worth of the book, yes. But . . ."
"But?"

"But I'm afraid the anniversary idea *is* marvelous publicity, and there's no question about it, the media does respond to that kind of thing."

"Well, the book will have to get by on its merits, then. I can't do everything we've agreed on and have it back so that you can go into production in a month and have it ready by the magic date. And I'm sure you know that as well as I."

I did. I also knew something else. If I let Adam go back to New Hampshire without suggesting that he stay in my house and thus speed up the revision of the book, Max would be, to put it mildly, not pleased. It might be stupid and commercial, but there was no getting around it, a publicity handle or lever such as Max envisioned could certainly attract more notice, and more notice often meant more sales.

"Is there something you want to say or ask me? We seem to be waiting for something," Adam said, standing still.

"Yes. There is. I . . . Ewen—my son—and I are about to move into a house in Brooklyn Heights. I inherited it recently, and it seems cheaper and pleasanter to be living there than in my present cramped apartment in one of New York's grimmer neighborhoods. Max thought . . . and I thought . . . it might save a lot of time if you'd care to rent the basement floor of this house. It's a self-contained apartment. If I listened to the tapes as you made your revisions, I could do some of the actual typing and one whole step could be saved, aside from the length of time in shipping tapes back and forward, and you touch-typing the changes."

There was a pause. Then Adam said in an odd, hard voice. "Whose idea was this—yours or Max's?"

"It was Max's. But it seems a feasible plan."

"Thanks. But I'd rather work at home."

Having been indignant that Max wanted to wish such a plot onto me, I now felt vaguely ruffled that it was being so brusquely refused. "As you wish," I said coolly.

"But thank you for the offer."

"As I told you, it was Max's idea. I can take no credit for it."

I went with Adam and Tania to the elevator without any further conversation and then returned to my office.

I was sitting in my office that afternoon proofreading some galleys when Max strolled in.

"I gather Adam doesn't think much of our idea of having him rent your basement apartment," he said, sitting down in my one free chair.

I turned to face him. "Not much. But it was more your idea than our idea."

"Yes, and apparently Adam saw it that way, too, my leaning on you to make you invite him. Which is too bad, because even with thinking the invitation came from you alone he'd be hard enough to convince."

"Why?"

"I told you," Max said with a certain grim patience. "He's fanatically independent. He wouldn't come stay at my apartment, and he certainly wasn't going to stay at yours with you acting under my whip, so to speak."

"Well, I'm sorry, Max, that I didn't do a better acting job. But maybe it's better this way. Having publication day on his anniversary was a neat idea, but I must say I agree with Adam, if it's a good book it's going to go over no matter when it's published."

"Quite true. But Len Gottfried over at the book club was holding a possible slot for him for next April, depending, of course, on how well he liked the novel when it came in. But the May, June and July selections are all just about sewed up with that big political novel from Random House, another by those two reporters and the new Greene. After that, the club goes into its summer selections, which are pretty much beach and hammock reading. Do you know what being a selection could mean to Adam?" He looked at me.

"Lots of money and lots of publicity."

"An opportunity to pay off those horrendous debts he acquired in the last years before his accident."

"I thought his wife paid those. I read somewhere that she did. And heaven knows she was rich enough."

"Oh, sure. She paid them. But he signed an agreement to repay her."

"How could she force him to do that?"

"I'm not sure she had to, considering how he felt when he came around and learned that he had killed a child and permanently injured its father. She had his guilt going for her, to say nothing of his fiendish pride."

"But . . . " Something struggled up in my memory from several years back. "There was that story in a news magazine . . . "

"Reporting on an item in a gossip column? Sally Pembroke Kingsley supports family whose father was permanently injured and baby brother killed in her divorced husband's drunken spree."

"Yes. That was it."

"Well, a lot of people saw that item, including three people from publishing who went after her to write a book—or allow somebody to write it for her. But I decided to go after Adam. You see, Sally Pembroke and I grew up together, and the whole picture of Sally Kingsley, noble wife, made me want to throw up. It didn't sound at all like the obnoxious child who pushed over my summer cool-drink stand, five cents a swallow from a free straw . . . "

He caught my bewildered eye and grinned. "The Pembrokes had a place in Maine next to ours. One summer when I was saving for a bicycle, I decided to avail myself of the free-enterprise system and set up a cool-drink stand where everybody coming off the bridge onto our island had to pass. Sally came along and said she wanted in. I told her to shove off. After all, she already had a bicycle. She promptly drove her bike into my stand and into me. I picked myself up and clouted her. When her father came up at that strategic moment, she told him how I had attacked her. He stormed off to see my father. The next day, the stand was hers."

I burst out laughing. "And on such cosmic events are publishing decisions made."

"That, plus the fact that I've always thought Adam's

Prize novel the best novel written in this country in the past half century. And I think *Journey*'s even better."

I didn't reply for a minute. In front of my mental eye was the memory of a golden-haired woman whose staggering beauty was as much a subject of campus comment as her husband's talent. Beside her, when they appeared in the college dining room at dinner, he looked large and clumsy, like a lumberjack who had just wandered in from the woods. Which was logical enough because I had read that at one point he had been a lumberjack . . .

"Antonia, are you listening to me?"

"Yes, Max." But there was something that didn't fit. "But do you mean that when you found Adam he told you this? About the agreement, I mean?"

"Oh, no. But I know a lot of people who know Sally; it was easy enough to dig out."

"Does Adam know you know this?"

"Yes—unfortunately. I was stupid enough to let him know I knew."

"And he told you to mind your own business?"

"With a few scathing adjectives attached. Which was why I thought I was being so clever in having you invite him to your basement apartment."

"Why didn't you tell me all this in the first place? I might have been able to put more oomph into my act."

He sighed. "I should have." He got up. "But that bucket of milk's already been kicked over."

"Max—what happened to the three publishers who went after Sally Kingsley?"

He was at the door, but he turned and grinned. "One of them got taken for a contract. He had everything all lined up, even somebody who would do the actual writing. And he gave her a hefty advance. But the time for the manuscript to be delivered came and went, and no book. The lawyers are still trying to get the advance back for nonfulfillment of contract."

"But why? Why did she even sign one if she had no intention of doing a book?"

"According to rumor, and the ghost who was lined up, there was not enough there for a book. What they wanted, of course, was the inside story of the marriage—you know, Adam's drinking, the fights, the other women, the car accident, all the dirt. But when it came to actually getting it down, she was a no show."

"I wonder why. The story of that marriage certainly left enough of a comet's trail on several continents."

"Well, there's another rumor about that: apparently Adam said that if she went to print with all of that, then he'd make public the fact that those touching stories about her supporting that family and paying his debts are phony; that he's paying back all she handed over."

"So then they're blackmailing each other."

"No. Because Adam quite voluntarily drew up that agreement long before the publishers came a-courting. I told you he had fiendish pride."

As he was about to go, I said, "I'm sorry, Max. I mean about not convincing Adam to stay in the apartment."

"Maybe you couldn't have anyway." He shrugged and walked out.

I was sitting, staring at the typewriter, when my telephone rang. Rather absent-mindedly I picked up the receiver. "Hello."

"This is Adam Kingsley," his voice said in its usual abrupt manner. "Is that offer of renting your basement still open?"

"Yes," I replied, surprised and surrendering to the inevitable. "Have you changed your mind?"

"No. But the man who owns the farm I've been living on has. I called him to tell him I was coming back and it threw him into a turmoil. Apparently he's been using my absence to have the cottage I live in renovated, painted and weather-stripped. He says the place is a shambles and will be for the next three weeks. He knew I had made a reservation at the hotel here for that long and snatched the opportunity."

"It's just as well. Max has been in here fuming over the extra delay."

"When do you plan to move in?"

"In about two weeks. Sooner, if possible. Somebody has discovered the house is empty and has been making him-, her- or themselves at home there."

"What are you charging for rent?"

My mind promptly went blank. "I don't know. I hadn't thought that far."

"You'll never get rich that way."

"I hadn't planned to. Anyway, it was . . . " I swallowed the rest of the sentence, but Adam finished it for me.

"Max's idea. Yes, I know. Let me know when you have decided on a rent." And he hung up.

"Yes, Sahib," I muttered to myself. Adam might be broke, in debt, disgraced and blind, but his arrogance seemed to have survived intact.

The next two weeks passed in a haze of packing, sorting, throwing away, almost daily trips to Brooklyn Heights, papers to sign, painters, paperhangers, plumbers and contractors.

Having on two previous occasions felt the necessity of sneaking out of the office, I now came in late, left early and absented myself whenever necessary. And Max, having gotten his way about Adam, looked on benignly.

Slowly the house took shape, or rather regained something of what must have been its original beauty and elegance. One morning when I arrived I found myself staring at the new shiny black paint of the front door, and for the first time I felt that the house was not a monster that had been wished on me and that I was moving into against my basic will. I looked down. Even the step had been scrubbed. And the short iron railings on either side of the stoop had been painted also.

"Looks a lot better, doesn't it?" A voice said behind me. I turned. There, with his bike, was the kid I had seen before, his light brown hair in a fuzzy halo around his square face.

"Yes, it does," I agreed.

Then I remembered the footsteps inside the house the day Ewen and I were there, and all the refuse that had been left. Evidently my unpleasant recollections started to show on my face, because my young companion started rapidly getting on his bicycle.

"Hey, wait a minute," I yelled, as he was about to ride off.

He paused, putting one foot down beside him. "Yeah?"

"What's your name?"

"Why d'ya wanna know?"

"Aren't we neighbors?"

"Yeah. But I don't want to take a lot of flak because people have been busting in the house. It wasn't me."

He had answered my question before I asked it. But I was intrigued by the fact that he knew it had been broken into.

"Well, I'm not going to give you a lot of flak. But I did wonder if you could tell me who'd been using it as a temporary shelter."

He shrugged. "How should I know?"

He was wary and hostile, just, I suddenly realized, the way Ewen might be if somebody were questioning him in this fashion.

"I'm sorry," I said. "I didn't mean to sound like the prosecuting attorney. I just thought . . . "

"What?"

"Well, maybe you saw somebody." I said it without a vestige of hope that he had, or that, if he had, he would tell me. But life was full of surprises.

"Well, if that's all—yeah, I did."

I was about to unlock the door, but I turned back fast. "You did?"

"Yeah. I mean I didn't see him breaking in or anything like that. Only he was walking up and down the street, like he was counting the houses. Then he came back to here and went up the steps. Only he didn't go in. Just put his hands on the front door. Then he came back down again."

I stared at him. "What—by the way, you still didn't tell me your name."

"It's Bonzo. Bonzo Malloy."

Diverted for a minute, I smiled. "Is Bonzo your real name, or is it a nickname?"

Red flowed into the square cheeks. For the first time he looked like a little boy rather than the neighborhood tough he was trying hard to appear.

"It's really Beverly. But who wants to be called that? Bonzo is what the kids at school call me."

"Okay, Bonzo. What did he look like? The man who walked up and down."

Bonzo chewed on some gum for a bit, Then, "He was tall and blond. Wore shades. Had a big dog."

Chapter 6

Ewen and I moved ten days later. It was a day of unspeakable confusion and noise, and threatened to end in calamity when we suddenly got into one of our rare fights right in the middle of the move.

Needless to say, it was over his animals, and occurred when the movers reached his room and started to move out his furniture. What with the noise of the dollies, the yells and heavy feet, Mr. Ears, the rabbit, almost threw his cage on the floor, rushing in fright from one corner to another, the gerbils and mice thrashed around, and high squeaks of panic punctuated hoarse instructions and periodic thuds. Wilma went under the bed from which she refused to emerge, and which the men refused to touch, since every time they did Wilma would utter one of her bone-chilling growls.

When I tried to tell them she was all show, the chief mover said, "You insured for dog bites, lady? Because I'm not, and I'm not having my men bit."

"Ewen," I said, my temper beginning to fray, "get Wilma out from under the bed. Now."

Ewen bent double. "Come on out, Wilma, old girl," he said cheerfully. "Nobody's going to hurt you."

Wilma barked, but showed no signs of moving.

Ewen straightened. "Why don't they finish with the rest of the moving, Mom? I want to get the animals calmed down anyway, and put Nemesis's harness on."

"We're behind time now," one of the men said, and started towards the bookcase. Unfortunately, the heavy rope he was carrying caught in Mr. Ears' cage and brought it crashing down.

Ewen gave a cry and bent down. There was a flash of white from Ewen's pocket.

"Hey, look at the rat," one of the men yelled.

"Get him!" another one cried.

"Don't you dare!" Ewen rose and charged the men, catching them off guard and pushing them out the door. Then he slammed it and stood in front of it, the men standing facing him.

"You better let us in, kid."

"If you don't move, we're going to move you."

"We didn't contract to move no menageries . . . "

Ewen, his eyes blazing, folded his arms. "Mom, tell these movers they can't come in my room until my animals have settled down. Ears has probably had a heart attack and I've got to find Einstein."

It had been a harrowing week, with long hours packing the boxes the movers left so as to cut down the cost. Furthermore, I had told Ewen to have his animals ready, of which I now reminded him. "You knew the movers were going to be here. I told you to have the cages stacked and ready. The men are already two hours overtime, and I am paying them by the hour. Get away from the door."

"Mom, if Einstein gets out, as tame as he is, he'll go up to anybody . . . some dog will . . . he'll get killed . . . " Suddenly Ewen's unpredictable voice shot up. His lips quivered before he tightened them.

"Lady, we move that furniture now or we quit."

I am ashamed of the fact that my temper snapped. "Ewen, if you don't stand away from that door, I'll tell the mover to move you."

The words were not out of my mouth before I realized how wrong I was, regardless of moving men or cost.

A bleak, stubborn look came down over Ewen's face. "Then they'll have to move me. Because I'm not opening the door."

"Ewen," I started, appalled at the look on his face, when a voice spoke from behind me. "Can I help?"

I swung around to see Max standing in the open doorway. Beside him stood Adam and Tania.

"I realize we couldn't have come at a worse time," Max said. "I didn't know you were moving today, or if I did, I'd forgotten. Somehow I thought it was next week. I brought Adam, who had some tapes he wanted to leave with you. Well, never mind that now. I couldn't help hearing some of all this. Would it help if Adam and I drove Ewen and his animals to Brooklyn? I have the station wagon outside."

"Would you?" Ewen burst out before I could answer. "That would be absolutely great!"

"Max," I said, feeling both grateful and tired, "this is my son, Ewen. As he says, it would be great if you would drive him and his zoo."

"Yeah, and what about all the time we're wasting," the chief mover started to say.

Max turned to him. "Then you will charge accordingly and it will be paid to you, and you will now be quiet," he said firmly. He looked at me. "Who is Einstein?"

"He's Ewen's white rat. He got excited and jumped out of Ewen's pocket."

Ewen, his voice angry, said, "To Mom and these men he's just a rodent. But to me he's, he's, well . . . he's my friend."

"Yes, well, women don't always see it that way," Max said, man to man. "Let's go in and see if we can find him." Ewen opened the door a small amount and they slipped through.

I turned to the movers. "I'm sorry," I started to say, despising myself for wishing I had another male chauvinist to take up the cudgels for me. To my surprise, Adam spoke. "Where is the chief mover?" he asked quietly.

"Here," one of the men growled.

Adam got a billfold out of his breast pocket and pulled out five dollar bills. "Why don't you have a short beer break. We'll have the animals downstairs and in the car by the time you come back and you can get on with the moving."

"Well, thanks." The mover turned to me. "Sorry about all that. It's just . . . "

"That's all right," I said quickly. "Go ahead and have your beer."

When they had gone Adam said, "It's amazing what a little money can do sometimes. Did they upset you?"

"No. I upset me. I shouldn't have spoken to Ewen that way, letting him think that I didn't feel Einstein was important."

"Do you?"

I sighed. "To be honest, no. But he is to Ewen. And therefore he *is* important and should be taken seriously." I paused. "Ewen finds it very hard to forgive people who don't value animals as much as humans. I have always understood this, but now he will think I was just putting it on and didn't really mean it and am therefore what he calls a fake, which is worse than being a pig of a pig. Because, after all, he likes pigs." I paused. "Would you care to join me in some coffee? There are two chairs left in the kitchen and I have clung onto the coffee pot."

"All right. Where is the kitchen?"

"Would you like me to lead you?"

"No, I would not. Just tell me where it is."

I bit my tongue to keep from apologizing again. I was tired of being in the wrong with all these males of different ages and conditions. "It's across the hall from where you're standing and about three feet to the left." And I left him and Tania to find their way.

"Sit," Adam said, when they had reached the kitchen and found the table and a chair. He patted the dog. "Good girl."

I poured coffee into two mugs and sat down. "When we all get moved in, you and Ewen and the animals should get on beautifully," I said bitterly.

"Leaving you on the cold outside, like the male chauvinist pigs we all are. Are all his animals males, too?"

I laughed. "No, there's Wilma, but she's a disgrace to her sex. She's large and black and fierce-looking and the moment there's the slightest threat she goes under the bed. How about Tania?"

He ran his hand down her head. "As long as she's working, she's immune to distractions. But she's not timid. Once, when we were out walking, and I heard a man's footsteps approaching, she growled, which is something she never does when she's in harness. Later, I was told by someone passing that the man had a knife."

"That's nice to know. That she'll defend you."

"Oh, yes." He took a swallow of his coffee. "I had a rat once. He wasn't white, but he was very tame and used to come when I whistled."

"You'll have to tell Ewen."

At that moment I heard Ewen's door open. Ewen and Max appeared in the doorway.

"Did you find Einstein?" I asked anxiously.

"Yes, thanks." Ewen didn't look at me. His eyes were on Tania. "That's a super dog," he said.

"Yes, she is." Adam got up. Tania stood up, too. He put his hand on her harness. "Are we ready?"

"We are," Max said. "The cages are stacked in the hall ready to go."

"Ewen," I said. But he had left.

"Max, I can't thank you enough."

"That's all right. Glad to be of service. We'll get over there and I'll leave Ewen and Adam to get the animals settled and will come back for you. Now, Ewen, let's get the zoo on the road."

The rest of the move passed without crisis. With all the animals gone the movers—soothed, no doubt, by their beer break—got the rest of Ewen's furniture down and finished carrying out the various odds and ends. With beautiful timing Max was back and within another hour the main part of the move—the actual transportation—was accomplished.

By late afternoon the movers had gone and Max and Adam were preparing to go when there was a ring at the front door.

"I'll see who it is," Ewen said.

He came back followed by Lance, who was carrying a large square box.

"He brought a pizza," Ewen said.

"Peace offering," Lance explained.

"Great," Ewen commented. "I'm starved.

I introduced Lance to Adam and Max. "Why are you bringing a peace offering?"

"Because out in your hall are two large boxes of Mrs.

Standish's papers. I'd like you to run through them and decide what you want to keep before they're thrown out."

"Why should I need to look at them? She was no relation to me."

"Because in view of her association with your aunt, they might mean more to you than anyone else."

"I don't see why, but all right."

"It'd be a favor. I'd really appreciate it. Now I've got to run."

"Don't you want some pizza?"

"Can't tonight. I'll take a raincheck."

After he'd left Max said, "I guess we'd better be pushing on."

"Stay and have some pizza."

"Yeah, there's lots here," Ewen added. "I thought . . . "

"What did you think?" I asked, still feeling as though I were trying to get myself back into Ewen's good graces.

"That maybe if Mr. Kingsley didn't mind I could ask him some questions about Tania."

There was a pause. Then, "I don't mind," Adam said abruptly. "But I think I may pass up the pizza."

Ewen led the way to the kitchen, and by the time the rest of us were assembled there, he had everything opened and had unpacked a few plates.

"Don't you like pizza, Mr. Kingsley?"

"It's a little unhandy for me to eat. And I'm not particularly hungry."

"Look," Ewen said, with a directness that I rarely heard from my reserved son, "if I'm being stupid just say so, but can I help you with the pizza?"

I took a breath, waiting for Adam's annihilating snub. My surprise was even greater than my relief when he said, "All right. If you cut the pizza piece in two and see that there are no long trailers of cheese, it will be a help."

"Sure."

We all sat down and I watched with some amazement while Ewen cut the pizza and trimmed it neatly. "Here," he said, putting the pieces on a plate and placing it in front of Adam. "It's on the plate in front of you, sort of to the right."

Adam put his hand out, and the long fingers sensitively touched the rim of the plate and moved in to the piecrust. "When I was being trained—rehabilitated as a blind person—I was told that one way to tell me where food is on the plate is to do it as though it were on a clock, such as, meat is at two o'clock, potatoes at four, string beans at nine."

"That's a neat idea," Ewen said, through a mouthful of pizza, "sort of like the Air Force. You know, planes at two o'clock, sir."

Adam grinned. "Yes, I know."

"Were you in the Air Force?"

The smile went. "No. But I've flown. Did you want to ask me about Tania?"

It was not really a rebuff, but the deliberate change of subject sounded that way. I saw Ewen withdraw behind his expressionless look, the warmth and openness shut off, and I felt a kind of angry relief. I didn't want to see Ewen pushed down and humiliated as I had been. In fact I would go to any lengths to prevent it.

"Don't ask so many questions, Ewen," I said coldly, because I was afraid. And I saw on his face surprise because I had never publicly chastised him before, followed by a flash of anger. I knew, as though I had gone inside his body, how he or any other child-adolescent would feel: outrage at injustice done. *Be nice to people, Ewen, show an interest.* How often had I said that? And now, when he did, coming out of his child's defenses, out of the solitariness that had worried me so much, I flicked him with the adult's favorite whip: authority. How could he know how many layers of fear and experience lay beneath my denigrating command?

"Ewen," I started.

"Sure. Sorry." He got up, picking up his empty plate, and went to the sink.

"Ewen," Adam said.

"Yes." Ewen turned water on the plate, his face a careful blank.

"I turned you off the subject of flying because I did it at a period of my life that I want to forget, or, at least, not to remember too much. I don't like to think about the kind of person I was at that time. I think your mother knew that, which was why she said what she did, not because you were doing anything wrong."

It was an astonishing statement. Over Max's face came a startled expression. I saw Ewen turn, the open look back on his face. "That's okay. I mean, I'm sorry . . . "

"You have no need to be sorry. Sometime, perhaps, I'll talk to you about flying, if you're interested in it. But I'd sooner now talk about Tania."

"Yeah. I'd like that. How long have you had her? Did you have to train her yourself? Or did you go to that Seeing Eye place?" Ewen, his dignity, or face, or perhaps just faith in the inhabitants of the adult world, restored, came back to the table, questions pouring out of him like peanuts from a vending machine.

And Adam answered them, at first with his usual brusqueness, but then, as Ewen said something to make him laugh, he relaxed and the talk became less question and answer and more conversation. Tania, lying back of Adam, nose on paws, seemed to follow what was going on, her intelligent golden eyes fixed on Adam's face, her sensitive ears turning as the voices came from first one side and then another.

"May I stroke her?" Ewen asked. He was sitting down beside Adam and looking down at the silvery black and brown dog between them.

"Not while she's working. She shouldn't be distracted. It confuses her and is bad for discipline."

"That sounds terribly structured. Like she was a soldier or something."

"Not a soldier. A working dog. While she's at work, she's at work. The way you are when you study or your mother is at her office or I am when I'm writing. When her harness is off she's free to be her doggy self. You can stroke her then, that is, if you and she become friends. But I'd rather you didn't feed her," he added, "because I'd just as soon not have to get up in the middle of the night and get dressed because I have to take her out to answer a call of nature."

"Oh," Ewen said, absorbing this. "I see. I mean, she takes in things on a regular basis, so she—er—"

"Can let them out on a regular basis."

Ewen grinned. "I get it. But look—don't be mad—what does she get out of this? I mean, she works almost all of the time."

"Love," Adam said simply. "I'm dependent on her, and she knows it. She also knows I give her friendship and affection. Once, when I had to go into hospital for a minor operation, I was taken back to the farm for a few hours while I was convalescing. But someone who knows Tania came and took her away while I was there, so she wouldn't have to go through the separation once again, it had upset her so much before. You know the traditional working dogs—the shepherds, the collies, the retrievers—not only enjoy work. They thrive on it. That's why they are chosen for guide work. Other breeds of dogs that are just as intelligent don't have that particular element in their nature. For example, a poodle—one of the most intelligent of dogs—was taken for training. But she could not be taught what the trainers call intelligent disobedience."

"What's that?"

"If I give Tania the command to go forward, but she sees an obstacle—say an open manhole—ahead, she doesn't go straight: she leads me around. The same if it's a ladder which she could walk under, but I couldn't. But the poodle, which is not and never has been trained as a working dog, could not get this. When told to go forward in front of a manhole, she'd simply jump over it. If she'd been guiding a blind person, he'd have fallen in."

"I see," Ewen said.

"Speaking of dogs," I asked, "where's Wilma?"

"Under the bed upstairs," Ewen said. "I closed her in."

"How did the ride go with Tania and the zoo traveling together?"

"Tania didn't even react," Ewen commented, almost aggrieved. "Wilma started whimpering, so I put her on the floor. And I kept Nemesis in his carrier, which he didn't like, because he bellowed all the way over here."

I glanced down at Tania. "And this well-bred lady didn't twitch an ear? It's hard to believe."

Adam smiled. "Not while she's working, but I wouldn't like to bet what she'd do off the harness. We'll have to work that out when I come here. While we're on the subject, when would it be convenient for me to move in?"

"As long as you don't mind a certain amount of confusion, any time."

"All right. How about a week from tomorrow? That'll give you time to get settled."

"Do you have enough stuff to furnish Adam's quarters?" Max asked. "Because if you don't, Betty and I have an attic full at our place in the country. Beds, carpets, chairs."

"Let me think," I said, and then after a minute. "If you have it, I could use an extra bed, an easy chair and a carpet. I was going to put Ewen's down there, because he can sleep on the cot he used to have and which he uses when his friends stay overnight, but having another bed would be better. Maybe I could buy it from you?"

"I'd be happy to donate it. Betty's been threatening a garage sale now for nearly a year. But being a packrat, I've been putting her off."

"Let me buy the bed," Adam said quickly.

"No, Adam," I said. "Because when you're not here I'd like to rent it out to someone else. I can use the income."

Ewen reverted to his favorite subject. "How old is Tania?"

While Adam was answering that I glanced at Max, who was quietly working on his third slice of pizza, a thoughtful look in his eyes. I wondered what he had made of the cat Adam had let out of the bag—that we had known one another before—but now was not the moment to find out.

New Yorkers were nicer than they had been given credit for, I thought about half an hour later as the doorbell rang and an attractive young woman who introduced herself as Susan Hirsch brought some fried chicken in a napkin. Within the next forty minutes two more neighbors showed up, one with a cheese and another with a casserole. When I expressed surprise and gratification to the last one to arrive, a Mrs. Cunningham, she grinned a little.

"We're very block conscious these days. Our children are into the community thing. But we're also happy to have the house bought and occupied."

"I didn't exactly buy it," I began, and saw the smile freeze on her face.

"You mean you've only rented it and might move out anytime? It still belongs to those awful people who let it run down and become practically a flophouse?"

"No," I said hastily. "It's mine. I inherited it."

"You *inherited* the old Standish house? How could that be? Are you a Standish?"

I had no idea of its cause, but I could not mistake the hostility in her voice. "I must get back," she said suddenly, and made for the front door.

Ewen's reaction was much quicker than mine. "We're not Standishes. We're Moncrieffs."

Mrs. Cunningham, a middle-aged, rather plain woman

with an oddly powerful face, hesitated at the front door. She half turned. "But you must be related to the Standishes, or you wouldn't inherit."

I put out a hand to Ewen, to forestall any further enlightening comment from him. "Why does it matter so much? What was wrong with the Standishes?"

Some darkness seemed to flicker over her features. "You should read their family history sometime. Their real history. Not the pap that was handed out to the historical society. Good night." And with that she was out and the door closed behind her.

"Fascinating," Max said. "I wonder if there's a—"

"Book there?" I finished for him.

He grinned at me. "No harm in finding out, Antonia."

"None at all. But I think I will establish myself as a non-Standish first."

Adam had stood up. "I think it's about time we shoved off, Max. Antonia and Ewen must be ready to collapse."

Max stood up. "Right. You must be. If you need us tomorrow, Antonia, give us a buzz and the station wagon will be right over."

Until that moment I hadn't realized just how tired I was. Thanking the men, I closed the front door after them. "Adam was right, Ewen. I'm not sure I can even make it upstairs. I'll leave the dishes to do tomorrow."

"Okay," Ewen agreed with alacrity. Quite naturally, he was never one to push housework, although he was good about helping me, if I reminded him once or twice. He went up the stairs two at a time. "I think I'll go fix and feed the animals. And I want to let Nemesis out to get acquainted with the house."

By this time, he was up two flights, one of his delights about the house being that he had a whole floor to himself. I turned out the lights and checked the locks on both the front door and, downstairs in the basement, the door leading to the cellar stairs. I knew I should go down one more flight, now that the stairs had been fixed, and check the door in the cellar out to the garden. But the thought of the crawling and scampering inhabitants I might encounter was more than I could face. Then I made my way slowly up to the parlor floor, locking the door to the basement stairs securely behind me, and then up to the second floor to the master bedroom at the back overlooking the garden.

It had been a long time since I had gone through the dislocations of moving and I had forgotten how depressing it is to go to bed in a strange place in the midst of unpacked cartons, especially if one has to dig into two or three boxes to find the necessaries for taking a bath. But finally I had the bed made, soaked for half an hour in a hot tub and gotten into bed for some soothing reading.

But even the P.G. Wodehouse I had picked to counter my growing depression didn't do the trick, nor did it distract my attention from the small but steady draft that seemed to come from somewhere. After a while I got up and went over to the windows. They were all shut and there was no air coming in. Then I wandered over to the fireplace. It was cooler there, but the fireplace itself was bricked up and my hand could find no moving air.

It has to be my imagination, I said to myself. I crawled back under the covers and gave myself up to the wafflings of Bertie Wooster. But what kept coming across my inner vision was Ewen's face in the other apartment when I had shown my basic indifference to Einstein's fate, and later when I rebuked him in front of the movers. I had always tried to make him feel that I was his first defender, in his corner at all times. Now I had, perhaps hopelessly, tarnished that record. A woman, I thought, weakly giving in to descending misery, should not attempt to bring up a young male alone. This kind of misunderstanding was bound to happen, and who knew what dreadful scars he would blame me for in later life? By this time my hand was clutching tissues from the box beside my bed, and the tears were running down my cheeks.

You're just sorry for yourself, I said to myself, and as I was about to abandon myself to a good cry, there was a knock on the door.

"Can I come in?" Ewen called.

"Of course," I said, and hastily blew my nose.

Ewen, in pajamas and robe and wet hair clinging to his neck, pushed the door open. Cuddled in his arm was Einstein.

"Hi," he said. "I wondered if you'd like to have Einstein for company."

Perhaps the company of a white rat is not every woman's idea of a comfort offering, but I was so touched I almost cried again. "Ewen, darling, how nice of you. I thought maybe you didn't think I—er—appreciated Einstein sufficiently."

Ewen grinned. "I didn't. But Mr. Bainbridge and Mr. Kingsley explained that it didn't have anything to do with how you felt about Einstein. Just that you were worried. And Einstein likes you. I mean, I would have brought Nemesis, but you know how he is."

I did indeed. Within two minutes of Ewen's leaving and closing the door behind him, Nemesis would make such a racket that I'd have to let him out.

"Yes, darling. I know how he is."

"The thing is, you ought to have an animal of your own."

I stared at Ewen a little mistily. "I do."

"You do?"

"Yes. You. You're my favorite . . . animal." Just at the last moment I avoided the yawning pit of calling Ewen my pet. Even so, he looked disgusted.

"Do you object to being called an animal?" I asked a little

timidly. "After all, that's what you assured me you were not long ago."

"No. It's just that I thought you were going to call me your pet or something."

I sighed. "I almost did. I suppose that deeply offends you."

"It's pretty sickening. Shall I leave Einstein?"

"I think he'd be happier with you, Ewen. Particularly in a strange house."

"Yeah, I guess. Well, good night."

"Good night." I thought about asking him to come over and give me a kiss, but felt too cowed to try. I was therefore almost undone when Ewen ambled over to the bed, and, putting his free arm around me, gave me a hug followed by a kiss on the cheek. He was still holding Einstein, so my other cheek was caressed by Einstein's whiskers, and I tried, almost successfully, to keep my mind off the proximity of Einstein's whiskers to Einstein's teeth.

"Thank you, darling," I said, returning his kiss.

Ewen straightened up. "You know, it's cold in here," he said. "You must have a window open."

"No, I don't. And what's more, the fireplace is bricked up. I don't know where that air is coming from."

Ewen went over to the fireplace and moved his hand around in front of it just as I had done. "You're right," he said. "It isn't coming from there. Maybe it's a ghost. They're suppose to turn everything cold."

"Where on earth did you get that?" I asked, not at all pleased.

"Some book on the occult that a kid had at school."

"Since the school is attached to the cathedral, I'm surprised they let you have books like that."

"Oh, they don't. It's part of our underground library."

"An underground library! What else is in it?"

Ewen grinned. "Porn."

I closed my eyes. "Go to bed, Ewen. I'm too young for all this."

He laughed and went out.

I turned off the light and, getting up, defiantly opened the window. "Now, ghost," I said more bravely than I felt, "do your worst!" That sounded so insanely challenging that I added, though, of course, I did not believe in ghosts, "No, never mind. I apologize. No offense meant!"

Having bitten off the large, initial bite of moving, everything after that seemed to settle more easily. The endless cartons slowly got unpacked. Bookshelves that I had ordered arrived and the books were put up in the living room downstairs, Ewen's bedroom and mine. A contractor turned up and unbricked all the fireplaces.

Five nights after we had moved in Ewen arrived home somewhat later than usual, having been to a meeting of his Naturalists Club.

"Hi," he said, tumbling all the books that had been on his arm onto a chair. He looked at the fire I had lit in the living room fireplace. "Hey, that's nice."

"Yes, isn't it," I said rather dreamily. Back in the kitchen a casserole was heating in the oven, the salad was made, ready for dressing and tossing, and I was taking my ease with a manuscript in front of the fire. "It makes me feel like a genuine, eighteen-carat lady."

Ewen strolled toward the fireplace. "I thought the word was banned by women's lib?" Predictably, Einstein was sticking his head out of Ewen's parka pocket. But I frowned a little at the cardboard box in his hand. "If there's anything we don't need, Ewen, it's another carton."

"This is a present for you."

My eyes fixed on the carton, which seemed, suddenly, to be jiggling about in an ominous fashion. "I can hardly wait. What is it?"

Ewen pushed aside the string, pulled the tops back, and lifted out a small furry bundle. "I call her Cleopatra," he said, and put a calico kitten down in my lap. The kitten and I stared at each other. A patch of black fur covered one eye, making her look as though her wig had slipped.

"Ewen," I said desperately.

At that moment, the kitten marched up my front, braced her back claws on my chest, and proceeded to inspect my face. And there we rested, nose to nose. Then she went up to my shoulder, went round and round in a circle, finding a comfortable position, and finally nestled into a ball, her nose breathing gently against my neck.

"Yes, Mom?"

"Thanks," I said.

He gave one of his rare, blinding smiles. "I thought you should have one of your own. You know, somebody to sleep with."

I considered disputing that comment, or perhaps going into the matter of preferences. Then I decided to leave it alone.

It was two days later that I encountered Bonzo again, when I got home from work.

"That guy was back again," he said, without preamble. "You know, the blond guy, the one with the dog."

"Thanks," I said, fitting in my key and going into the front door. I felt mean not inviting him in and letting him meet Ewen when he got home. But for one thing, I didn't think Ewen liked to be presented with somebody already in his own kitchen. For another, I had a hard time warming to Bonzo. His tough-guy stance was, I suspected, mostly façade, but it was a convincing one.

But, once in, I decided to telephone Adam. I had been meaning to find out at what hour he was arriving the following Sunday.

"How about the afternoon," Adam said. "Max said he'd drive me."

"Fine. By the way, my spies have informed me that you and Tania have been over here casing the street twice, the last time this afternoon. Why didn't you hang around longer, you might have been invited in to have a drink?" The last was added because I didn't want to sound like I was investigating his movements. But then I got a shock.

"Well, I don't know who's been telling you what, Antonia. But except for the day you moved and I went over with Max and Ewen, I've never been in Brooklyn Heights to my knowledge in my life."

I sat there at the hall table after I had put down the receiver. It was very plain: either Adam was lying, or . . . My resistance to the thought that Adam was lying was oddly strong, far stronger than common sense would have indicated. After all, people do lie. But why should Adam bother to hide the fact that he might have wanted to vet the streets before moving here permanently? For a blind man it wouldn't even rank as eccentric—surely the most natural act. Then why deny it?

I played with the idea for a while, keeping my attention on Adam's possible motives for evading the truth, telling myself that lying was not, by most people, considered the arch sin I had been brought up to believe it was. In fact, I looked at anything rather than confront the alternative: that it was another man, a fair-haired man, with, most mysteriously, a dog, who had walked up and down inspecting the house. But, eventually, I could no longer evade what the alternative might be. Or rather, who.

There was only one other man I had ever known, who had invaded and changed my life, whose fair hair—far lighter than Adam's dark wheat-colored head—made him noticeable at a distance, and that was Dauntry Leigh.

Dauntry, with his silvery blond hair and gray eyes and athlete's graceful body, was far handsomer than Adam even before the accident that had scarred the latter's face and destroyed his eyes. Dauntry's looks and charm were such as would attract the notice of anybody, certainly the impressionable Bonzo, loitering on the street. After all, why not? I had seen a whole roomful of people turn and fall silent as they looked at Dauntry, lost in the kind of wonder and attraction that even the most insensitive feel in the presence of great beauty, whether male or female, and this without Dauntry making a move, with no beckoning smile on his finely chiseled features.

But if it were Dauntry ... My stomach quite literally contracted at the thought. When, twelve and a half years before, I had been thrown out of our apartment by Dauntry and, disgraced and humiliated, had fled the campus without even packing all my clothes, I had assumed that Dauntry would continue on his successful, brilliant way and end up where he was obviously headed, as the chief of some exalted laboratory on the West Coast.

Lifting the receiver again, I dialed Laurence Metcalf's number.

"Hi," he said, with his customary cheer. "How does it feel to be a householder?"

"Tiring."

"Once you've settled all the stuff and cleared out the

garbage you'll love it. There's nothing like having one of those great brownstones of one's own. Apartment living can't compare to it."

"Don't you live in an apartment?"

"That's different. I'm a bachelor."

"I see. I didn't realize it made that much difference." There was no way I could ask the question filling my mind except straight out. So I said baldly, "Lance, is Dauntry Leigh in the vicinity?"

"Why do you ask?"

"Because it has twice been reported to me from our local wire service—a small boy who keeps tabs on the neighborhood—that a fair-haired man with dark glasses and a dog has been seen casing the street, my house in particular."

"That could be—" He stopped short.

"That could be who?" I said, a funny alarm going off in my mind.

"That could be Dauntry," he said easily. "He's come east for some scientists' conference or other."

I didn't know which sent more alarm signals through me: the fact that Dauntry was here or that Lance had so obviously started to say something else.

"But why would he wear dark glasses and have a dog with him?" I knew the obvious answer: to impersonate Adam. But I waited painfully to see if Lance said it.

"Antonia, you are really . . ."

"What?"

"Well, I was about to say paranoid, but I don't think it would sound polite."

"Don't let that stand in the way of truth."

"What truth? As long as I've known Dauntry, he's always had a dog. And you must know as well as I that no Californian would go out even in a dense fog without dark glasses."

148

I laughed. "All right, Lance. But I wish you'd let me know about Dauntry's being here."

"Why? You're divorced, and it wasn't even a friendly divorce."

It was all so plausible. Why, indeed, should he have told me? Yet, in some strange way, I knew I was beginning to feel encircled: the house, Adam, Dauntry, all from a past I was determined to forget, a self I wanted never again to think about . . .

I had hung up and was sitting there, only vaguely aware that Cleopatra was trying to climb up the leg of my pants suit, when the front door opened and Ewen walked in.

I turned and stared at him. Standing there, his pale hair looked almost silvery in the afternoon light streaming through the door.

"Why are you looking at me like that?" Ewen asked.

"Like what?" I played for time, trying to still the pounding of my heart.

"Like I was a ghost or something."

"You are," I said. "A ghost from the past."

"What past? Who's past?"

"Yours. Mine. Your father's." The minute I said that I knew I had made a mistake.

"What about my father?" Ewen asked, alerted.

"Just that you look like him."

"You've never said that before. Not that I looked like him."

"Maybe it's simply that you're getting older. After all, I only knew him as a man. And you're getting to look more like a man yourself."

He was pleased at that. I could tell by the way he flushed.

I got up, feeling suddenly tired. Emotion can be wearing, especially if it's fear.

"You do like Cleopatra, don't you?" Ewen asked, looking

now not like his father, but like the boy he was, a little anxious that I was not cherishing his gift, partly because it was his gift, but mostly because he worried about his animals all the time.

"Of course I like Cleopatra. How could I not when she let me have some of her pillow last night?"

"What pillow?"

"My pillow, dunce. What other pillow is there on my bed? She appropriated it immediately and never left except in those moments when she got right under the covers and reminded herself of her mother by kneading her claws on my back."

"Oh, that means she liked you. I thought for a moment there, when I saw your face, that you were sorry I had brought her."

I bent and picked Cleo up. A loud purr vibrated her ribs. "We're great friends," I said, and was rewarded by seeing the anxious look disappear from his face.

"Well," he said, "what were you thinking about before, when I came in?"

"Why do you keep asking that? Did I look strange?"

"I'll say. Like you'd been fired or something."

"I was probably wondering what we're going to eat for supper, in view of the fact that I forgot to unfreeze our chicken this morning."

Which just shows how quickly a lie is born, because I had been thinking about his father.

Chapter 7

Dauntry telephoned the next morning at the office.

"How are you?" he said, with his old, easy charm, precisely as though we had been exchanging good will for the past twelve and a half years.

"Just fine, thanks. How are you?"

"The same."

I tried to get some grip on my jangling nerves. Perhaps, I thought, he is really just calling to say hello, to say, in effect, no hard feelings . . .

"I said I'd like to have lunch with you today, Antonia. That is what you're calling yourself, now, isn't it?"

"Yes." The lunch invitation itself was common enough. There was no reason for my heart to freeze, then pound like a rabbit's. "I'm afraid I can't today, Dauntry," I said, staring at my blank calendar page. "Another time, perhaps."

"No, Antonia. I think it has to be today. There's something I want to talk to you about."

"Oh, what?"

"Something I think you wouldn't want discussed on the telephone. You know how these switchboards are."

"There's nothing we have to discuss, Dauntry."

"Now that's where you're wrong. I'd rather it be in a civilized way, over lunch. But if you really can't make it, then I can come to your office, or perhaps to your new home—in Brooklyn Heights, isn't it?"

It was all I could do to prevent my teeth from chattering as they used to. It was one of my humiliations that when Dauntry started, in that light, almost idle voice, to indulge his anger, or cruelty, or even just amusement, I could no more stop my teeth from their reflex chattering than I could prevent my eye from blinking over a caught eyelash.

But I made a huge effort, and to say something, commented, "Well, you should know. You've been hovering around there with your shades and your dog—although I can't imagine why."

"My dear Antonia, so your paranoid fanatsies—or perhaps not so much paranoid as wistful fantasies—have not ceased after all. Why should I lurk like some policeman in clumsy disguise around your house?"

"I have no idea. But I was definitely told that a blond man with dark glasses and a dog had been seen there twice." Too late, I remembered that it was never wise to answer him back.

"Then it must have been your other boyfriend. Tut, Antonia! Fancy not being able to tell the difference."

"But you always have dogs," I said rather desperately, repeating Lance's statement.

"Back in California I have two. And if you're about to tell me that all Californians take their showers wearing dark glasses, I'll agree with you. But I have not been around your house. Nor indeed in Brooklyn Heights."

"But—"

"And you should know that I don't lie," he said gently. "I have never once lied to you."

Technically—as far as I knew—he was telling the truth. "Our whole life was a lie," I said with a bitterness I thought I had left behind. "And that includes your courtship, our marriage, and everything that followed."

"But not our son," he said smoothly. "Meet me for lunch today, or I will have a talk with him, and I don't think you'd like that. The Algonquin Hotel. Twelve thirty." And he hung up.

For about ten minutes I just sat there without moving. Then I got up, went to the ladies' room and was vilely sick. I had rinsed out my mouth with the corporation mouthwash supplied by the management and was washing my face in cold water when Melissa came in. "Greetings," she said cheerfully. "Have you heard the latest?"

"No," I muttered, keeping my head well down in the wash basin.

"Well . . ."

To this day I don't remember, if I actually heard, what tidbit she was passing on. Whatever it was slid through my mind and out the other side until I caught the words, "What's he really like, Antonia?"

"Who?" I said, talking through the water, though I knew.

"Adam Kingsley, of course, you nut! Who else would it be? The receptionist said he's really badly banged up. And when I asked her if he tried to flirt with her, she acted as though I had said the funniest thing on earth. Apparently he came over like the height of austerity. I must say it says worlds for our prison reform system . . . " She rattled on and on while I kept washing and rewashing my face, hoping to slap some color into it. But I couldn't run the water for ever. Eventually I had to stand up.

" . . . and as for that dog of his . . . Hey, Antonia, you look terrible."

"Thanks so much. You're too kind." I bent forward and looked in the mirror that runs along the top of the basins. Melissa was right. My face was gray behind my few remaining freckles. Feeling like Scarlett O'Hara, I pinched my cheeks and a little pale rose came up and started immediately to recede.

"Are you sick?" Melissa asked abruptly.

"Well, I just threw up."

"Been out on the town? No—you're not the type to have a hangover."

For some reason I found myself resenting this. "How do you know?"

"Because although you have the kind of undernourished good looks that I'm sorry to say are the height of fashion—I could starve myself for *weeks* and not get those interesting hollows under my cheekbones—they seem to be wasted on you. Why aren't you more—er—liberated?"

"How do you know I'm not?"

"I don't know how I know but I know. There's something about you of the unbreached citadel." She saw me wince. "Sorry about the ghastly pun and all that. But I do know several of our macho males, including the patrician Max, have made one or two unsuccessful attempts on your virginity."

"My virginity? With a twelve-year-old son clumping around the place?"

"That's what I mean. Despite your clumping son—and I resent that description on behalf of Ewen, who will one day

154

break hearts—you remain the snow queen, beautiful but remote behind the castle walls and the fence of thorns. It's not at all modern or in keeping with the times."

"Melissa—you talk more nonsense than any six people I have ever known."

"It's not nonsense. Simple envy." She looked at me a moment. "What is it, love? Anything to do with Ewen?"

Everything to do with Ewen, though I was determined not to say so. Melissa meant well. But her probing curiosity occasionally amounted to a disease. "Nothing at all, Melissa." I raked around in my mind for an acceptable excuse. "I think it's all the furor of moving. It's been upsetting, to say the least."

"Oh. Sure, I guess so." She accepted that statement, and her visible disappointment that it was not scandalous or titillating was almost ludicrous.

I turned to go. As I got to the door, Melissa said, "You haven't said what he's like."

"Who?"

She sighed. "Who do you think? Our Big Author. Mr. Mysterious. Adam Kingsley. I think it's damn funny you've been so close about it. And Max won't even let me put out a release yet. Not until Kingsley goes back to his country retreat."

"He's right, Melissa. You know how the papers and radio and TV would be. Better save it for publication time."

"I suppose so. But you'd think, the way you're being so chesty with it, that he's your long-lost love or something . . . ye gods!"

The red was in my face before I had the wit to turn away.

"So that's it!" she said, much as a miner might exclaim over the gold he'd long been panning for. "Well, well, well . . . who'd have thunk it!"

I went out, slamming the door.

At twelve I left the office and started to walk slowly over to the Algonquin. As I passed the various restaurants and storefronts, I caught sight of my reflection and once, in front of a particularly dark pane, giving back a clear mirror-image, I hesitated and stopped. Would Dauntry recognize me? And as I thought that, staring at the tall, spare, fashionable woman reflected in the store window, I saw, as vividly as though she were standing beside me, my younger self, seventeen-year-old Mary Antonia Moncrieff, as she arrived at the little college and how she must have struck its most glamorous inhabitant, Dauntry Leigh.

Those were the early sixties, but the characteristic sixties look—the natural hair, straight or frizzy—had not yet broken over the campuses. We were still, in spirit, in the fifties, and judged by the standards of that particular era, my straight, thick, coarse red hair was a disaster. Therefore, just before embarking on my new life away from home at college, I had treated myself to a cheap home permanent. Even I, bent on curls—and the more the better—knew when I had finished that something had gone wrong, so I oiled and watered and flattened it, and was passably pleased with the results. My soul lusted after sweaters and skirts, the uniform then of all college girls, but what I wore were hand-me-downs from my stepmother and other ladies of the parish. Since the clothes had been altered and made over, I didn't think they looked too bad. It had taken an overheard remark from one of the wittier sorority girls to set me right: "My dear, pure mid-century mission barrel! You'd think—" But at that moment she caught sight of me and swallowed the rest of what she was going to say.

So, in addition to my part-time job at the library, I took another washing dishes at a nearby beanery, and instead of paying the next installment on my tuition, bought the most expensive sweater and skirt I could find. When I later had to appeal to my parents for the money to stay in college for the next quarter, I received a four-page reproach on succumbing to the fleshpots of the world. But because I had, by then, attracted the notice of the college's most shining bachelor, with his rich, eastern panache, I considered the cost well worth it.

He had come to the college when I did, only he came as one of the few graduate students, doing his thesis, he told me, in psychology. It never occurred to me to question such a project, any more than I questioned what such a swan as Dauntry was doing among all us geese in that church-oriented college in the first place. And if his faculty advisor thought to query him, he was undoubtedly discouraged. The new little college, desperately seeking status, was bent on encouraging its fledgling graduate department.

That such a man should notice me was incredible, that he should take me out and pay me court, a dream come true. My experience of men had been zero. In most ways I had been brought up like a girl of a much earlier era. Our tiny community was a theocracy run by my father, the pastor, and the elders of his rigidly fundamentalist church. There were no television, movies, drinking or card games. In addition to that, my stepmother, her sense of duty unencumbered by natural affection, made it her main project to see that I entered adulthood as pure as chaperonage and a nine-o'clock curfew could keep me. And, finally, I was, as daughter of the manse, considered out of bounds for any buckish impulses on the part of our rather cowed population of young males.

I had made up for these deficiencies by a long and rich fantasy life, in and out of which walked male figures fashioned by the kind of literature I was allowed to read: Sir Launcelot, The Green Knight, Mr. D'Arcy, Mr. Rochester.... The trouble with that became immediately apparent: the boys on the campus looked just like the boys at home—gauche, callow, inept, inarticulate. In addition to that, they found me totally resistible. My virtue was secure.

And then I met Dauntry.

The fact that he was sought after by every female in that corner of the state just added to his aura. And when he came across the gym floor—we were having a midterm dance—to where I sat in my stiff black organdy, and asked me to dance, it was simply the story of Cinderella all over again. Then he took me home, kissed me and asked me out for the following day. And I was lost.

Two months later, in secret, we were married, and I embarked on marriage convinced that the prince had found me, the slipper had fit my foot, and that I would live happily ever after.

Within the first twenty-four hours that illusion had gone forever. Porn, or near-porn, had not yet become accessible, at least not to us. My ideas of what a wedding night should be were exceedingly dim, culled from vaguely worded allusions, romantic hints, and no facts. I was eager but ignorant. But ignorant as I was, I knew that the whole fumbling, embarrassing episode was by any definition a disaster. The next morning, my bridegroom, changed within a few hours from the knight of love to an icy-voiced stranger, let me know that the failures of the marriage bed had been entirely my responsibility; that a man had a right to expect certain things from his wife, however unskilled, and that I had lamentably failed in every respect.

"What things?" I cried, desperate for practical information, and defenseless against any and all accusations.

But he never told me. A curtain came down between us at that point, and he became, to all intents and purposes, another man, as different from the solicitous, affectionate lover of our premarital days as snow from fire. Having paid me the first compliments I had ever received and built up my almost nonexistent self-confidence, he now systematically tore it to shreds, and my last state was worse than my first, because I had lived, for a few short weeks, in the land of the loved and wanted, a country as removed from any I had ever known as the moon itself.

I had always felt the mockery and contempt of my classmates, but from a reasonably humane distance. Now I lived with it, and

Dauntry's tongue was far more sophisticated and barbed than any bred and schooled locally.

One of his favorite taunts was over my lack of feminine curves—then still fashionable.

"I could sue you for misrepresentation," he said lightly one morning, as I slipped out of my nightgown. "You and the foam-rubber manufacturers. You must have been one of their best customers."

I stood there, fighting tears, inarticulate as I always became when wounded.

But I remember, even at that terrible moment, being puzzled. A look came over his face, a look I had come to know well: it meant more and worse was coming, his words and tone no longer just flicking at my thin skin, but gouging. But in the few dispassionate seconds before pain and rage closed in, I remember being bewildered at his obvious anger. I had done nothing, said nothing: just stood there naked, vulnerable and ashamed.

He continued, his voice almost shaking. "You're about as female as a neutered boy. How I—" But he then surprised me by stalking out of our one-room apartment, and I didn't see him for several days.

I lived like that for almost a year, a prisoner of my own neurosis as much as Dauntry's contempt because, befuddled as I was, I honestly believed the whole thing was my fault, springing directly from some basic failure as a female, all the more frightening to me for my not knowing what it was. If my life had not been wrenched into another path I might have ended up killing Dauntry or committing suicide or both.

I could have stood on the sidewalk staring into the dark glass of a restaurant windowpane for another hour, if an indignant lunchgoer had not all but knocked me over and muttered something about "Wyncha buy yourself a mirror, lady?"

"Sorry," I said, and laughed. Then I turned towards the hotel and Dauntry.

I am not sure what I expected—probably that Dauntry would look exactly the same as when I had last seen him, standing like a silver angel at the door of our apartment, ordering me out in the best tradition of husbandly outrage.

I saw him immediately I entered the hotel dining room, and my first reaction was that he had shrunk. Then he stood up, and though he still seemed diminished, I saw he was still tall and slender, though underneath his belt was the beginning of a thin man's paunch.

"Antonia," he said. "It's good to see you." And to my astonishment leaned over the table and kissed me on the cheek.

"Hello, Dauntry," I said drily. "You're full of surprises."

His light gray eyes looked at me critically. "You've changed," he said. "You've grown attractive. Even beautiful."

"Oh?" Out of old habit (and it was amazing how quickly it came back), I made myself noncommittal, presenting as small an area as possible for his shafts.

"Yes." His smile was secretive and sarcastic, as though he knew much I didn't know, and in a flash the dining room with its chic clientele vanished and I was back thirteen years.

"Well, well," Dauntry had said, as I came home one after-noon, starry-eyed after a class of that not-to-be-forgotten summer school creative writing course, "and how is the great man, your hero, the New England balladeer, Adam Kingsley? Still sending up your girlish blood pressure? You should really put yourself in for some of those private tutoring hours he is so free with—among the prettier students, that is, which is perhaps why he hasn't suggested a session for you. His wife must be very complacent, or possibly she

knows that since she has the money, she has nothing to fear." And there, on Dauntry's much younger face, was the same small, slightly sarcastic smile.

I fell into his trap, of course. I always did. "That's not true."

The pale brows rose. "What's not true? That he married a rich wife? Or that he tumbles every girl who comes to his studio for special counseling—that is, if he's not too drunk?"

"Neither," I said hotly, desperately afraid that Dauntry's sneers were all too true.

And then he threw back his head and laughed and laughed . . .

That memory was more than thirteen years old, but it sent a shiver of remembered pain through me. "Perhaps I have changed, Dauntry. I hope so. God knows there was room. But I don't think you have."

The smile went, then. And, for the first time since I had sat down, I noticed small things: that his face was tired and the lines unusually deep for a man who was not more than in his middle thirties. There wasn't a gray hair among the pale gold, but his hairline was higher and uneven. Even so, or perhaps because of it, he was even better-looking than he had been. He had the kind of looks that often become very early what is generally called distinguished.

He looked at me. "Let's order and get that over, shall we? What will you have to drink?"

"Nothing, thank you. I don't like to drink during the day." And also, although I didn't want to say so, I intended to keep my wits about me.

"How puritanical of you, my dear." He beckoned the waiter. "I'll have an extra dry martini, please."

After his drink had arrived he lit a cigarette, and, as an afterthought, offered me one. "No, thanks."

"You don't smoke either, I take it."

"That's right, Dauntry. I still don't smoke, but spare me the predictable cracks about the daughter of the manse, I've heard them all. And you'd be amazed at the number of people even in chic Manhattan who prefer going back to their desks with clear heads."

"Still on the defensive?"

It was the smile that did it. Suddenly, as though it were a play about someone else, I saw what had always happened: he acted, I reacted; he poked, I jumped. I was the perpetual marionette waiting, tense and frightened, for him to pull my string. He had known that, and that was the way he controlled me, and what he was doing now with his smiles and digs was reestablishing his control. It was as though a fog had rolled away and I saw us both clearly. I took a breath.

"Oh, no, you don't, Dauntry. No more games. You're right. I've changed. Now tell me what it is you want."

He gulped the rest of his drink and gestured to the waiter to bring him another. "Nothing that should bring you any grief. I've been appointed head of the physics lab at the university." He paused.

"Congratulations," I said. "But where do I come in?"

"Before the appointment is final and an announcement made to the press, there is a routine investigation. Defense contracts are involved. They aren't quite as heavy-handed about such things as they used to be. Nevertheless, they don't like having unknown quantities in jobs involving a lot of classified data."

"So?" I was puzzled. By abandoning his needling, Dauntry had revealed something that startled me: that he himself was both nervous and on the defensive.

"Though people are a lot less—primitive—in their attitudes towards . . . well, sexual preferences . . . "

His voice ran down again. I stared at him, and, after a moment, he looked up and stared at me. It suddenly occurred to me that for the first time since I had known him I was seeing him without the shield of one of his numerous façades and without being distracted by the slashes of his wicked tongue.

"You must know what I am talking about, Antonia. You were a stupid and ignorant child when we married. But it—the state of affairs between us—must surely have occurred to you since."

The astonishing part was that it hadn't. I had been too preoccupied, first, with my conviction of failure in our life together, and second, with my own dramatic fall from grace.

It was surprising how, with that one fact about Dauntry finally clear, everything else fell into place.

"Good heavens!" I said slowly.

"You mean you hadn't guessed?"

"No."

"Then you *are* stupid."

The knives were all there, in his voice, but freed now from my sense of being a puppet, I heard the pain behind the hostility.

"I'm sure I am. But why on earth did you marry me, if you were a homosexual?"

The lines about his mouth became marked. "I thought marriage might—change me. You have to remember that this was before everyone started coming out of the closet."

"No," I said finally. "I can't buy that. If you wanted marriage to act as some kind of solution, why pick me? As you were the first to point out, after we were married, not only was I then not attractive, even less was I skilled or knowledgeable in any way that could help you."

"I grant you it was a mistake to marry you. But suppose I had married one of the campus beauties? If what happened between you and me had happened with a self-confident, sought-after girl, what do you suppose she'd do? Keep quiet and put up with it? Not on your life. There would have been an annulment as fast as Daddy and a righteous set of lawyers could arrange it. And the news would be out."

"I see. But with me you could be fairly sure that sheer timidity and a willingness to believe the whole mess was my fault would keep me quiet while you experimented?"

"Well, it worked, didn't it?"

"Didn't it ever occur to you that what you did was the act of a selfish, cold-blooded bastard?"

The old Dauntry flicked out again. "It didn't hurt you that much. You got yourself a lot of kudos by marrying me. And it got you Adam, didn't it? What happened between you and Adam would never have happened except for me. You wouldn't have had the guts. But you were so desperate you went straight from my arms into his—much good it did you." His eyes glinted. "But it did, after all, get you Ewen, didn't it?"

It was then I remembered his threat over the telephone to turn up at my house.

"I keep forgetting," I said.

"Forgetting what?"

"How vicious you can be. All your motives and impulses seem to come equipped with knives."

"How else do you get people to . . . behave generously?"

"That's a revealing statement. I think you were about to say, 'do as you want,' weren't you?"

"It's the same thing—most of the time."

"You don't fit the standard portrait of a deprived person."

"Don't I? Not all deprivation comes from a slum or a ghetto."

"It's hard for me to associate any kind of hardship with my memory of the eastern . . . " Suddenly, I recalled what Laurence Metcalf had told me, and was stunned that it had slipped to the back of my mind. "Dauntry, I didn't know you were related to the Standishes."

He stared at me. "Why should you know or care? I told you my mother came from an old New York family. Did the name of Standish mean anything to you when you were in college? Had you ever heard of it?"

At the moment, sitting there, something very strange happened. It was like a parting of a curtain, a split in the familiar surfaces of my mind: Just suddenly I saw my house, but not as I had come to know it in the past. There was something different about it . . . And then it was gone.

"No," I said slowly. "I don't think the name meant anything to me."

"But you're not sure?"

"Just suddenly . . . "

"Suddenly what?" he asked, and there was a tenseness about him that I put down to his usual impatience with my slower reactions.

"Suddenly I seemed to see my house, but not as it is now. There was a difference . . . "

"What?"

"I don't know."

He made an impatient sound and turned to the waiter, who had been hovering. "What do you want to eat, Antonia?"

We ordered, and when the waiter had gone he said, "Haven't you heard of *déjà vu?*"

"Yes," I said, and was surprised to find myself relieved. "It must be that."

The food came and we both made fairly half-hearted efforts to eat.

"By the way," I asked, "how did you find me?"

He put down his knife and fork, and with half the food still on his plate lit a cigarette. "It wasn't difficult. I hired a detective and he did it."

I, too, suddenly found my *truite almandine* uninteresting. "Which brings me back to my original question: What do you want?"

He was smoking rapidly, dragging in the smoke, the lines in his face deep. Then he started to put out his cigarette. "You said that I always got what I wanted by having a knife in my hand."

"Metaphorically. Your tongue has always served as a very effective knife."

"All right. I'll try it the nice way first. I told you I will be investigated as a result of becoming chief at the lab out in Santa Barbara. I've already been questioned—very gently, of course—by the vice-chancellor of the university. All gentlemen together and all that. The subject of homosexuality has already come up. Obviously they picked up some rumors. I denied it. They asked why you left me. I told them that we had had a marital spat and that you had walked out and that I didn't know you were pregnant, otherwise, of course, I would have wanted to see my son, contributed to his support, and so on. I made out I was delighted to find you and would see you here while I came east for the convention."

I held my hands together in my lap to keep them from shaking. "Why on earth did you tell them that rigamarole, Dauntry? As you yourself pointed out to me, one of the things you aren't is a liar. Why build such an elaborate tale that is bound to get knocked over?"

"Because it's not going to be knocked over. That's why." He looked at me out of a white, bitter face. "You of all people should understand why I lied. Have you ever handled a disagreeable situation by confronting it? You ran away from an unpleasant home. When we got married we had to do it secretly. When we finally got found out did you go home and tell them why you did what you did? Of course not. You skulked at college and made me confront them. When you got pregnant did you stay and cope with that—?"

"You threw me out!"

"I told you you were a lying, cheating little bitch—"

"Which in view of our nonconsummated marriage was a pretty funny thing for you to be mad about."

"But instead of standing and having it out with me, you ran. When your boss on one of your following jobs discovered you were not married, though obviously pregnant, you didn't wait to see what he'd do. You got on the nearest Greyhound bus and ran. Have you ever in your life stood still and fought?"

"Yes. Here. And if you think bringing up a boy in New York all alone is easy—"

"And what have you told him about his father, Antonia?"

Afterwards, when I went over our conversation, line by line, as though it were dialogue in a play, I could see how cleverly he had placed that question; how artfully he had arranged the context so that I would blurt out the truth, or start to.

"I told him that his father was dead."

Dauntry leaned across the table. "And how dead, my dear? How did he die?"

I stared at Dauntry, saying nothing.

He went on. "When the detective brought me back the result of his inquiries, he told me that in the two places you had lived before you finally got to New York, and later here, you were known as a war widow. That your husband was killed in Vietnam, very early on, of course, well before the escalation, when being a war widow was something nobody would be tactless enough to question." He smiled a little. "I wonder if you have since regretted that. In a previous generation any son could feel unreserved reverence for a father he had never seen who was killed in the service of his country, etcetera, etcetera. How does Ewen, of the anti-war generation, feel about his war-hero father? I'm afraid, my dear, you just might have got caught in one of history's little ironies."

For a minute I couldn't say anything. So many of Dauntry's jibes had been well founded, particularly the one about running away. I took a deep breath. "So far it hasn't been any real problem. He's asked me once or twice what his father thought of the war, and I said that he was a . . . a reserve officer who had to go. That this was before the controversy . . . "

"Nothing simple like a private soldier for Ewen, eh?"

I blushed. "All right, Dauntry. In addition to my other sins I was a snob. I wouldn't do the same now. But it's done . . . "

"And you think you can keep it done, as he gets older and wants more facts? Do you really think you can keep up that pretense?"

There were indeed some things I had not wanted to face. Part of Ewen's passion for animals was a sort of extended pacifism. And as I sat there, I also knew that the story about his father had produced in him conflicts that he otherwise wouldn't have had. What does a pacifist do with the memory of a war-hero father? Perhaps his pacifism had come from that. There'd been one teacher at his school—a fanatic anti-war activist of the sixties—who had thrown some barbed comments at Ewen about his father. He'd been made to apologize by the headmaster. But at the time it happened I knew I had made a mistake and wished I had chosen some other fiction about his father. And although I didn't like to think it, he seemed to become a little more solitary after that. Ewen was popular, but many of the boys felt the way the teacher did, and for a while he came home with a rash of black eyes. But when I questioned him, he gave vague answers.

"All right, Dauntry. I should have told him some version of the truth, I suppose. But what would that have been? That he was your son? And leave him with the knowledge that a father alive and well didn't even bother to come and see him? That he was Adam's son, and then explain that Adam was not my husband, and that he—Ewen—was the result of one night's drunken roll in the hay; and that, incidentally, his real father, who didn't know he existed, had spent some months in the pokey for hit-and-run drunken driving and killing a child? Those choices aren't exactly attractive."

Dauntry lit another cigarette. "I'll offer you an out. If you will back up my claim that he is my son when and if the investigators come calling, I'll tell him that the whole thing was my fault, that I left you before I knew you were pregnant, that I had gone into the army (which I did), and that you were informed that I had been missing in action. It's fairly full of holes, but will hold together for long enough to let him grow up."

"And if I refuse?"

"Then I shall find Ewen and tell him the truth myself, and in such a way that no matter how loyal he may be to you, he will never be able to look at you in quite the same way again. How old is he? Twelve, going on thirteen? That's a tricky age, even with no complications."

I opened my mouth and closed it again. Then I said, "My God, Dauntry! There's nothing you won't do, is there?"

"There's no way you could stop me, you know."

"I could tell him myself as soon as I get home tonight."

"Oh, yes. You could tell him your version. And you could tell him about our conversation. But I could tell him details that he would not like . . . or forget, and that would be very off-putting to a sensitive boy. I would tell him who his real father is, and what a coast-to-coast swinger he had been and so on and so forth. And don't imagine, Antonia, that you could prevent me from getting to him. You couldn't. I am a scientist of some reputation. If I went to his school—I know his science teacher, by the way—and offered to lecture they'd jump at it. If you raised some kind of fuss, you'd look foolish, not I. Oh, yes, you could damage me. But I could damage you more, because I could really damage Ewen . . . "

As I sat there staring at him, even knowing that a lot of what he said was bluff, I also saw Ewen's face, his worry over his animals, his life, a rather solitary life, becoming more so. I knew that his anguish over every abandoned stray sprang from identification on a deep, unacknowledged level. Ewen, brought up in New York, was intelligent with a lot of street know-how. But I could also imagine what anything Dauntry chose to tell him would do to him.

Dauntry had never taken his eyes off me. "It really isn't worth it, Antonia. And what I ask is not that far out. I won't bother you and him."

"And you think that is a solution—to have you acknowledged as his father, and then to abandon him again?"

"I'm perfectly willing to establish a relationship with him."

Dauntry made a mistake in saying that. Until that moment I had, against all my revulsion, considered accepting his bargain. But when he said those words he triggered my alarm system. Something in his tone—a little less guarded, perhaps, relaxed, within sight of his goal—reminded me of the Dauntry I had always known. The one who always got his way.

I got up and was almost surprised to feel my legs steady. "I'll have to think about it, Dauntry. I'll let you know."

"Yes, do. Soon. I'm staying at the Hilton. Don't wait too long."

I knew then, as I walked out, that I was right. For purposes of his own Dauntry might have put away his knife. But it was still there, and he was still dangerous.

I went back to the office and spent most of the afternoon staring out the window.

Dauntry was absolutely right about one thing, I thought: in the choice between fight and flight, I had always chosen flight, and now every impulse within me tended towards doing exactly the same thing again—picking up Ewen and going anywhere. But picking up a one-year-old infant and picking up an independent, stubborn twelve-year-old boy were two entirely different things. There was absolutely no way I could flee the locale without bringing on what I was willing to pay almost any price to avoid: explanations.

I then thought about Adam, mentally bending and twisting every imagined circumstance to see if I could avoid his moving in. Certainly Dauntry would discover his being there. However absurd it might seem in view of the circumstances of our marriage, there was no question but that Adam aroused in him some kind of demon of jealousy. Would this precipitate his revelation to Ewen of all I did not want Ewen to know?

I put my hand on the telephone receiver to call Adam and tell him not to come. I would say that Ewen had measles or mumps, that there was no furniture for the basement apartment (no, that wouldn't do; Max had offered furniture from his own house). I could say that it seemed less and less a good idea to have us living there together while working on his book, but then I realized I had forgotten Adam's blindness; not to work together would mean that the book would never make the anniversary which Max was so determined to observe. I took my hand off the phone. Eventually I put on my coat and went home. There was nothing at all I could do about the whole matter, and I knew it, and the powerlessness of my position frightened me.

The following Saturday Max brought various oddments from his house—a studio bed, a carpet, bookshelves and a couple of chairs, lugging them in a small van he had borrowed from somewhere. The next day he returned in his car with Adam, dropped him and drove off for a dinner appointment.

By this time I had worked up two fairly active resentments against Adam. One was that he was there in the first place. It was through no will of mine, and I felt trapped.

The second was that between Adam and Dauntry, each disclaiming that he had been in the vicinity as seen by Bonzo, it seemed to me obvious that Adam was lying. My reasons for this choice resisted any and all attempts at analysis. But they were nonetheless firm for all that.

I took Adam down to his apartment in the basement on the floor above the cellar, using the separate entrance in the area way. Other than being on the dark side, which, of course, would not disturb Adam, the apartment was self-contained and attractive, the rooms large and well shaped and the kitchen small but fully equipped. With the pieces Max had supplied, it looked more completely furnished than any other part of the house.

"Shall I tell you the layout?" I asked him when we were inside.

"All right. Then I'll go around and inspect everything for myself."

So I described the rooms and the way the furniture was arranged.

"You have a door into the garden through the kitchen," I said, "which might be nice for Tania. And, of course, you have your own two front doors into the area way. You can lock the door to the stairs leading up to the rest of the house, and the other door to the stairs leading down to the cellar. Here are the keys." I stopped, aware that I hadn't thought ahead of time how to tell him to tell the keys apart.

He held out his hand and I put them into it. "How are you going to tell them apart?" I asked. "By shape?"

"Yes. Or I might paste rough paper or sandpaper in different shapes on them. There are all kinds of ways."

"I should have thought of that." I felt a little guilty. For the first time it was beginning to strike me that there were a number of details I had taken for granted all my life that were for him, and for all blind people, puzzles to solve.

"Why?" The harshness of his voice reminded me of the sandpaper he was talking about.

"It might have shown some consideration for you . . . " Too late I saw how patronizing it sounded. "I mean . . . "

"I know exactly what you mean, Antonia, and I am delighted to have this opportunity of settling now, at the beginning, that kind of unwelcome sympathy. I don't desire or need or deserve your pity. I don't want to be helped over curbs or out of doors or onto public conveyances. I have been trained and have trained myself to manage very well. I'm not an invalid and I'm not feeble-minded. Is that clear?"

"Very clear, Adam. And you didn't have to bite my head off. If there's anything further you want, let me know." And I left him standing in the middle of the floor and went up the stairs.

Ewen was waiting when I got to the top. "Is he okay? I mean, does he need any help?"

"No, Ewen, he doesn't. I asked him exactly that question and got a lecture from him on how he doesn't need to be treated like an invalid. I want you to leave him alone."

"Oh, Mom! For Pete's sake. I like him. And I think he likes me."

"I mean it, Ewen. Please remember that the reason he's here is that he and I are going to have to work on his book, so the more professional and the less personal we keep it, the better." And then I added, not thinking, "He's never been the sort of person who is either kind or considerate on a one-to-one basis."

"You mean you knew him before? Where? Why didn't you tell me?"

By this time Ewen and I had progressed to the kitchen. As I made a to-do about getting out pots and the broiling rack,

I kicked myself for my loose tongue and reflected that in my concern over someone else spilling the beans, I had overlooked myself.

"He taught for a while out at a summer school I attended when I was at college. I didn't—" But I choked on the words, *I didn't know him well.* In one way, of course, it was entirely true. What I saw and fell in love with and was seduced by was a writer burning himself out in the best romantic Fitzgerald-Hemingway tradition, and using his extraordinary and compelling personality as both a trap and a shield. Probably, I thought, as I clattered about the stove, he was as much a prisoner of his charisma as those caught in its fascination.

I tuned back into Ewen's voice as he was saying, " . . . what was he like, then? I mean, I was talking to some of the teachers at school and they said he was very brilliant and . . . and unstable and had some kind of a breakdown. Was that true?"

I hadn't, consciously, planned to say what I said then. It just came—out of the depths, perhaps, of some deep anger.

"I wouldn't call it a breakdown. He was put in prison for a hit-and-run killing of a child and injuring his father."

I heard my own words and it was as though they came from someone else. Nor could I pretend that I didn't know what effect they would have on Ewen. His first dog, a mutt named Muffin, was killed on Riverside Drive by a driver who neither swerved nor stopped.

For a minute Ewen and I faced each other in silence. Then he said, "I'd better take Wilma out before dinner," and left.

Dinner itself was a silent meal. I could, at least, I thought, tell him that Adam was drunk when he did his hit-and-run killing. But I didn't. For all his popularity, Ewen had few close friends. He took to even fewer people. Obviously he had liked Adam, helped, no doubt, by Adam's interesting and unusual relationship with his guide dog. Well, I had fixed that. My son was both sensitive and idealistic, and I had shown him an Adam with not only feet, but a whole body, of clay. It wasn't a very nice thing to do, but I didn't want him going down to Adam's apartment with enthusiastic offers of help that would earn him nothing but one of Adam's corrosive snubs. It was better this way.

After dinner Ewen said, "Mom, can I be excused? The animals' cages need cleaning."

"Sure. Go ahead."

I heard his feet pounding up the flights as I washed the few dishes we had used. It was entirely possible that the animals' cages did need cleaning. Especially Mr. Ears'. But one of the things about Ewen that I had had to accept was that when he was upset he went to his zoo for comfort, not to me.

Chapter 8

It was four nights later that I woke suddenly. I had no idea what time it was. A pale light from a high, distant moon was filtering through the window. Nor did I know why I woke. Yet I knew that I was frightened and that my heart was pounding. The room was very cold. I had, always, left the window partly open and I could see the blind moving a little from the air. But the cold was not coming from that direction.

Not since I was a ghost-haunted child had I lain stiffly in bed, too afraid to move. Yet I lay rigid, on my side, my eyes trying to probe the shadows in the room. What light there was couldn't penetrate them. The room was too big. Someone or something could be there.

Ashamed of lying in a sweat of panic, I decided I had gone mad and regressed to childhood. But I could no more move than if I had been strapped. My sense of isolation was total, something I had never felt in our highly insecure New York West Side apartment. There, Ewen was in the room next door. At night sometimes, when I woke, I could hear the sounds of his animals, either playing with their exercise wheels, or moving around their cages, or communicating with one another in a series of muffled noises or squeaks. And, of course, there was Cleo, who should have been there in bed with me, curled into a ball somewhere between my shoulder and my pillow. But though I couldn't move to verify it, my conviction was that she wasn't on the bed or in the room. I sent her out a silent message, *Wherever you are, I need you,* and decided, my heart thudding against my back, that at this point I would even be glad to see Einstein. That idea amused me so much that I relaxed and moved my cramped leg. As I did so, there was a sound, and my heart gave a sickening thud and started racing again. And as I lay there, paralysed, the cold seemed to intensify and spread over me. There was a slight sound. I closed my eyes and repeated, silently, the prayers of childhood. Then, suddenly, it was all over. The room was much warmer, the shadows no longer contained something frightening and alien. I sat up in bed, as astounded at my lack of fear as I had been before of my terror. I heard far away the noise of trucks starting up. Nearer there was another one. Ordinary, mechanical sounds. Comforting sounds. And through the window came the salty freshness of morning and sea—I was inclined to forget that Brooklyn Heights was right over the New York Harbor.

I snapped on a light, swung my legs out of bed and rummaged around for my slippers. Then I slipped on a robe and went upstairs. Moving as softly as possible, I pushed Ewen's door open and went in.

It smelled, as it always did, of animals, even though Ewen kept his cages and boxes as clean as he could. But I found, with my experience of the past half hour fresh in my mind, that I didn't object to animal odors nearly as much as I used to. Ewen's room, directly over mine and the same size, was also large, so I didn't see until I got quite close to the bed that it was empty.

"Ewen," I said sharply, and turned on the light by his bed. Wilma's rear, protruding from under the bed, quivered.

"Why did you have to do that, Mom?" Ewen said, poking his head through his bathroom door. "Now you're going to wake the zoo and make them think it's morning and breakfast."

"What are you doing?"

"I got up to give Ears a pill."

"What's the matter with him?"

"I don't know. He got scared or something. All of a sudden he went around the cage as though he'd gone crazy."

"What kind of a pill is that?"

"Just a tranquilizer. The vet gave it to me for the moving."

I looked at the black-and-white rabbit lying along Ewen's arm, and saw, or thought I saw, the terror in its eyes. "What bothered it, Ewen?"

"I don't know. I woke up to hear him squeaking and running."

"Where are the other animals?"

"Nemesis is in the bed; Einstein's in my pocket. The mice and the gerbils are in their cages. Wilma's under the bed."

"Yes. I saw her. My, she's a good guard dog."

"Being a guard dog isn't her thing. She's got other qualities."

"Name two."

"She's loyal and affectionate and she's good with the other animals."

"You mean she doesn't actively persecute them."

By this time Ears was looking more placid. His ears lay back, his nose wiggled contentedly.

"Ewen, did you hear anything tonight?"

"No, first thing I heard was Ears. Why, did you?"

"Yes. Something woke me up. Also there was a cold wind or something."

Ewen looked at me quickly. Sometimes I forgot what quick and perceptive ears he has. "Were you scared?"

"Yes. I was. I think I must be the Compleat Coward."

"Then maybe you can understand better how Wilma feels."

It was debilitating. What I had hoped for was a pat on the back. "Perhaps I should join her, under the bed, that is."

Then Ewen grinned. Those aqua-blue eyes, so like Adam's as I remembered them, came alive. "I could let you both have a blanket." He stroked Ears for a while and went back into the bedroom with me following. Ears hopped off and placed himself near the pillow. From somewhere near the foot of the bed a lump moved slowly up and Nemesis' black head emerged.

"Your bed is quite heavily populated," I said. "Doesn't Wilma feel out of it?"

"Oh, she'll get on as soon as I do." He gave me a sly look. "Like to join us?"

"Where? Lying at the foot?"

He laughed, took off his robe and climbed into bed, pulling up the blankets. Sure enough, Wilma pulled herself out backwards, then got onto the bed and lay full length on Ewen's other side. "Do you suppose," he asked slowly, in the academic manner he sometimes had, "that that cold you felt was from a ghost or psychic manifestation?"

"What a comfort you are. I thought it might be just a plain old burglar."

"How would he get in?"

I had wondered about that. "He might get in through the cellar."

"Then he'd have to go past the basement apartment. Mr. ... Mr. Kingsley or Tania would hear, wouldn't they? Especially Tania."

"Possibly. Probably. By the way, have you seen Cleo?"

"No. I thought she slept with you."

"She usually does. But she's not there tonight."

Ewen sat up. "When did you last see her?"

I thought, and the thought did nothing to comfort me. "When I went to bed."

"Where was she?"

"On the bed, beside my pillow, where she always is."

"Maybe she got hungry in the middle of the night and went down to the kitchen."

"Yes. I guess that's it."

"Has she ever done that before?"

"No. But there's always a first time."

Ewen pushed back the covers and stood up. "I'm going down to see if she's there."

"I can look for her, darling. There's no reason for you to get up."

But I was talking to the air. I could hear Ewen's bare feet on the stairs. With no other option left me, I followed him. By the time I got downstairs he was in the kitchen. A few minutes later he said, "She's not down here."

"She could be hiding. She's still pretty small."

"I've looked everywhere. But I'll do it again."

This time he and I opened all closets, cupboards, drawers and looked behind pieces of furniture. Then together we went up to my floor and looked everywhere there. Then we looked on the third floor and in the attic. She wasn't anywhere.

"I'm going down to Mr. Kingsley's apartment," Ewen said.

"No, Ewen. I don't think anything can have happened to

her and I don't want you waking him up. Wherever Cleo is, she'll be all right."

"That's what people always say. Animals don't matter."

"I didn't say that, so don't accuse me of it."

"If it was me you wouldn't mind waking anybody up. You'd wake up the whole street if you had to."

"That's different, Ewen. You know it is."

"Not to me."

"Well, what could happen to her down there?"

"Tania could go after her."

"But you saw Tania with the other animals. She didn't move a muscle."

"That was because she was in her harness. She was working. Don't you remember him explaining that? That when she was working she didn't do anything like running after a cat or another dog the way she would if she was just being herself?"

"Yes, but—"

"And she wouldn't be in harness now. And if Cleo got down there, there'd be no reason she wouldn't take off after her. And Cleo doesn't weigh two pounds."

"Well, Adam would stop her, Ewen."

"Yeah? A guy who wouldn't stop when he'd hit a kid?"

Ewen and I were on the third-floor landing, staring at each other. Ewen turned and started down.

"Ewen. Please stop. There's something I have to explain. About Adam."

Ewen half turned. "What?"

"He had a drinking problem. He was drunk when he did that. In a blackout. It came out at the trial and was in all the papers. I doubt if he has drunk for a long time. I know he didn't when we had lunch."

"Does that make it okay? You have an ounce of grass and

you're stuck in jail forever. But a guy gets drunk and runs over a kid or a dog and doesn't stop and it's okay. Nothing wrong with drinking."

"I don't think going to jail could be called everything being okay. And right after hitting the child, he ran into a concrete embankment and the crash blinded him. I wouldn't say Adam hasn't paid."

"Why are you sticking up for him? I thought you didn't like him. When I did—before I knew about his hit and run —you didn't want me around him. I can't figure you out, Mom." And with that he went towards the door leading to the basement stairs.

"Where are you going?"

"To see if Cleo is downstairs. If she's in the cellar, a rat could get her. Maybe you don't care about her—I guess you didn't want a cat—but I do."

With that he tried to open the door, which, of course, was locked.

By this time I was suffering what Melissa calls one of my motherhood depressions. I could see all too clearly that, from Ewen's point of view, I was not only being unfairly inconsistent, I was showing indifference to his present, which happened also to be an animal.

"All right, Ewen. The key's here." I opened the drawer of the small hall table and took it out. Ewen fitted it in the lock, opened the door and turned on the light down the stairs and then proceeded to go down. Feeling defeated on every score, I followed. Down at the bottom was another door, also locked, but with a bell beside it. Without a moment's hesitation, Ewen rang it. I waited with considerable interest to see how an author, and a blind one at that, would react to being awakened in the middle of the night over the whereabouts of a kitten who, in my opinion, could not possibly have gotten into his apartment.

182

There was a firm tread on the other side of the door. Then I heard the lock turn and the door opened. Adam, a dark robe over pajamas, stood there, with Tania, unharnessed, sitting beside him. He was without his glasses. One eye, the aquamarine iris undamaged, looked normal. The other eye socket was empty.

"Looking for your cat?"

I think the eyeless socket shook Ewen a little, because he waited half a second before answering. Then he said, "Yes. It's Mom's kitten, Cleo."

"All right. Come in." He stood aside.

"Were you expecting us?" I asked, walking through the door. "You answered the ring awfully fast."

"Yes. When I woke up and eventually discovered I had a kitten on the bed with me, that seemed the logical explanation, although I have no idea how she got here. Have you?"

By this time we were in his living room. Through the big double doors was his bedroom and I could see the studio bed with the covers thrown back. Sitting up, licking her paws, was Cleo.

Tania also saw her, because she gave a plaintive whimper.

"Since Tania is off her harness she's feeling frustrated that I won't let her follow her natural instincts and give chase."

Ewen gave me a quick glance, as though to say, I told you so. Then he said gruffly, "Thanks. Can I go and get her?"

"Of course."

Adam and I waited while Ewen went into the bedroom, scooped Cleo up and strode past us both back into Adam's hall and up the stairs.

Tania, I decided, was not the only one to be frustrated. Ewen, unforgiving of Adam's hit-and-run killing, was holding himself aloof from asking questions and sharing speculations about how Cleo got down, an exchange that would normally lead to other reminiscences about animals. Nevertheless, and no matter how he felt, he should have apolizized to Adam for hauling him out of bed at what I could see by Adam's clock to be 4:00 A.M. Hastily, as Ewen went up the basement stairs, I tried to remedy this omission.

"I'm terribly sorry, Adam, to get you out of bed at this hour. Truthfully, I would have waited, but Ewen gets so exercised about his—or my—animals that he was down here before I could stop him." (Which was true in spirit, if a slight bending of fact.)

"I understand that," Adam said abruptly. "The cat could have gotten out or Tania could have eaten it alive, practically."

"Would she?"

Adam put his hands in his robe pockets. "When she's out of harness she's all dog, in every sense of the word, and she's been known to chase cats, or start to."

"How did you know Cleo was down here?"

"Tania barked. Your kitten—what's her name? Cleo?—hissed. It was a small hiss, but I was awake by then and heard it, and told Tania to sit. After that it was just a matter of time until any normal, curious kitten would come over to inspect me."

"And all that time Tania just sat?"

"Every now and then she gave a whine of pure frustration. But she didn't move."

"She's marvelous," I said. I looked at the longish coat and friendly eyes, "Is she pure bred?"

"Not quite. There's something there other than shepherd. Guide dogs are chosen for character rather than pedigree."

"She has a lovely one. Can I stroke her?"

"Of course. She's out of harness."

"Come here, Tania."

She got up, came over, sniffed me, wagged her plumy tail and jumped up and down. Then she went over to Adam and rubbed against him and licked his hand.

"Do all guide dogs have this come-hitherness?"

He laughed. "No. I learned from one of the trainers that they try to suit the dog and the man by matching opposites. An outgoing, exuberant man will often be given a rather reserved dog. A reserved man will have a friendly dog." He rubbed the top of Tania's head. "Tania's excellent disposition reveals the fact that the school considered me on the surly side."

I turned. "Good night, Adam. And thanks again."

I was almost through the door and starting up the stairs when Adam said, "What's Ewen angry about?"

"What . . . what made you think he was?"

"Step. Voice. Manner. He's always been friendly to me."

I hesitated. Dauntry said I had always run from the truth, so this time I gave it a half-second's consideration before deciding that there was no way I could deal with it in pieces. And there was no way I could contemplate telling Adam all of the truth. "He's angry with me, Adam. I think he feels I do not sufficiently appreciate Cleo. Now I have to go up and convince him I do. Good night."

And I pulled the door closed after me.

When I got up to my bedroom I glanced in. Cleo wasn't there. So I mounted to the next floor and knocked on Ewen's door.

"Come in."

I went in. Ewen was sitting up in bed, holding Cleo, whose ears were back. Einstein was sitting up on the blanket cleaning his whiskers. Ears was nowhere to be seen, and Wilma was again under the bed.

"She doesn't understand about the other animals yet," Ewen explained.

"Well, you can go over it with her tomorrow. I came to get her."

"You don't have to take her if you don't want to."

I went over and lifted Cleo out of his arms. "She's my cat. I like her very much and I do want to. So there." I stood there for a minute, holding her in one arm while I tickled her chin. "Ewen, do you have any idea how she got down there? That door was locked."

"I know, I was thinking about that. I suppose she could have got out of a window and then got into the basement apartment through another one."

"But there's not a window open downstairs. I checked."

"Well, your window was open. Maybe there's a vine or creeper outside."

"For this kitten? No, Ewen. She'd never try anything like that. I'm sure of it."

"Then how do you think she got down? What other way could she?"

"I don't know."

"Did—er—Mr. Kingsley have any idea?"

"I forgot to ask him."

"How could you forget something important like that?"

"Because I was rather upset at your abruptness with him. After all, you got him out of bed—"

"He looked as if he had been up for a while."

"Well, as a matter of fact, he had." And I told about Cleo's arrival. "But he noticed your manner towards him and asked me what you were angry about."

Ewen looked up at me. "Did you tell him?"

Was that eagerness I detected in his face and voice? I asked slowly, "Did you want me to?"

He shrugged, a gesture that has always irritated me.

"Please answer me, Ewen."

"I don't care. And anyway, you didn't answer my question."

"No, I didn't tell him why . . . why you felt the way you do. I said you were upset with me because you thought I didn't appreciate Cleo enough and had been careless with her."

"Well, that much is true. Animals need to feel *loved.*"

I sat down on his bed and put Cleo temporarily on the eiderdown. "Do you feel loved, Ewen? Because you are."

"Sure I do. That's not what I'm talking about." He scooped up Cleo and put her back in my arms. "Maybe you better get some sleep. You have to be at the office tomorrow."

"How true!" I stood, cradling Cleo and trying hard not to show my sense of being rebuffed. I went to the door. For a second I hesitated there, unhappy over our unfinished conversation, over having been, in effect, dismissed. But there was no way I could state this, I decided, without violating that strong wall of privacy that Ewen had wrapped around himself. "Good night," I said, and went out.

It was three days after that that Adam telephoned me at the office and formally asked for a book conference. He had completed two tapes of revisions and wanted to discuss them.

"You better let me have the tapes, Adam. I'll listen to them first, but since it's easier for me to read than listen, I'll have them typed up later and then we can talk."

I hesitated on the brink of asking him to dinner, and then refrained. I was sorry now I had told Ewen about Adam's accident. But it was done. I couldn't undo it, and to sit with Ewen aggressively silent and Adam puzzled as to why was more than my nervous system could tolerate—or so I told myself.

"What time would you like to come up?"

"Eight o'clock?"

"Fine."

At dinner I said to Ewen, "Adam is coming in at eight to bring some tapes and talk about the revisions to his book. If you can't be civil then maybe you'd better be upstairs when he arrives."

"What are you trying to do, keep us apart?"

"I thought he had developed feet, legs and chest of clay in your perfectionist sight."

Ewen didn't say anything. But he went upstairs shortly before eight.

Promptly on the hour the front doorbell rang. I was surprised. For some reason I thought he'd come up the basement stairs straight into the back hall, and told him so when I opened the front door.

"I didn't think you'd be expecting me there," Adam said, coming through the door with Tania. "Besides, I wasn't sure you'd hear me."

I had brought my recorder home, and played some of the tapes, while Adam and I sat in the living room and listened.

When I was finished Adam said, "I know you want to have them typed and read them first, but do you have any initial reaction to what I've done, and if so, what?"

My initial reaction was that he had done very well indeed, far better than I had hoped, but there were still one or two points that I was ready to argue.

At the end of several spirited discussions that once or twice became very lively indeed I looked up to see Ewen coming down the stairs.

"Oh," he said. "I thought Mr. Kingsley had gone."

I am rarely seriously displeased with Ewen, but this time I was, and surprised. He is seldom gratuitously rude or unkind, yet I thought he was being both. "Go back upstairs at once, Ewen," I said, angrier than I had been in a long time.

Adam got up. "No, it's later than I realized." I saw his finger open the glass front to his watch and touch the dial. "It's after ten thirty," he said. "I'm sorry I stayed so long."

"It's not that late, Adam. We haven't finished. Please don't go."

He felt for Tania's harness. "Tomorrow is another day. And besides, we should wait until you've had a chance to read the transcript." He bent a little and patted Tania. "Come along, girl. Forward."

But when he got to the front door, opposite to the stairs, he turned. "Ewen," he said. "Are you still there?"

"Yes."

"I don't know what I've done to offend you. Would you care to tell me what it is?"

An entirely involuntary surge of admiration for Adam went through me. The dark glasses were facing up the stairs, waiting. I wondered if Ewen could meet such candor with equal candor.

"Mother said you hit a kid and killed him and didn't even stop because you were drunk. That's what happened to my first dog, Muffin. The man didn't even stop, and Muffin just lay there, with all his insides broken and squashed. Maybe killing him was an accident. But you should have stopped."

Adam's face was as white as the newly papered wall. "You're absolutely right. I should have. And I shouldn't have been driving drunk, or I might not have run over the boy at all."

"Well, why did you run away? I mean, what were you thinking about?"

"Since I don't remember anything about the accident, I can't tell you. Probably—I'd prefer to think—that being drunk I didn't even know I had hit anyone. I'm sorry about your dog. Nor do I blame you for feeling the way you do. So would I.

Good night, Antonia. Let me know when you want to talk again. I put my phone number on that slip of paper there on the coffee table."

Ewen's face was as white as Adam's had been. I had quite a lot of things to tell Ewen about his hastiness in judging others, but I decided it could wait. Instead I went to the kitchen and started cleaning up the remainder of the dinner pots and pans that hadn't been finished. By the time I was ready for bed, Ewen had disappeared. When I went upstairs to say good night to him and knocked on the door, there was no answer. I pushed the door open a trifle. The room was dark.

"Ewen?" I said softly.

No answer.

I was reasonably sure he was not asleep. I didn't turn on the light, but, leaving the door open so I could get a glimmer from the landing and not fall over something, I went over to the bed and sat down.

"Wanna talk?" I asked.

"No," came the muffled reply.

"I'm sorry, Ewen. I shouldn't have told you the way I did. It's partly my fault. I didn't realize how much you'd grown to like him."

He didn't say anything for a moment. Then, "Mom, please don't be upset, but I'd like to be alone."

I sighed. "All right. Good night, Ewen." And then, whether he liked it or not, I groped for his head, bent down and gave him a kiss on the cheek. What I got in return was a slight grunt.

I spent the next two days getting the tapes typed up and studying them. They were as good as I thought they were and I called Adam up and told him.

"That's good news," he said. "Especially as there's a lot more to be done. I'll have another couple of tapes ready for you in a day or so." He produced them the following evening and, while Ewen was upstairs doing his homework, talked and argued about the revisions yet to come.

For the next two weeks the discussions occurred nightly. Once or twice I came back home after lunch and Adam and I talked all afternoon. They were extraordinary sessions, extraordinary because it was hard for me to remember that the quiet, thin-faced man in dark glasses was the wild, reckless, dazzling teacher with whom I had once fallen flat on my face in love. The one link with that man of which I was constantly conscious was his writing. Of all his facets that was the only one that had remained consistent, although it had, in the intervening time and with all that had happened to him, developed greater depth and dimension.

One afternoon I said impulsively, "You know, you waited a long time to write another book, Adam. But it was worth it. You're a much better writer."

I had thrown the remark out without thinking. He was silent for a moment, a stiff, strained look on his face.

"Did I say something wrong?"

Had my tactless mention of his long silence touched a raw nerve? I was kicking myself for clumsiness when he said, "No, Antonia. On the contrary. In fact, you've . . ." He put his hands up to his temples for a moment, then dropped them. He took a breath. "You just removed my major worry, or at least one of them. Sometimes, when I was dictating, I thought . . . I was afraid that whatever talent I had had was gone. I'm grateful."

Till that moment I had been oblivious of what must have been—could hardly have failed to be—a painful worry to a man who had been through what he had and had not written for so long. Having worked with writers, I should have known from the beginning that that particular anxiety was nagging him. And then, with an odd stab, I remembered his words, "*You've just removed my major worry, or at least one of them."* To as gifted a writer as Adam Kingsley, what other than his work could be listed as a "major worry"? Except, of course, love.

Was he still in love with Sally Kingsley, who, by this time, I seemed to have read somewhere, had had two more husbands? Especially in view of the fact that he was supposed to have married her for her handsome inheritance, or so Dauntry had said. Even the thought of Dauntry's name was a dark shadow, and I thrust it away. Then I looked at Adam and forgot about Dauntry.

"There's no need to be grateful, Adam. I was only saying what I truly thought. Besides, Max says so, too."

"Yes. But though I am in debt to Max for his kindness in keeping in touch and coming to dig me out, I don't think he's primarily an editor. And he'd be the first to agree with me."

I couldn't help but be pleased myself. There was nothing like being considered better than one's boss.

"Now I'm grateful," I said lightly. And we sat there for a minute or two in my living room, far closer than the few feet that divided our chairs.

Then Adam said, "I must go. Tania needs the second half of her exercise." He stood and then rocked a little as his shoe slid on the fringes of the carpet.

"Steady," I said, grasping his arm.

"I'm all right," he said quickly.

"Yes, sorry." I dropped his arm as though it were a live coal, and moved away.

"Antonia," he said. "I'm the one who's sorry. In the words of a therapist I've worked with, blind people tend to become fanatically independent sometimes."

"It's all right."

"No. You offered kindness and I pushed you away. Please forgive me. I've lived alone too long." He was holding out his hand. I couldn't not take it, I told myself. And I moved back towards him and grasped his hand.

"I understand. Truly."

I don't know exactly what happened then, but his arms were around me and his mouth on mine and I felt weak and on fire all at the same time. A few seconds of eternity passed, and then his arms tightened. I could feel the powerful muscles against my ribs, the warmth of his lips and the quickening thud, thud of his heart against mine. And then something very strange occurred. We were no longer standing in my living room. We were in the studio the college had lent him for his summer course.

He had pulled the pins out of my hair, which was spilling over his hands, cupped around my head. "Copperhead," he said thickly, and laughed. His eyes were blazing with what I wanted desperately to believe was passion, and the smell of whiskey on his breath was overpowering. "Why do you frizz it like that?"

Then his hands were pulling at my clothes and mine at his. I remembered catching my fingers in the chain he wore around his neck and under his shirt.

"What's that?" I asked, looking at the curious, rough circlet at the end.

"A mystery," he said, laughing again and pushing my straps down.

"What do you mean, a mystery?" I asked with great dignity, and then spoiled it by hiccuping.

"The mystery of who I am." He pushed me down on the divan. "Now stop talking."

I thrust Adam away and walked across the room, my own heart racing with strange, feathery beats that made me breathless, whether with fear or desire I couldn't exactly tell, but I thought fear.

"Let's not complicate things," I said as evenly as I could, so that he wouldn't hear my voice shaking. "I don't think that's in the script." My voice came thinly through my inner turmoil. I wondered if it sounded as cold to him as it did to me.

He said as though absolutely nothing had happened, "I'll have another tape for you by tomorrow. Forward, Tania."

So he hasn't changed after all, I thought, after he had closed the front door. And thinking that was worse than anger. It was pain.

Dauntry called the following morning. "I've been waiting to hear from you," he said without preamble.

And with those words I realized how much I had been running true to form: Since I had had lunch with Dauntry I had pushed him to the back of my mind, along with the fact that I was supposed to let him know whether or not I was going to cooperate with his idea of allowing him to claim Ewen as his son. Caught in a bind between permitting Dauntry to claim Ewen and telling my son the facts about his birth, I had followed my characteristic habit pattern: I had hoped the whole thing would go away . . .

"I'm sorry, Dauntry. I've been busy."

"So I gather."

"Your spies keeping you well informed?"

He ignored that. "Have you decided whether you're going to make things easy for all of us and do them my way?"

Until that moment I had pretty much decided to do exactly that. But the words of agreement wouldn't come.

"Well?"

"I need more time to think," I blurted out finally.

"I told you what the alternative was."

"That's blackmail, Dauntry."

"If you want to call it that."

I didn't say anything.

"All right. I'll give you until day after tomorrow morning. That's far longer than I had originally planned. There's no point whatsoever in your saying no. But I'd rather you realized that for yourself."

"Thanks."

He laughed. "*De nada.*" And hung up.

That afternoon I went home early, more or less expecting Adam's appearance with another tape. But though I sat there scanning what I had brought home and rereading the typed manuscript version of his revisions, there was no ring on the doorbell. The only person to arrive was Ewen.

I had expected his commuting up to Manhattan's Upper West Side to be far more of a complicated deal than it had turned out to be.

"You're sure it isn't tiring?" I asked him.

"No. Of course not. Besides, I get half an hour extra reading time in the morning."

"You haven't had any trouble of any kind on the subway, have you?"

"No. What kind of trouble? There are always a lot of people around when I'm on the train."

Still, I thought he was looking a little more tired than he had when school was only three blocks away.

"Are you feeling all right?"

"Yes, I'm feeling all right. Stop fussing."

The next day I knew there was a meeting of the Naturalists Club of which he was a member and which sometimes concluded its rites by a trip to the Museum of Natural History, where one of the assistant curators was honorary counselor to the club. So I wasn't particularly worried when I arrived home at five twenty to find no Ewen. He had started the Naturalists Club and was its prime mover and was liable to arrive home late and exhilarated.

At six I called the museum. But the young assistant curator, who was almost as enthusiastic about the club as was Ewen, was on a field trip, and no one seemed to know whether the boys had been there or not. That is, a sympathetic curator told me, there had indeed been groups of boys in and out, but he couldn't say whether or not they were the ones I was looking for.

By this time it was six thirty. I called the school, but it was a day school and there was no answer. At seven I telephoned the headmaster at his home. His wife answered and couldn't have been more understanding. She promised to have her husband return my call as soon as he returned from a drug clinic where he worked two evenings a week. She added apologetically, "I can't really call him there, Mrs. Moncrieff. There's only one phone and they try and keep the line open as much as possible for emergencies."

I stifled the impulse to tell her that this was an emergency. It wasn't that—yet. At seven thirty I tried to call her back to tell her that by now Ewen's whereabouts ranked as a full-blown emergency. But there was no answer.

I called the police. The sergeant who answered was also sympathetic, but pointed out that Ewen had been missing only a few hours.

"He could have gone to a movie with friends or just be playing hooky, Mrs. Moncrieff."

"But Ewen would never do that without at least telling me. He knows how I worry."

"Even the best kids sometimes do that, ma'am." He told me to call back in a couple of hours if Ewen hadn't returned. By this time it was almost eight.

Then the telephone rang. I snatched off the receiver. "Ewen? Where are you?"

"I'm sorry," Adam's voice said. "Is Ewen late getting home?"

"Yes." My voice was doing strange things. I took a deep breath. "Adam do you mind if I call you back later? I want to keep the telephone open. In case . . . if . . ." I put down the receiver, hoping he would understand, but past caring.

A few minutes later there was a knock at the front door. "It's Adam," his voice said from the other side of the door.

"I don't want to be a nuisance," he said when he and Tania came in. "But I thought I would come and lend you moral support since I know you haven't been here long enough to develop any friends in the neighborhood. But if you'd rather be alone, say so."

As a matter of fact I was glad to see him. Like my son, I was inclined to be solitary. In the past few hours I had learned the drawbacks to that.

"No, Adam. I'm glad you're here."

We went into the living room and sat beside the fire where, partly to make the house seem less empty, I had lit a small fire soon after I came in.

"It may be a stupid question," Adam said, directing Tania with his hand to a place a little back of his chair, "but have you thought of every possible place he could be? I mean, including any activity he could legitimately be engaged in that you have forgotten about?"

I shook my head. "I wasn't worried when I came home because he was going to a meeting of his Naturalists Club—that's a club he started with a friend or two and is his ruling hobby. But when he didn't come home I called the natural history museum—one of the staff there has a kind of counseling or supervisory function with the club—but he seems to be away on a field trip, nobody answers at the school and the headmaster is out at a drug clinic." And at that point, to my horror, I burst into tears.

"I'm sorry, Adam," I said, groping in my handbag for some tissues. "It's just nerves."

"I know. Do you want a handkerchief?"

"I've got tissues somewhere."

"Here." He put his hand in his inside breast pocket, pulled out a folded white handkerchief and tossed it over to me with remarkable accuracy.

"Thanks," I said. "How can you manage to be so accurate, Adam? That landed right in my lap."

"I could judge where you were by the sound of your voice."

"I must say you're remarkably adept."

"I have to be, if I'm going to live anything remotely like a normal life."

"Yes. I suppose so. Nevertheless, I think you're very brave."

"Antonia, the only alternative is to be institutionalized or totally dependent on a paid servant. I've been through that and I'd rather be dead. Courage is often just a matter of choices. It's either/or. So, you choose the least unpalatable."

I stared down at the wet handkerchief in my hand. "Maybe. Recently . . . someone . . . said I had always dealt with every problem by running away." And with that I remembered Dauntry. "Oh, God!"

"What? What's the matter?"

"I just remembered . . ."

"What? Where Ewen is? Somewhere he was going tonight?"

"No." I got up and started walking around. But Dauntry had given me until tomorrow. Would he jump the gun on me tonight? Why—

There was the sound of a key in the front door and Ewen walked in.

"Hi," he said. "I'm a bit later than I said, but you weren't worried, were you?"

"Worried?" I repeated. And then, hearing my voice rise and unable to stop it, "Ewen, where have you been for the past four hours?"

"At the science show." He was standing at the edge of the living room, his pea jacket half open, frowning. "Didn't somebody call you? He said he would."

"Who said?"

"Dr. Leigh. He's a friend of the science teacher, and arranged for the club to see the biology film they showed at the science convention. We were late for the film, so he got our telephone numbers and arranged to have somebody call the parents."

And don't imagine you could prevent me from getting to him . . . I know his science teacher, by the way . . .

So Dauntry was giving me a demonstration. Relief from fear was followed by another, greater fear, with the usual result—irritation.

"You should have called me yourself, Ewen. For four hours I haven't known where you were or what might have happened to you. You shouldn't have just delegated that so easily to somebody else. You—"

Adam spoke from behind me. "He's all right, Antonia. And he did think someone had called."

His voice calmed me. "Yes, that's true. I'm sorry, Ewen. Did you have a good time?"

"Yes," he said. "Until now."

Adam spoke again. "Four hours not knowing what's happened can be a long time, Ewen."

"Yeah, I guess. I think I'll go upstairs. I've still got some work to do."

I asked, "Did you get anything to eat?"

"Yeah. We got some burgers after the show." And he started up the stairs. "Oh, by the way, Mom. Dr. Leigh said he knew you in college."

"Dr. Leigh?" Adam said sharply.

"Yeah. Dauntry Leigh, I think."

"Yes, I knew him," I said as steadily as I could. "I'll come up after a while, Ewen."

When he had gone, Adam said, "Is there more to this than some kind of coincidence? Wasn't Leigh your husband?"

"Yes," I said. "There is. Dauntry is trying to force my hand. This evening's adventure was his way of showing a little muscle." A distant part of my mind seemed to find it extraordinary I should be telling Adam this. But it was so distant as to seem totally irrelevent.

"I know this is none of my business. But that . . . demonstration . . . strikes me as a particularly brutal one. You don't have to answer this if you don't want to. But I'm curious to know what Dauntry Leigh wants you to do."

I was silent for a minute, then I said, "Did you ever meet him, Adam?"

"Once. I think he brought you to a seminar or something."

"What did you think of him?"

"It's hard to say. My self-preoccupation in those days was almost total." He frowned. "He was a notably good-looking young man, but in an almost inhuman way. For some reason what leaps to my mind is the Apollo Belvedere."

And the moment he said that I saw Dauntry. Not the rather tired-looking, young middle-aged man that I had had lunch with, but as I saw him first coming across the dance floor towards me. "Yes," I agreed. "He would have looked very well in a Greek tunic."

I paused on the brink of continuing, of telling Adam what Dauntry wanted. But at that moment what flashed through my mind was the memory of Adam's arms around me, not only recently, but thirteen years before. And the treachery of a man who could love me so tenderly one long summer night and, then, the following afternoon, pass me by without even a flicker of recognition, stopped the words in my mouth. I thought I had forgotten that pain, buried it deep. But there it was, like my most intimate ancient monster, alive and well, pouring acid over my heart and laughing harder than ever.

I said, "What Dauntry wants is . . . well, it's something rather confidential. I'm afraid I'm not really free to discuss it."

Later I went up to see Ewen and knocked on his door. "Come in."

Responding to that was a little more difficult than could be normally expected. Ewen's door opened in, and what immediately confronted me was a plywood barrier, knee-high, three sides of a square, the fourth being the door. On the other side of it, all over the floor, ran Ewen's white mice. Ewen was over in the corner, cleaning out the mice's pen, a four-by-four enclosure made of more knee-high plywood and on top of that a specially built cage high enough for Ewen to stand up in. The floor of the pen was filled with wheels and small mazes and bits of shrubbery and little houses and rocks and various minute toys—all the impedimenta of life which delight the heart of white mice.

"Where's Nemesis?" I asked.

"In the bathroom. He's pretty good most of the time, but there's no use straining his nervous system."

"No, indeed. To say nothing of the mice. Heaven knows what Nemesis might do to their nervous systems, especially if they were inside him."

Ewen grinned.

"I'm sorry I was angry when you got home."

"It's okay."

I strolled over to the pen. "Did Dauntry . . . Dr. Leigh say anything about me?"

Ewen turned his head and looked at me. "Only that he knew you. Why? What was there to say?"

I decided not to answer that question. "Did you like him?"

"He was okay, I guess. I don't think he likes animals."

"What makes you say that?"

"Well, Einstein happened to look out of my pocket just as we got there, and Dr. Leigh really backed off and gave me a pretty funny look. Like he didn't like him. Mr. Perkins, the teacher, said was it okay to bring Einstein along. So I said if it wasn't I'd just truck on home. And he—Dr. Leigh—gave a sort of laugh and slapped me on the back, which I didn't care for, and when he got anywhere near me I could see him staring at my pocket."

"Yes. I remember now. Dauntry hated rats. He always said that that was the reason he didn't go into behavioral psychology." I watched Ewen spread fresh newspaper on the floor. "How was the rest of it?"

"The movie was good. Dr. Leigh then gave us a short talk on physics and math and how they can be useful to make social conditions better. When he talks about things like isotopes he's all right. At least, I guess so, I'm not up on those things. There was one thing he said that sounded way out. I asked Mr. Perkins and he said he'd check it."

"What's an isotope?"

Ewen, who was rolling up the soiled newspaper, looked back at me over his shoulder. "Do you really want to know?"

"Is it something you're passionately interested in?"

"Not as much as other things. I don't want to be a physicist. I'm going to be a vet."

"Well, then, in that case I think I'll stay with my ignorance. But if you're not hot about isotopes, then why did you like Dauntry better when he was talking about them?"

"I dunno. He sounded like he knew more about them. Not as phony as when he tried to talk about animals to me, which he did, pretending he'd once had a rat, which I didn't believe, and now I know's not true because you said he hated rats. Why'd he bother?" He stood up. "What was he like when you knew him?"

The words rang at me in all their unthinking irony. *When you knew him.* The urge to say, *Ewen, I didn't know him. I was married to him and I still didn't know him,* was overwhelming. But for the second time in one evening I drew back.

"It's hard to say, darling. He . . . he wasn't an easy man to know. I think the real person lives far inside the outside one." So far as it went, that was the truth.

"Yeah. That sounds like it's for real." He went over and put the rolled up paper in a paper bag then came back and straightened the fresh paper on the floor with his foot. "I'll put the family back in now."

"The family?"

"Mr. and Mrs. Mouse." He bent and picked up two fairly large mice. "These are the parents." He put them into the pen. Then he collected the others one by one. "And here are Alice, Beatrice, Carl, Dennis and Kingsley."

I went over the names in my mind. "I see, alphabetical for the children. That is, until you got to Kingsley." I gave Ewen's averted face a look. "Did you name the youngest after Adam?"

"Yeah."

I tried to think of something to say. But there was nothing to say now. I had already said it.

"One funny thing," Ewen said suddenly. "That Dr.

Leigh asked how was my father? I told him my father'd died in the war over in Vietnam. He said the usual nothing . . . I'm sorry, or something. But he was smiling. Like I'd just said something funny."

Chapter 9

The next morning when I had been in the office about half an hour, the telephone rang. I picked up the receiver and said, "Hello."

"Mrs. Moncrieff?" asked a man's voice.

I could feel my muscles tighten. "Yes?"

"This is Charles Barrett of the FBI. I wonder if I could come and talk to you, either at your office or your home."

My mind felt like one of the mice that had scuttered away in fright when I stepped into the room. "What is it you want to talk about?" I asked, to play for time, although I knew.

"I'd rather discuss that with you in person."

"Well, I can't see you in my house, because my son Ewen is there." Too late I saw that I had revealed that I knew what the Federal Bureau wanted to discuss with me.

"So you have, at least, an idea of the subject we're concerned with."

"Yes. I suppose so. But you can't see me here, either. The office is cramped and the partitions are thin."

"Then what would you suggest?"

Silence.

"Surely your son is in school during the afternoon?"

"Yes. He is." It would be better to have the FBI man there in the afternoon when I would at least have privacy. "You'd better come then, some afternoon when Ewen is in school."

"How about this afternoon?"

"I have a business appointment this afternoon."

"Then how about tomorrow?"

It was as smooth and relentless as an ocean breaker. If I thought of an excuse for the next afternoon, then he would suggest the one after that, and after that, and after that . . .

"All right, Mr.—er—"

"Barrett," he supplied.

"All right, Mr. Barrett. Tomorrow afternoon. Two o'clock. My son gets home shortly after four."

"Very well, Mrs. Moncrieff. I'll see you then."

The following thirty-six hours were among the worst I have ever lived through. My choices were simple and unacceptable: Either I supported Dauntry's story about his being Ewen's father, or I put Ewen in danger, because I was now quite convinced that if I did not do what Dauntry wanted, he would not hesitate to hurt my son in one way or another. That little demonstration was to prove that.

And this is the man you're going to acknowledge as your son's father? a quiet but very distinct inner voice said to me as I got out of the subway the following afternoon and started to walk home.

What choices do I have? I asked that inner woman.

You could tell Ewen yourself, came the answer.

Would that stop Dauntry?

The thought that no matter what I did Ewen might be in danger had not occurred to me. But now, walking home along the Esplanade as I always did, it sprang from some hidden recess where it had been all along, waiting for me to notice it.

If defeated by my telling Ewen the truth, would Dauntry give me the chivalric loser's salute and go out of my life? Not likely. Not Dauntry, who could be spiteful for spite's sake, whose reserve of bitterness carried enough poison to justify—in his own eyes, anyway—any vindictive act.

That realization made me feel queasy with fear. Without thinking, I went over to the railing to stare at a view that somehow had always calmed me. I had not been in Brooklyn Heights long enough to have become used to or blasé about one of the most beautiful sights in the city: the island of Manhattan across the river. Even now, in the peak of the early afternoon, it was an astounding view, with the silver perpendicular buildings soaring to the sky and the patch of green like a neat apron around the western edge. Far to the left was the New Jersey shore. Over the waters in between, boats and ferries plied back and forth. And a huge liner, doubtless embarking on its spring cruise, made its stately way towards the open sea.

But if it was beautiful now, at dusk, when I usually passed this way going home, it was staggering—still light enough to see the silver shapes of the buildings, yet dark enough for their lights to be coming on.

At dusk, of course, I thought idly, moving on, there were more people about, workers like myself coming home. Now there seemed to be very few: one of the community's elderly seated on a bench, taking handfuls of something out of a paper bag and offering them to a set of assertive and greedy pigeons. At the far end of the Esplanade was a man and a dog. There were footsteps behind me . . .

The moment I registered that, I knew that I had been

aware of those steps now for quite a while and that there was something odd about them. I slowed down, veering to the left where, on the other side of iron railings, were the gardens of the great mansions built in the eighteen twenties and thirties by merchant princes like the Standishes.

Pretending to look into the long narrow gardens, I listened, and knew that the footsteps I had been aware of had also slowed. I turned quickly. A young man with long hair, in jeans and a pea coat, was also looking through the railings, some thirty feet behind me. But it was ludicrous to suspect that this fuzzy representative of the counterculture, busily sketching onto a pad, and looking up constantly at the iron-lace grillwork of one of the houses, could either be following me, or in any way be a threat. These houses were famous. Tours were conducted along the Esplanade, artists or would-be artists could be seen there almost any day.

Nevertheless, for the first time along this elegant parade, I felt uneasy. The old man, friend of pigeons, had gone. So had the man and the dog at the other end.

You've always known you were a moral coward, I said severely to myself. Now you discover you're a physical one as well. Don't be so paranoid. I increased my pace and moved briskly along the wide promenade, forcing my attention to the ferry, about to dock below, to the Manhattan Bridge, just back and to the right, and to the twin towers of the World Trade Center on the other side of Manhattan Island.

But the steps had quickened, too. I turned.

Where the young man had stashed the pad and pencil I don't know. They weren't visible about the lanky figure much closer behind me. Over his eyes were dark glasses. He was much nearer to me, and gaining.

From somewhere I got the nerve to say loudly, "Are you following me?"

His mouth opened on white teeth. "Sure I am. How did you guess?" And he suddenly came at me in a run.

At school one of my few distinctions was winning the hundred-yard dash. I turned and ran. But I was older now than the child in gym shoes that I had been, and not dressed for sprinting, whereas my pursuer was.

I was running as fast as I could, making for one of the entrances to the Esplanade. But he was gaining on me rapidly. I was about to muster my breath for a scream, when the break in the railings came. There was a short path into the street, and coming towards me were Adam and Tania.

It made no sense, of course, to call out to him, since he was blind. But I did. "Adam," I cried, without thinking.

I saw him stop and heard the feet behind me slow.

"Antonia, come here and get behind me," Adam said quickly.

Then I remembered that he couldn't see, and my fear veered towards what the nut behind me would do. "Adam, he's dangerous," I yelled.

"I told you to get behind me."

The feet had slowed and then picked up again. He was only a few feet back of me.

It was at that point that Tania growled. Her lips lifted from her teeth. Then the steps stopped. I glanced behind.

The man took a knife from his belt.

"Adam, he has a knife. Don't let him get Tania."

"Don't worry. Tania will get him before he can move his hand. And if he gets near enough, I can add my measure."

Whether it was Tania's growl, combined with the display of her excellent teeth, or what Adam said, I don't know. But as suddenly as he had come towards me, the young man turned and ran, not back onto the Esplanade, but off to the side, where he could get to the road.

"Thank you, Adam, and thank you, Tania," I said. And oblivious of any rules about touching Tania when she was in harness, I bet down and gave her a hug. A warm tongue licked my cheek.

"Who was that?" Adam asked abruptly. "Have you seen him anywhere before?"

"No. Nowhere."

"Do you have any reason to think it's anybody but some stray thug on the prowl?"

"No," I said, and knew that rarely had I ever wanted so much to believe anything.

There was a short pause, then Adam said, "All right. Are you on your way home?"

"Yes." Then remembering how early it was and for what reason I had come home, I said, "I'm expecting a business call at home."

"I see."

We turned towards my street. Thank heaven, I thought, for conventional politeness: the kind of barrier that would prevent Adam from saying, *What business appointment?*

"What kind of business appointment?" Adam asked. And then, as I could feel myself jump at this accurate bit of mind-reading, "And why are you so tense?"

"I react badly to probing personal questions."

"Yes, so do I. Most people do. My justification is my . . . concern for you and Ewen. You're as jumpy as a cat, and there's an odd atmosphere in the house, to say nothing of a cold draft that seems to emanate from the walls themselves. Are you having some kind of psychic manifestation?"

"That's funny. That's what Ewen asked."

"Well?"

"There is a cold draft, only I thought it was only in my room."

"Well, it's in my apartment, too. I've felt it twice. The

first time was when your kitten arrived in my bedroom." We walked on for a bit. "To go back to my impertinent question, I won't push for an answer. But be careful."

A little chill went over me. "Why do you say that?"

"I have a feeling you're in some kind of danger. And being the way I am, there's nothing much I can do to help you."

It was absurd, that little jump or flutter somewhere in the direction of my stomach or diaphragm . . . or heart. I swallowed an overwhelming desire to say, Do you want to help me, Adam?

Instead I asked, "Is there . . . is there any reason you have for saying that?"

"You mean, any material or factual evidence that I can offer?"

"Yes, I suppose so."

"You'll be convinced I'm paranoiac, but I've been sure once or twice that someone is following me. And I live in your house."

"Couldn't you be mistaken?"

"No. I don't think so. As I told you, the so-called acute hearing of the blind is actually just concentrated listening, learning to distinguish between and among sounds. On several occasions there were footsteps behind that accommodated themselves to mine. And Tania has been aware of them, too."

"How can you tell?"

"I feel her tension through the harness. Twice she growled. The first time it was too low for anyone but me to hear. But the second time her growl was more than audible, and the steps definitely stopped, then faded away."

More absurd than absurd was the spurt of alarm I felt, different from the panic of half an hour before with the mugger after me. (I had by now decided he was definitely a mugger, a breed with which, unfortunately, New Yorkers are intimately acquainted.) This chilling fear was what I usually felt on behalf of Ewen. Only this time it was on behalf of Adam. I managed not to take his arm. But I couldn't stop myself from saying, "Please be careful, Adam. I don't mean to tread on your independence—I know how you feel about it—but . . . I worry," I finished lamely.

He was silent for a minute. We turned the corner into our street. I kicked myself for impinging on his prized privacy.

"Do you, Antonia? Worry about me, I mean?"

"I shouldn't have said that. I know how you feel . . ."

"Do you? I suppose it must be obvious. Does it bother you? Would you prefer me to move out? I'd rather not, because even the way I am, I can keep on eye on you, metaphorically speaking. And Tania is an excellent guard dog."

And then, as my heart was thumping and my throat grew tight, that old treacherous picture, like a film seen again and again, flashed across my mind.

Adam, his blue-green eyes bloodshot, the vertical lines of dissipation gouged deep in his face, walking straight past me less than twelve hours after we had lain naked and on fire, on the divan in his studio. I, too, had drunk far too much that evening at the farewell party the English Department had thrown for Adam and Sally Kingsley, and, with my inhibitions gone, had not only responded to Adam's skilled and practiced flirting but had blurted out the dismal story of my failed marriage.

"It didn't fail," I wept. "It never started."

That was when he put his arm around me and slid me gently and (I fondly thought) invisibly from the party.

The next day I waited at first eagerly, then despairingly, for his call. Finally, I ventured out onto the campus looking for him, and that was when he passed me. The day after that he and his wife were gone.

And, naturally, it never occurred to me that all the tenderness and passion that had happened between us had been lost for him in an alcoholic blackout. What was it he had said about the party that day at the restaurant? "I remember the beginning of it, but, as usual, I was drunk pretty much all of the time then, before, during and after, and I don't remember the end of it. . . . What happened?"

And my reply, "Nothing much. You talked to me and other adoring fans, then my husband came and took me away . . ."

". . . I said what's the matter?" Adam's voice, sharp and urgent, broke through the umpteenth running of that scenario. With his free right hand he had grasped my arm. "This is the second or third time you've done that."

"What?" Although I knew.

"Gone away from me. Back into some hole or cave. That day in your living room. I realize . . . I have to face the fact that being blind and scarred . . ."

"It's not that," I said quickly, and then instantly saw what I had admitted. "I mean . . ."

"Then what is it?" His hand was still around my arm.

"Adam, not here in the street." I watched a familiar figure with his reddish brown afro approach. And then Adam and I both spoke.

I said, "There's that—"

He said, "There are those—"

And we both stopped. Adam said, "What were you going to say?"

"I just said, there's that boy, Bonzo. Let's . . . let's go in."

There was a fraction of a pause. "All right."

"Now," he said, when we were in the living room and Tania was lying at the edge of the carpet near the chair he usually sat in. But he had not sat down. And when I started to move away across the room, he reached out and grasped both of my arms. "Now. What happened to you when you freaked out?"

But I had had time to think. What he wanted to know—the reason why I always withdrew from him—was locked inside his own head, hidden away, encapsulated in a bubble of alcoholic amnesia. But who knew what might activate that memory? The smallest explanation might jar everything loose, including the fact that Ewen was his son. If he knew that, there would be no question of my playing along with Dauntry. And Dauntry would get to Ewen.

"I told you, Adam. Let's not complicate things. And"—I glanced at my clock—"I have an appointment here, that business appointment I mentioned to you, in about five minutes. Please go."

The urgency in my voice was quite sincere. I did not want Adam anywhere near or within hearing when the FBI man arrived. "You can go through the basement stairs. You have your own key to the door at the bottom."

"Antonia—"

"No, Adam. No."

I could see then his own withdrawal behind that scarred face. He bent down. "Tania!"

He went out the front door, anyway, before I could stop him, and I watched, seeing Bonzo strolling along, minus bike, across the street, and another man turning the corner at the far end.

Less than five minutes after Adam's own front door closed down in the area way, there was a ring at my bell.

The man that stood there was one of the most unnoticeable people I had ever seen: medium everything—height, weight, hair color, eyes, and so on. "Charles Barrett," he said. He produced from his palm an identification card case and flashed it briefly. Then he smiled. "May I come in?"

I stepped back.

"All right, Mr. Barrett," I said, when we were both in the living room. "What is all this about?"

He smiled again, and I liked it even less than the first time. "But you know, don't you, Mrs. Leigh?"

"I took back my maiden name," I said.

"But not legally."

"No."

"So that all documents, social security and so on that you have signed by your maiden name are invalid."

It was not a question, I noticed. It was a statement.

"I don't know. Perhaps you're right. I would have to ask a lawyer about that."

"But I am a lawyer, and I know."

I remembered then I had read somewhere that most FBI agents were lawyers or accountants or both. Was it their usual custom to start exerting pressure immediately?

"All right, Mr. Barrett, so then?"

Again the smile. He had a false front tooth, I noticed. Perhaps it was that that gave the smile such a phony quality. "So nothing, Mrs.—er—Moncrieff. That was just to let you know that we have investigated you thoroughly."

"And will pass on these various tidbits of information to the agencies that might refuse me unemployment insurance or social security on the ground that all my signatures were invalid?"

"Not necessarily. If you will cooperate with us in our investigation of your divorced husband, Dauntry Leigh."

"That's blackmail."

"We don't use those terms."

"Whether you use them or not doesn't alter the fact that that's what it is."

He didn't reply to that. "All we need is your confirmation that Ewen Moncrieff Leigh—because since your name is legally Leigh so is his—is Dauntry Leigh's son."

I reminded myself that I didn't have to like all government employees even though I was, as a citizen, paying his salary. Still, beyond my simple dislike of the man interrogating me and the manner of his interrogation, there was something odd. I was trying to define it when he said, "I asked that you confirm the fact that your son Ewen is also Dauntry Leigh's son."

"And if I do?"

"Why then there will be no trouble about his appointment to head up that new laboratory."

I don't know what made me say it, but I asked quickly, "The one in Oakland?"

He was getting a paper out of his pocket and a ballpoint pen. "Yes, that's right. Now if you'll just sign this statement here, affirming that Ewen is Dauntry's son . . ."

I knew then that, whatever he was, he was not an FBI agent. But if I had had a brain in my head, I would have kept that flash of illumination to myself.

Instead, I said, "I thought the lab was in Santa Barbara. By the way, may I see your identification again? You flashed it so fast out there on the steps that I didn't get a chance to read it properly."

I realized at once what insanity it was for me to say that. He looked at me, and I knew that he knew I knew . . .

I turned to run. If I could just get to the street, I thought—and that was the last I remember.

I awoke with a grinding headache and an unpleasant feeling of nausea.

"Ouch!" I said, as I opened my eyes.

"Mom, are you okay? What happened? How do you feel?"

Ewen was standing beside me, and at the other end of the living room sofa where I was lying was Adam.

I started to sit up. There was a sharp pain at the back of my head, the nausea got suddenly worse, and there was an interesting display of fireworks in front of my eyes.

"Better not sit up yet," Adam said.

"How did you know I was?" I asked rather crossly.

"The sofa springs."

"I'm not that heavy."

To my surprise the strained look on his face was replaced by a half smile. "I'm quite sure you're not. In fact, I'd say you were quite light."

I was opening my mouth to say, And how do you know that? when I suddenly realized exactly how he knew. Who else could have carried me to the sofa? And hadn't his arms been around me? I decided I didn't wish to discuss the matter in front of Ewen. However, Adam's advice seemed good. I lay down again.

"Mom, what happened to you? I came home early because the last class was cancelled, and you were lying there on the floor."

This time I sat up more slowly. "Did you go and get Ad—Mr. Kingsley?" I asked, playing for time.

"He telephoned me," Adam said briefly. "I, too, would like to know what happened to you. When I left earlier you were about to have a business appointment. Did he do this? If so, I want to know his name and what you were about to see him for, so we can tell the police, and the sooner the better."

By this time I had had time to think. "Oh, he came and went, and it was in coming back from seeing him out that I tripped and fell, and, I guess, hit my head. How stupid can I be?"

"Tripped on what, for gosh sake?" Ewen asked, disbelief written clearly on his face.

"On that small throw rug," I said, and remembered then that it was at the cleaners.

"That's at the cleaners."

"Then obviously it was something else."

Ewen, looking like a miniature version of the tall man standing beside him said slowly, "Mr. Kingsley told me about the man who was chasing you this afternoon. Twice in one day seems a little heavy to me. There's something you're not telling me."

"I could wish Mr. Kingsley had kept his mouth shut."

"Why?" Adam asked. "Ewen's not a small child. He has a right to know if you're in any kind of trouble."

"Look, Adam," I said more sharply than I had intended. "This is none of your affair. I wish you'd stay out of it. And I wish you'd leave me alone."

That last sentence just added itself without any volition on my part, and it had nothing to do with the events of that afternoon or the two men who seemed bent on getting rid of me. And in that second I knew that it was an unfinished sentence, and that it was also, on a deeper level, a plea: *I wish you'd leave me alone because . . . because what? Because I need you?* Unthinkable to say such a thing. I must have been more shaken than I thought, because I completed my performance by bursting into tears.

Adam bent and took Tania's harness. "By all means. Ewen, let me know if you need me. And call a doctor." And he and Tania left.

After the door had closed behind them Ewen said slowly, "I thought you were all for politeness and civility and all that garbage. Boy, you sure turned him off in a hurry."

"I know. I'm sorry." I put my feet on the floor and looked around for my handbag.

"Why were you so lousy to him? I mean, you've always liked him. And you were mad at me for being turned off by his accident."

I tried to think of something to say that would make sense to Ewen. But absolutely nothing came to mind. Finally I said the only thing I could. "I'm sorry, Ewen, it's a long story."

"He likes you a lot, you know."

I looked up sharply at him. "How do you know? Did he tell you?"

"No. But I'm not six years old. And when you're together, there's something . . . well, like an *atmosphere* . . ." His voice faded.

"Does that make you unhappy, Ewen?"

"No. If I just knew what was going on."

"I thought you had decided you didn't like him."

"Yeah, well. I looked up alcoholism in a big medical dictionary we have at school and talked to our science teacher about it. They—he and the dictionary—both say it's a disease, and blackouts are like amnesia. So it's not really his fault in the same way."

"Did you tell him?"

"No. I haven't gotten around to it yet." He paused. Underneath the floppy yellow hair his face looked peaked. "I thought maybe I ought to give him time to forget how mean I was to him. And . . ."

All of a sudden there was a mature look on his little boy's face. I put out my hand and pulled him towards me. "What's the matter, Ewen, love? Tell me."

Those blue-green eyes suddenly lifted to mine. "Mom, is he my father?"

We must have sat there for a full two minutes, my own eyes locked with his, before I could unfreeze my tongue.

"What on earth makes you say that, Ewen?"

"I don't know. I guess I'm crazy or something."

"But what made you say it?"

"Well, I mean, just look at him. That night we went down looking for Cleo, he didn't have his dark glasses on. His one eye is exactly the same color as mine, and I haven't ever seen anybody who's got the same bluish-greenish-color eye. And my nose looks like his. And . . . and I don't know, Mom, but there's something about the two of you together that made me think of it."

Funny, I thought, sitting there. The thing I had always run away from: that Ewen should know this, the truth I couldn't face, the confrontation I didn't dare risk. What had I been saving at the expense of everything else?

"Is it true?"

"Yes, Ewen. It's true."

"Well, why did you tell me all this crap about my father being killed in Vietnam?"

"Because I was afraid you . . . you wouldn't respect me, you wouldn't love me, if you knew how it . . . how you happened."

"Well, how did I happen?"

"All right. I'll tell you. But let's go into the kitchen. I'd like some tea."

"Okay. Only I think I ought to call a doctor."

"Do you know one?"

"Only Dr. Sommers."

"He's your pediatrician."

"Maybe he knows somebody."

"Yes. He probably does. On the Upper West Side of Manhattan. No doctor's going to make a house call from there to Brooklyn Heights. And I sure don't feel like hopping a subway up there."

"Okay. But I bet he'd know how to find somebody over here."

"All right, Ewen. Later. When I feel up to talking to him."

So, sitting in the kitchen while I had tea and he had cocoa, I told him everything, right from the beginning, as I should have long before.

After a while Ewen said, "So Dr. Leigh was your husband?"

"Yes."

He took Einstein out of his pocket, holding and stroking him and then cradling him in his arms. "Well, I can see why you don't think much of him. I mean . . . apart from him being . . . the way he was when you were married."

"There's more, Ewen. Dauntry . . . Dr. Leigh wants to claim you as his son."

"Why? I don't want to be his son."

"Because . . . well, he has been appointed head of some kind of lab doing defense work or something. Anyway, he says he's being investigated, and that he said you were his son as some kind of proof that he wasn't a homosexual. And now he wants me to back him up."

"That's pretty silly. Lots of gays are married."

I stared at my worldly-wise son. "How do you know that?"

He stared back at me, as though I had asked an idiot question. "Everybody does. All you have to do is read the papers or go to the movies. Even on television they talk about it. You know, Mom, I've often thought you were pretty old-fashioned."

"I guess you're right, Ewen." I stirred my tea. "How do you feel about . . . do you mind Adam being your father?"

"No. I like him. I'd a lot rather have him for a father than some war hero."

"You don't think much of war heros, do you?"

"No. They kill."

"Suppose you'd come home and found that man beating me up. What would you do, just stand there?"

"No, of course not. I'd . . . I'd . . . I'd call the police."

"Who would arrive, armed. And what if the man refused to stop beating me, and the only way they could make him stop was to kill him?"

"Okay. So I'd rather they'd kill him. I could do it myself. But that's not the same as dropping bombs on villagers."

"All right, then, Ewen. I just mean that pacifism isn't that simple. I'm glad you'd defend me even to the death. And I'm glad you don't mind having Adam for a father."

He was bright pink. "*Of course* I'd defend you. Did you think I wouldn't?"

"I just wondered. Maybe I'm having an attack of insecurity. It was that man, by the way, who hit me on the head."

"Well, why didn't you say so? I'm going to go call the police."

"No, Ewen. Stop. Let me explain. Dauntry said that a man from the FBI was going to call on me to confirm what he had told them about your being his son. So when a man called me at the office yesterday and said he was from the FBI, I didn't question it. And I arranged to see him here this afternoon when I was sure you'd be out. You see, my thinking I would go along with Dauntry was because I didn't want you to know . . . anything."

I glanced up at Ewen. He didn't say anything.

"Anyway, the man came and flashed his badge at the front door and I let him in. But there must have been something about him that put me on guard. Because I set a trap for him—Dauntry had told me that his lab was in Santa Barbara. So when the man mentioned it, I said, all innocent,

Oh, is that the lab in Oakland? And he agreed. And started hauling out a paper for me to sign saying that I definitely confirmed Dauntry's statement about your being his son. So I knew he wasn't from the FBI. I asked him if I could see his badge again. He realized then that I had begun to suspect him. I tried to run to the door, but he got me before I had taken a couple of of steps."

"But *why?* Why didn't you tell Dr. Leigh to go shove it?"

"Because I was trying to protect you from knowing who you were and who your father was and all that. Yes, I know, Ewen. You think I'm out of the ark. But please remember I grew up before the sexual revolution and in an area and among people for whom practically everything was forbidden. I was still very much under that influence when you were born and for several years afterwards. Lately, in the last few years, I've begun to see what a mistake I made in telling you what I had. But it was done, and I didn't know how to undo it without shaking your faith in me. And I was afraid to do that. I'm sorry. I'm really sorry."

"It's all right. I understand. I think. But who's going to tell my . . . Mr. Kingsley? About me." And he blushed.

"I will. I made this neat little mess. And I'm going to have to unravel it."

"I'll help. If you like."

"Thanks, Ewen. You always help. Just by being."

He blushed again. Then he grinned. Then he put Einstein away and came over and kissed me. "You know you don't have to be Mrs. Perfect. I like you anyway. Are you going to call the cops about that guy? And what about the guy who chased you on the Esplanade?"

"I think they're both little messengers from Dauntry. So I'll tell him you know all about my spotted past and to call off his hounds." As I said that a little chill went through me. "Ewen, I told him once that I would spike his guns by telling

223

you everything myself and he said he'd still get to you and tell you . . . unpleasant things . . . about me." I looked over at him. "There's nothing left to tell, Ewen. Truly. But there's nothing to prevent him making something up, or twisting something I've already told you. He threatened he would get to you, and he did, by going to your science master and taking you to the film and not phoning me. So you will be careful, won't you, darling? Don't accept any unusual invitations for a while. Please. He is a bitter man and a dangerous one."

"Yeah. Okay. There's something else. You know the science master seemed a little surprised at some of the things Dr. Leigh said. One of the kids wrote down something he'd said after the film and brought it up in class the next day. And Mr. Perkins said maybe he, Dr. Leigh, had been thinking about something else because it wasn't quite right."

"But I thought Mr. Perkins had known Dauntry at school."

"Yeah, he had. But only as a freshman, or something."

"Oh. You mean he implied that Dauntry isn't quite the scientific hotshot he claimed to be."

"Something like that. Perkins is very relaxed about degrees and that kind of thing. But I think he thought something was fishy." There was a pause, then Ewen asked, "When are you going to talk to Mr. Kingsley?"

"Tomorrow maybe."

"Okay. I think I'll go up and do some studying."

When he had gone I glanced at the clock. More, much more, than I had allowed myself to show Ewen, I was frightened. I wasn't sure that Dauntry wanted to do any more than just terrorize me into acquiescing to his plans. But a blow on the head went far beyond that. I felt as though I had lived at least two days since I had left the office, but it was only five in the afternoon. I went to the telephone and called Dauntry, deliberately turning my fear into anger so that I could use it. I half expected him to be out, but he answered on the second ring, as though he had been waiting.

"Dauntry," I said, after his hello, "I have told Ewen everything. So you can no longer hold that over my head, and you can call off your would-be muggers and your phony FBI men. And don't bother to tell me that you can make things up to tell Ewen or get to him in some other way. I have warned him about you." And then, for the second time in one day, I committed a gross stupidity. "There's no way you can get to me through him or get to him. And if you make a move towards either one of us, I shall go to the police."

"Have you told Adam that he is a father?"

"No. Not yet. Why?"

"No reason. It doesn't matter. If you don't somebody will, given the resemblance. Isn't it just like Adam to have a son his spitting image." Then Dauntry laughed. "Well, that would seem to be that, wouldn't it?"

"It would and is. Good-bye, Dauntry."

And I hung up, feeling a huge load roll off my shoulders, happily unaware that I had just signed my own death warrant.

Chapter 10

That pleasant oblivion faded somewhat as the evening wore on. Perhaps it was because the day's adventures had left me with a nasty, nagging headache that refused to respond to any of the usual household remedies. Maybe, I thought, after Ewen and I had had a rather silent dinner, he and Adam were right: I should have dug up a doctor from somewhere. In my dismal mood, everything I had ever heard about brain damage and spinal injury flitted across my mind.

Another possible explanation for my depressed condition was the realization that tomorrow I would have to redeem my promise to Ewen and remind Adam of a night long ago that he had forgotten or blacked out, and of which Ewen was the result. For some reason it was not the thought of presenting him with Ewen as a son that bothered me. I was serenely convinced that he and Ewen were quite up to handling that. It was what it would tell him about me . . .

But behind all that was another unease which I didn't

identify until Cleo and I climbed into bed, or rather, until I climbed into a bed in the middle of which Cleo, all two pounds of her, had staked out her permanent claim.

"Move over," I said.

She looked up from the task that was absorbing her, an intimate and thorough spit bath.

"You heard me," I said, and slid over next to her.

With a treble squeak, she bounced off the bed.

"I didn't say you had to get off altogether. Come here," and I patted the quilt.

When she refused to be courted, I threw down a cellophane ball I had tied on the end of a string, and for a few minutes we played bat and ball. Then I got up, Scotch-taped the string to the wide mantel jutting out into the room, and got back into bed.

"If that's the way you feel," I said to Cleo, who was looking positively bored as she watched the widely swinging toy, "then don't bother to join me. I can live without you."

Then I turned off the bedside light and snuggled down. Before I drifted off to sleep I knew what was bothering me: Dauntry's apparent willingness to accept defeat. His words, *"then that would appear to be that,"* mocked me. Such acquiescence was totally unlike every experience I had had of him. The moment that came to the surface of my mind I was awake.

When Dauntry wanted something, he didn't fool around with any nonsense about Queensbury rules. Dauntry played to win, always. If stymied, he simply regrouped and attacked from another angle. I sat up, hugging my knees, shivering, whether with cold or fright I didn't pause to consider.

If Dauntry were mounting another assault, what would it be? I didn't know, but whatever it was, it would be aimed at either Ewen or me, or, I was amazed to find myself thinking, at Adam. Why that conviction was so strong I didn't know.

In that case, I would have to have my talk with Adam in

the morning. I couldn't leave him, blind and defenseless, before the malignant twists of Dauntry's imagination.

All this gloomy cogitation was chilling to the blood, I decided, and lay back down again, idly taking in the fact that Cleo's cellophane toy was still swinging in its wide arc. She must have come off her dignity and played with it after all. But where had she gone to?

Oh, well, I thought, burrowing down among the covers, she was old enough to take care of herself.

But the next morning my midnight cogitations over Dauntry seemed melodramatic and unreal. Besides which, Ewen spent his breakfast fussing over Einstein who, he said, was not feeling well.

"How do you know he's not feeling well?"

"Well, look at him, Mom. His fur's spikey and his eyes don't look right." Ewen took Einstein out of his pocket and put him on the breakfast table.

Einstein, a fairly large white laboratory rat that Ewen had been allowed to take home one summer vacation, and which he had then bought from the school, was certainly not looking his usual self. His fur had lost its gloss and his nose was running.

"What do you suppose is the matter with him?"

"Well, I was looking in this book on rats. Either he has a cold or, it sounds crazy, he could have eaten some poisoned food. But I've had him with me all the time. Where could he get poisoned food?"

"I don't know, Ewen. But . . . since he's on the breakfast table . . . I have a feeling . . . I think you'd better put him on the floor, Ewen. Here, here's some newspaper."

My instincts proved to be entirely justified. Among his other symptoms, Einstein was having diarrhea.

Ewen cleaned up the accident, held Einstein in his arm,

went to the hall closet, and got out a sweater of his. Then he lovingly wrapped him in it. Then he sat there staring at him. It was difficult to say who looked more miserable: Ewen or his rat.

"Mom, I can't take him on the subway today. I should put him in the sick bay and stay beside him. Rats shouldn't be handled too much when they're sick. But I think he'd want me to be with him."

"You can't miss school, Ewen."

"Why not? I miss it easy enough when I have to go and have some stupid shot that doesn't do me any good. It's just like I always said, you don't care about Einstein. I'm not going." And with that he took the afflicted and bundled up Einstein out into the hall.

The next thing I heard was the telephone being dialed.

I went out. "Who are you calling?"

"Mr. Perkins. He can tell me what should be done."

But there seemed to be no answer. "I guess he's left home. I'm going to try the school." And he dialed again. Again there was no answer.

"Ewen—"

He turned. "I'm not going anywhere until I find out what to do about Einstein." And he went upstairs.

I went back to the kitchen. What do you do with a near-thirteen-year-old boy, almost as tall as yourself, who's much too big to spank, and much too big to make do anything he doesn't want to do? I couldn't take him by the hand and force him out of the house and onto the subway and up to school. What had happened to my authority? Would I use it now if I had it? And then, as clear as though it were a motion picture, I could see Ewen as he would be the rest of the day if he were in school: worrying, probably not taking in much. And how would he be if the wretched rat died?

I wondered then what other parents would do, and passed

on from there to one of my more frequent ponderings: was Ewen's mania for his animals some kind of way of filling the empty spaces of his life? With no father . . .

And then, I remembered Adam's voice saying, "*I had a rat once. He wasn't white, but he was very tame and used to come when I whistled.*"

For a moment I hesitated. What, other than an exchange of vital information about rats, would a meeting between Ewen and Adam produce? Wouldn't it be easier to let him stay home?

I went out into the hall. "Ewen, please come to the head of the stairs. There's something I have to tell you."

After a minute I called again, making enormous efforts not to sound impatient. "Ewen! Please!"

"What is it?" Ewen's head appeared over the banister. "I'm very busy Mom, looking up to see what I should be doing for Einstein."

"Adam, Mr. Kingsley, told me the day we moved that he once had a pet rat. Not a white one. But he came when Adam whistled, so they must have known one another pretty well."

The smile on Ewen's face was like seeing sunshine after days of gray. "Can I call him? Can I ask him to come here? Einstein is very sick and I don't want to move him. Please!"

To deny him, particularly in view of all that he knew about Adam, was ridiculous. "All right. Would you like me to call him?"

"Please, Mom. I have to go back to Einstein."

So I called Adam and asked him to come and lend advice about the care and medical approach to rats. "You did say you once had a rat," I justified myself.

"I did indeed. I'll come up and talk to Ewen."

"How will Tania feel about Einstein?"

"Since she'll be working she'll have to keep her feelings to herself, whatever they are."

When Adam arrived at the front door I simply said,

remembering his dislike of unnecessary instructions, "Ewen's room is up two flights."

"What about his school?" Adam asked, coming inside.

"School? You must be joking. What's an education beside a rat?"

When he laughed I said, a little defensively, "I suppose you think I sound just like a mother."

"No, I don't think that, because I don't know how a mother sounds, not having had one, or, I suppose to be accurate, not remembering mine."

"I'd forgotten about your orphan days. There are times when I think Ewen might consider you lucky. But those are only on our bad days."

"I'm sure," he said, turning towards the staircase, "Ewen doesn't think anything of the kind." He hesitated. "I take it you're feeling better. How's your head?"

"Fine."

He was silent.

"Really, Adam. It's okay. As a matter of fact, what with Einstein I had forgotten about it. We can't have two invalids at once."

"All right." He turned back to the stairs. "Forward, Tania."

Curious to see how Adam, blind, could diagnose Einstein, I followed.

We found Ewen crouched over a small cage he called the sick bay. Inside, Einstein was huddled up, looking unlike his usual friendly assertive self.

"Einstein's worse," Ewen said in that controlled, unexpressive voice that meant he was upset.

Adam and Tania advanced slowly to the cage. "Tell me, in detail, about his symptoms," Adam said.

When Ewen had finished his medical report, Adam said, "May I hold him?"

"Sure." Ewen added a little doubtfully, "he sometimes

bites, but only if he feels insecure or nervous."

"In that case I hope Einstein finds me soothing. But you take him out."

Very gently, and talking to him in a low voice, Ewen took the rat out of his cage. "I've got him now."

Adam reached over with astonishing accuracy and touched Einstein, who seemed to accept him without fuss. Then Adam gently took him from Ewen and held him, stroking his fur. Einstein, whom I have seen visibly withdraw into himself when strangers were even in the same room, seemed to relax. Adam's fingers probed gently.

"I think," he said slowly, "he just has a cold. But it would be a good idea if he could see a vet. Do you know one?"

"Our vet is in Manhattan," Ewen said. "At the animal hospital. And I hate to take Einstein on the subway if he's not feeling well."

"Do you know one here?"

"No. And a new vet . . . well, some of them don't feel too friendly to rats."

"You want to go to the one you know at the hospital?"

"It would be great, but how?"

"By taxi. I'll take you. And then I can bring him home if he's all right and you can go on to school."

I left as Ewen was repudiating the whole idea of school and Adam was gently but firmly insisting that he go.

When I got down I called the school and told them Ewen would be late.

"I hope he's all right," the nice receptionist said.

"He's fine. It's his rat who's feeling poorly and I can't seem to make Ewen realize that he should go to school anyway."

The receptionist, who was fairly new and unaccustomed to boy-logic, was a trifle shocked. "He should talk to Mr. Perkins about it, then. He'd know what to do."

"Ewen tried to call him at home but he had left."

"Well, he just walked in. I'll get him."

When he got to the telephone, Mr. Perkins was as sympathetic as Ewen would have wanted him to be. "Let me talk to him," he said. "I've had sick rats."

"Well, right now he's talking to . . . er . . . our tenant, who also had a rat at some point."

"You mean the writer, Adam Kingsley? Ewen told me about him. He seems to think the world of him."

"Yes it is, and yes he does. But I'll call Ewen anyway. I'm sure he'd want to talk to you."

The upshot of all this was that Adam and Ewen were going to take Einstein, well wrapped up, in a taxi to the Manhattan animal hospital. Adam would stay, if necessary, and bring Einstein back and sit with him.

"And he said we could drop you off at your office on our way," Ewen added kindly.

"How nice of you both." I tried to sound sincere and grateful.

Ewen, carefully holding Einstein in his cage, which was half wrapped in a blanket, threw me a sharp look.

"But," Adam turned his head towards me, "we don't want you to think that every time Einstein takes a taxi to Manhattan, you get a free ride."

"You mean I should keep my head under this deluge of flattery and consideration."

"Something like that."

"And when you get back with the patient, where are you going to sit holding his paw? Down in your apartment?"

"I suppose so. But that cold we were talking about, well, it's still there, only it's more like a draft."

"In that case, here's an extra set of house keys. Upper and lower front-door locks. You'd better take him to the living room or Ewen's room."

"That's funny," Ewen turned from opening the front door. "I've been thinking what you said about Einstein's having a cold. His cage, where he sometimes sleeps when he isn't in my bed, is in the corner by the fireplace—you know that deep corner, Mom, like the one in your room, with the angle from the other corner? Well, he was there this morning, and there was a cold wind coming from somewhere. If I hadn't been so upset, I would have mentioned it." He glanced at Adam. "Maybe if you could put his cage on the other side of the room. . . ?"

We were halfway over the Manhattan Bridge when I asked Ewen, "That cold draft, have you felt it before in your room? You never mentioned it."

"No. It's only been in yours and . . . er . . . Mr. Kingsley's."

Adam, of course, couldn't see the surge of red in Ewen's cheeks, but he could undoubtedly hear the hesitation. I wondered what he would make of it.

"You can call me Adam, if you like," he said.

"Oh. That's not . . . I mean, it wasn't that . . . Thanks," Ewen finished lamely. I got an alarmed stare from my son's strangely colored, but quite beautiful eyes.

As promised, they dropped me off, assuring me that one of them would telephone Einstein's prognosis.

A lot of busy work had piled up on my desk while I had been going over the typescript of Adam's book. So, after handing my secretary the newest tapes to transcribe, I settled down to clean it off. I had been at it for about an hour when Lance Metcalf called.

"How goes it?" he asked. "All well?"

"If you except one sick white rat, the answer would be yes."

"White rat? What white rat? You aren't a secret drinker, are you?"

"I don't think so. Why? Am I showing alarming symptoms?"

"White rats are even larger than white mice, although not as outstanding as pink elephants."

"No, Einstein—that's the rat's name—is not a symptom. He is the apple of Ewen's eye, and we have just conveyed him by personal ambulance to the animal hospital." And I told him the story, mostly because the more I thought about it, the more hilarious the picture grew: the three of us, cruising into Manhattan via expensive taxi, bearing a white rat with a bad cold, wrapped up like a papoose.

"A cold did you say? From a draft? I thought the theory of colds coming from drafts went the way of hot mustard baths."

"It's obvious you have not lived intimately with a rat."

"Obvious. I've often wondered what the void in my life was. Now I know. Speaking of drafts, has Ewen been leaving the window open?"

"Yes. He always opens his window, being something of a fresh-air buff. But the draft didn't come from the window."

"The previous tenants were always griping about drafts, but I put it down to propaganda aimed towards keeping the rent down."

"Well, there is a draft, and not only in Ewen's room. There's one in mine and one in the basement apartment, and they all seem to emanate from the same corner of where that funny angle cuts into the room. Ewen leans towards the psychic phenomena theory."

There was a short silence. "Was it always there?"

"No. It comes and goes."

There was a pause.

"What can I do for you?" I asked.

"Nothing. Shoe's on the other foot. The contractor who renovated your apartment is free again. He mentioned you said you might have something more. If so, the time to grab him is now."

"Thanks. I can't think of anything."

"Haven't found any old paintings, have you?"

"You mean the famous missing paintings?"

"The same. That's an old tired joke, by the way."

"You don't sound very amused."

"To anyone connected with the Standish estate, it's not an amusing story. I told you that. You read about the West German collection?"

"The one that's about to open?"

"Yes. It's not only the Standish collection that's missing—what's left of it: a couple of Early American paintings, a Guardi, a Sargent; old Mrs. Standish sold the others off one by one to pay the costs of finding her daughter Susan—but also three Harbachs."

Something stirred in my memory. "Harbach," I repeated.

His voice sharpened. "The name means something to you? I mean, other than that he was one of the pre-war painters?"

"I don't know," I said slowly. "Did you mention his name before, when you first told me about the paintings?"

His voice seemed to relax. "Perhaps. I guess I must have."

"If you did, everything, other than his name, must have gone in one ear and out the other. Who was he?"

"Egon von Harbach was the youngest son of some Prussian Junker aristocrat and generally considered the family black sheep. Whether out of rebelliousness against his stiff-rumped relatives or conviction or both, he got mixed up with the young communists when he was in university and was one of the first to oppose the Nazis. To do the family justice, I don't know whether they objected to this as strenuously as

they did to other things about him: One was that he was a
painter and lived a rather disorderly and bohemian life, and the
other was that he married an American—Susan Standish.
After the Nazis came to power he was arrested, tried for
crimes against the government or some such trumped up
idiocy, sent to concentration camp and was never heard of
afterwards. But he left some paintings which achieved instant
fame by being confiscated by the authorities because they did
not reflect the national spirit of the fatherland. Before they
were pronounced subversive, they had been considered quite
good by some major critics in Europe. Afterwards, they were
held to be works of genius. Those that are left are now
collectors' items. There are only about six, and they are in this
West German collection that is coming to the Met. Harbach
produced, or at least sold, thirty canvases. Six are in the
collection, twenty were taken by the SS. There are three
unaccounted for. Those are the ones Susan smuggled out to
her mother. The trouble is, we don't know whether she
received them or not, or, if she did, where they would be. The
Germans think they arrived over here. They say they have
some letter saying so. The only reference we could find was in
the diary of old Mrs. Standish—'Received package today from
Susan. Do hope she and Jonnie can get out and over here to
safety.' And that's all. What nobody knows is whether or not
the 'package' she referred to contained the three Harbach
paintings, if it did, what she did with them and, incidentally,
what happened to the four other remaining canvases of the
Standish collection."

"Well, she died in 1949. Surely if they were anywhere in
the house at all, you—or somebody—would have found them.
You must have been over every nook and cranny."

"Every crevice or mousehold, or so I would have sworn.
That's why it's such an old tired joke. But there's no record of
them anywhere."

"They must be worth a great deal of money."

"You could say that."

"What do you think has happened to them?"

He hesitated. Then, "I have absolutely nothing but a hunch to go on, but if I had to make book on it, I'd say she sold them."

"But wouldn't somebody have heard about it, somebody in the art world?"

"If she had sold them to the usual collector, or gallery or museum, yes. But I'm sure you know there are secret collectors. Their collections are never seen. They're open to nobody. And this kind of collector pays very well indeed—he has to, to compete with the legitimate collectors."

"I see. If they were found, by the way, who would they belong to?"

"You."

For some reason I was surprised. I was quite sure that if she hadn't sold them, old Mrs. Standish would have left them to a museum rather than to her housekeeper. "I don't suppose," I said slowly, "you could hazard a guess as to what they'd be worth?"

"Oh, yes. I've had to calculate their worth while administering the will. All together they'd bring around three quarters of a million dollars."

Above a certain sum—say about one hundred thousand dollars—my mind refuses to function. It might just as well have been the national debt. "Good heavens," I said weakly. And then added with a lamentable lack of originality, "That's a lot of money."

"Yes. It's a lot of money." There was an odd note in his voice, one I found hard to define. "Well," he said after a minute. "If you can't use the contractor, then I'll tell him to go on to the next customer in line. I don't suppose you've had time to go through that trunk of papers."

238

"Good lord, no. Is it crucial?"

"Until you see them, who knows?"

"You mean I might fall on unexpected treasure?"

"There's always the possibility. It looks like I've got another call coming in. Keep in touch."

I sat there for a while and thought about the name Harbach, saying it over in my mind. It was as though it had echoes that went far back, and all of a sudden, I saw my house again, as I had once before, and knew, again, that there was something different about it. This time the knowledge was much stronger than it had been. And there was emotion with it, a kind of sadness and . . . fear.

And then it was gone. Completely.

Not altogether sorry that that vision or whatever it was had gone, I went back to the mounds of paper work and correspondence.

Half an hour later Ewen called to say that the vet thought there wasn't much wrong with Einstein other than a cold, but that he wanted to keep him for a few hours' observation. And that he and Adam would bring Einstein home after school.

"Is Adam going home in the meanwhile?"

"Yes. Then he'll come back to the hospital and meet me there."

"That's pretty nice of him."

"Yeah. It is."

"I'm glad Einstein has nothing worse than a cold."

"So'm I."

After that I worked steadily through the lunch hour, ordering a sandwich at my desk, grateful that the phone, for once, was still.

It must have been about two o'clock that it rang again. Well, I thought, peace was too good to last. With my finger marking the place on some proof I was going through, I picked up the receiver with the other hand. "Hello?"

Silence.

"Hello?" I repeated.

Still silence. But I was quite sure that there was somebody at the other end. "Hello?" I said, more loudly.

Then it came: the softly exhaled breath.

"Who's that?" I asked sharply, angry at myself for the fear that quivered through me.

There was a click. Whoever it was had hung up.

To calm myself I considered the fact that it might have been a wrong number; that whoever it was took a minute to register the fact that he or she didn't recognize my voice and was too lazy or too much in a hurry to say, "Sorry, wrong number." After all, that had happened to me. But such comfort was brief. We had a switchboard. I picked up the receiver again and jiggled for our switchboard operator.

"Maggie," I said when she answered, "did you just get an outside call for me?"

"Yes. Why, were you disconnected?"

"No. He hung up." Why was I so sure it was a man? Whatever the reason, I had no doubt that it was.

Maggie confirmed it. "That's funny. He certainly asked for you by name."

"Did he sound uncertain? As though . . . oh, as though somebody had referred him and he wasn't sure, ·or something?"

"No, Antonia. He said your name as clear as anything. Excuse me—" and she was off answering another call, which was not surprising. At times our switchboard looks like a Christmas tree hung with blinking lights.

Then she was back. "Antonia. There was something— Just a minute." And she was off again. I hung on for a while, then decided to go out and talk to her.

After standing at her desk for a minute or two, I asked Sue, her lunch replacement, to step in for a minute. "Now," I said, when I got Maggie alone. "What did you think was funny?"

"I'm sorry, Antonia. I can't remember. I did register that there was something odd about the voice or what he said or something. But there were a dozen calls coming in and I was too busy to think about it. And now I can't for the life of me get it out of my memory bank, wherever that is."

"Try, Maggie. Please. It's important. And if you should remember after the office is closed, call me at home, would you?"

"Sure. I have your home number. Is anything wrong?"

I thought about the man who followed me on the Esplanade. I thought about the phony FBI agent and the crack on the head he left me. "Could be," I said, and went back to my office.

I sat there for a long time staring at the top of the Empire State Building a few blocks away. Always supposing the worst, I thought, why would someone call me and then hang up? The answer, from a dozen movies and television mysteries, to say nothing of countless suspense novels, came readily enough: to make sure I wasn't at home. And if the house were empty—what then? It wasn't as though there were anything there of value. Except Adam.

Don't be melodramatic, I said to myself. Why should Dauntry want to hurt Adam? Because he'd always hated him. Because other than Ewen and me Dauntry was the only person who knew that Adam was Ewen's father, and in his distorted and hate-filled mind that might well be reason enough.

Then I remembered Dauntry's question: "Does Adam know he's Ewen's father?"

And I, idiot that I was, said no, thereby putting Adam in danger. Because if Adam had known, others by now might have been told, either by Adam or me. If, on the other hand, Adam was still ignorant, then, dead, he would cease to be a threat: all proof that Ewen was not Dauntry's son would be removed. Further, with Adam gone, Ewen and I might be more amenable to Dauntry's wishes . . . He might . . . But madness lay in trying to second guess Dauntry's sick reasoning. When fear and hatred become strong enough, they become their own reasons and need no others.

For half an hour longer I sat there trying to work. Then I telephoned Adam. There was no answer. In case there had been a change of plan I called my own home number. He might be there baby-sitting with Einstein. But there was no answer there, either. He could, of course, be on the way into town to meet Ewen at the animal hospital. I called the school. Ewen was in class. After that they said he would be in gym and after that there was a student body meeting. On the other hand, I thought, he might skip that to pick up Einstein . . .

I fought the good fight for rational behavior for another half hour. Then I put on my coat and collected the manuscript pages of Adam's book that the typist had been able to do that morning. Then I told Maggie that I would be working at home and left.

Afterwards I figured that it may have been about forty-five minutes after the man had hung up on me. Forty-five minutes of patient waiting for me to respond exactly as I was doing on the part of . . . someone.

Both the Lexington and Seventh Avenue subways stop in Brooklyn Heights. I decided on the Lexington and went to the Forty-Second Street subway station under Grand Central Station to catch it. My mind, rather like Einstein on his exercise wheel, was going over that telephone call and all it might mean. I wasn't paying attention as I stood there on the express platform waiting for the train. At that hour, in the middle of the afternoon, there is a much longer wait between trains than at the rush hours. Used to battling rush hour crowds I stood, as I always did, near the edge of the platform.

At five o'clock, if you stand modestly back, the crowd surges past and you can miss train after train. So, my mind on its problem, I waited for the express train with my toes a few inches from the platform's edge.

Is there ESP? Are we all part of some collective unconscious and thus vibrate to the thoughts and intentions towards us of others? After what happened then I think my answer would be yes. I heard the train coming up from the tunnel and saw its square front emerge with a whoosh. At that second I looked back and saw the hands coming at me and behind them the face of the phony FBI agent. I screamed as I felt the shove and knew I was falling in front of the train. Then there was a huge tug on my arm and I was being hauled back, my arm almost wrenched out of its socket. Then the other arm was caught and I was pulled back onto the platform as the train hurtled past.

It all happened so fast. Dauntry's friend, the spurious agent, had tried to kill me, and somebody else had saved my life, and almost nobody noticed, although they all heard the scream.

"What's the matter, lady?" The transit cop was standing there in front of the train. A small crowd had gathered around us. "You screamed," he went on patiently. "What happened?"

I got to my feet. "You didn't see anything?"

"I was at the other end of the platform. Anybody else see anything?"

There was a general murmur. Then a man said, "I heard her scream and saw her down on her knees on the platform just as the train came through."

"You trying to jump?" the cop asked me accusingly.

"No," I said and was about to add, "Somebody pushed me," when I knew that that would mean I would be taken to some precinct and questioned about who and why for the rest of the day, while Adam and later Ewen would be in the house

243

and maybe each of them at different times so that either one could be alone. I had to get back there. Something was going to happen and this was an attempt to stop me from finding out. Quickly I glanced around. Neither my attacker nor my rescuer was there. I would like to have poured out my boundless gratitude to the man who had pulled me back to safety, and it struck me as extremely odd that he had not waited to see how I fared and to get his thanks. But right now, although feeling shivery and sick in the aftermath of my near-death, I clung to the knowledge that I had to get home. And that meant I had to shake off the policeman.

"You trying to jump?" he asked me again.

"No, officer," I said, making a lame effort to dust off my torn stockings. "I . . . slipped. I wasn't thinking, and when the train came in I stepped back and turned my foot."

"I think maybe I should take you to the hospital and then to the precinct."

The train gave a sort of sigh and the doors started to close. The thought of getting on that train was not at all attractive. But if I waited and went up to take a taxi, then he might indeed decide I belonged in Bellevue.

"I'm fine, officer. Really. And my little boy is alone at home." I stuck my foot in the door and it opened again. "I'll be all right, really," I said, and slipped inside the coach.

That ride was the most uncomfortable I have ever had in my life. I sat there, trying not to shake too visibly, aware that not only was I the target of sidelong glances (I think my fellow passengers agreed with the cop: I belonged in Bellevue) but I didn't know whether the man who pushed me was on the train and would have another try at the other end, or perhaps follow me home. A shudder went through me. I glanced up. There were, by my count, twenty-one other people in the car, most of them sitting across from me, and they were all looking at me. I quickly lowered my own gaze.

In addition to everything else, I ached all over and the pain in my arm was getting steadily worse. That Dauntry was behind this I didn't doubt. But why? Did he hire both the pusher and the rescuer to give me yet another example of his clout? Was his determination to get that job on the West Coast that unstoppable? If so, why? It didn't make sense. I might not be able to prove anything, but I could make a lot of accusations, and if his future employer out at the laboratory were as supersensitive as Dauntry claimed about his sexual life, if they demanded so much purity, then they would certainly be put off by what I had to say, proven or not. Surely, beyond a certain point, all this terrorizing would be counterproductive.

As I put up my hand and tentatively felt my wrenched arm, it occurred to me for the first time that there might be some other reason; that within and beneath the causes and motives I had accepted, however much I may have fought them, there was something else, deeper and more dangerous. And again, there was that flash in my mind, like a shutter that opened. And I saw my house, blazing sunshine on the walls, white on the ground . . .

White on the ground . . . white . . . snow. Frantically I clawed at the memory. And, of course, it slipped away. Scenes buried deep in the past didn't respond to that kind of pressure. I closed my eyes and clasped my hands and forced my mind to drift . . . drift.

"Miss, are you all right?"

I opened my eyes. A short, stocky woman in suit and tailored hat was standing in front of me.

"Yes, I'm all right, truly. I was just relaxing."

"You turned awfully white."

"I'm a little tired. That's all."

"I don't want to intrude, but—"

"It's all right." I achieved a smile. New Yorkers are

much nicer than the world at large, and particularly their own countrymen, gave them credit for being. "I'm fine. Really."

She went back, visibly rebuffed. I was sorry, but my mind was seething. Snow, I said to myself, white snow on the ground. And suddenly the mists rolled back. Dressed in boots and a snow suit I was going up the front steps of the house, my mittened hand firmly in my mother's. I couldn't have been more than four. Having been brought up in the moist, temperate climate of the West Coast, I had never seen snow up close, and to me it was a joy and an astonishment. And there was another scene surrounded by snow: A boy, much older, about nine perhaps, his tow hair under a wool cap, standing straddle-legged in the snow. There had been some kind of battle over a toboggan. The boy had been forced to allow me to ride. His voice came to me over the years.

"Who wants you, anyway? It's going to be my house and when I have it you're never coming in."

Chapter 11

When I got out at Borough Hall I looked very carefully around and behind me. I saw no one I had ever seen before. And although the face of my rescuer was fairly blurred in my mind, I was quite sure he wasn't there either.

I walked the few blocks quickly. As I turned into my street, I saw the ubiquitous Bonzo, who had been loitering on the sidewalk across from the house, suddenly climb his bike and pedal hell-for-leather in the opposite direction.

I heard the barking while I was still thirty feet from the house. Wilma? I didn't think so. This was a deeper, throatier bark, and there was a note of desperation in it. Then, as I neared the house, the bark turned into a cry, the high-pitched cry of a dog in terrible pain or distress.

Tania, I thought, and rushed down the stairs of the area way. I didn't have keys to Adam's front door, of course. I rang twice. The barking, interspersed with howling, rose to a crescendo. I knew now it was Tania. "Adam," I called out, and then saw it was useless. If Adam were alive and conscious and free, he would have answered that bell. I turned to go up to the front door, and as I did so, smelled smoke. The cries rose to a new pitch.

I tore up the stoop with my hand groping in my bag for keys. As soon as I thrust open the front door I could smell the smoke more strongly. Running to the hall table in the back, I yanked out the keys to the basement, opened the door to the basement stairs and was met by more smoke. I hesitated, then I ran to the hall telephone to call the fire department. The phone was dead. I stood there staring at it stupidly. Then I picked up the wire which dangled, cut, two feet from the telephone. That meant that somebody had started the fire and anticipated my call, which meant . . .

But I had to get Adam and Tania out. And then, as I turned towards the basement stairs, towards the barks and howls that were getting more and more frantic, some sanity took hold of my mind without my volition. I ran to the front-room window and threw it open. Bonzo, with bike, was back, loitering across the street.

"Bonzo," I yelled. "Call the fire department. Go to one of the houses . . ." Providence was watching over us. The front door of the house across the street opened and one of my neighbors came out.

"Fire!" I yelled as loudly as I could. "Call the fire department!"

Then I ran back towards the stairs. That Adam was downstairs I had no doubt at all. If Tania were there, Adam would be there. He would never go out without her. It was possible that somewhere in the house there was someone who had probably knocked out Adam—not too difficult with a blind man, even as alert a one as Adam—locked the door, cut the telephone wire and was waiting to lock me down there, too.

Far away I could hear some sirens. The sensible thing to do was to stay where I was until they arrived. Instead, I picked up the nearest heavy object, a hockey stick belonging to Ewen, and went downstairs. I unlocked the door and then stood back against the wall and opened it. A shot rang out and something whizzed past me. The smoke was so thick I couldn't see. Then a figure moved to the door opening and started to come upstairs. I had the stick raised, waiting. As he came level on the first step, I lowered it as hard as I could. Unfortunately, he had moved just beyond, so his head didn't get the crack it should have. Instead, the stick came down on his shoulder. At this point the sirens were roaring into the street. The man half turned, then fled upstairs. I ran into Adam's apartment. The cries, half stifled now, were coming from his living room. I opened the door, expecting Tania to come rushing past me, but she was sitting beside Adam, who was lying face down on the floor. I rushed to the front door.

"Here," I called to the firemen who were jumping from the fire engine. The next thing I knew two huge men in helmets were following me back into the basement. They carried Adam on a stretcher, with Tania following, out into the area way, but they didn't have to resuscitate him. The fresh air did that. In a few seconds he came to.

"What—?" He sat up. Then he said, "Tania," and was reassured by a wet tongue over his face. "Who's there?"

I had explained to the firemen by this time that he was blind and that Tania was his guide dog.

"There was a fire," one of the men explained. "Somebody called in an alarm and we got you out. How do you feel? You and your dog must have gotten a lot of that smoke." But apparently, because they had been close to the floor, they weren't in such bad shape.

By this time the firemen had located and put out the fire,

which had started in the kitchen among some newspapers.

"But I don't take newspapers," Adam said, and then, "My God—my tapes!"

"What tapes?" the fireman asked.

"The tapes of the book he was writing," I explained. "Where are they, Adam?"

"In the living room. On the shelf behind my chair."

Luckily, since the fire had been contained in the kitchen, the living room, though wet, was not soaked, and I found the tapes in their boxes on the shelf. "They're okay," I said to Adam, who had come back in.

"Good," he said. And I could hear the relief in his voice. "Antonia, have they moved the furniture around much? I know exactly where everything is, if it's still there."

I looked around. The firemen were leaving, pulling their fire hose with them. "Things look pretty much where they were when I last saw them. All except the kitchen, which is a shambles. You'll have to eat upstairs with us for a while, I'm afraid."

The fire captain was coming up. "Do you know how the fire started, sir?" he asked Adam.

"Yes. Somebody rang the front-door bell down here. I'd forgotten that in New York it's better to find out who's on the other side of a door. So I opened it, and that's the last I remember." He reached down to Tania, who was not in harness, but was staying very close to him and rubbed her head. "I'm just grateful that he didn't do anything to my dog. He could have the rest, including the tapes. But, of course, it's easy for me to say that. The house isn't mine. And I knew that neither Mrs. Moncrieff nor her son was at home."

"Did you know who he was?" The fireman asked. "I mean"—he looked flustered for a minute—"did you recognize his voice?"

There was a fraction of a pause. Then Adam said, "No, I didn't."

I stood there, thinking about the shot and the figure that had gone past me up the stairs. I knew now, beyond any doubt, that Dauntry had passed over some line into insanity and that the police would have to know or we would never be safe. But I didn't want to confide in this fireman now, with Adam, all unprepared, standing there. So I said nothing about the shot. But I did say, because I thought Dauntry, or someone he had hired, might still be upstairs, "Do you think you and one of your men could look upstairs for me? He might have gone up there."

"'We'll look," the fireman said, with a glance at Adam and me that clearly spoke his chivalry towards a woman and a blind man. "But it's the police you want." .

"Yes. I'll call them as soon as I get upstairs." Then I remembered the dead phone. "At least, the telephone was dead—the line was cut—when I tried to call you before. That was why I yelled to the neighbor."

"By the way," the captain said, "there's a hole in the kitchen wall behind the stove. Not a big hole, but I'm pretty sure it was there before. I don't think the fire did it—nor did the fire department."

"Thanks," I said. "So much for honest labor. That was probably something the contractors thought I wouldn't see—or maybe they didn't bother to move the stove."

The captain grinned. "Probably not." Then he and another fireman went up the basement stairs. I could hear them moving around and mounting the other flights.

Adam was standing very still beside his chair, his hand touching Tania's neck.

"You know," I said, "you and Tania remind me of Ewen and Einstein. Not that I'm making comparisons between what Tania does and Einstein does."

"It's all right. I understand. And you're right. I'm dependent on Tania in a way that Ewen is not on Einstein. In fact, it's more the other way around with them. But there's affection and understanding that goes beyond dependency."

"Nobody upstairs," the captain said, coming back into the room with his confederate. "But you're right about your telephone line. It's been cut. Whoever came in wanted a clear road. We'll report this to the police, and I suggest that you do, too."

After they had gone Adam said quietly, "Now I'd like to know what the hell's going on?"

"What . . . exactly . . . do you mean?"

"Because if that was a thief, he was no ordinary burglar. The reason I opened the door was because his voice sounded familiar."

My heart skipped a beat and then pounded. "You mean you knew who it was?"

"No . . . not quite. As I said, his voice was familiar, but I couldn't and can't place it. I've known for a while, in fact almost since I came here, that something was bothering you badly. That's true, isn't it?"

I didn't answer.

"Isn't it? Answer me, Antonia. Considering what just happened to me, and the fact that I might have burned to death, I think I have a right to know."

I let out my breath. "All right, Adam. But let's sit down."

And so, sitting there, I told him about Dauntry, and the job for which he said he was being investigated, and his blackmailing attempt to have me verify to any investigator that Ewen was his son.

"Isn't he?" Adam asked.

"No. The marriage between Dauntry and me was never properly consummated. He . . . Ewen . . . is somebody else's son." I waited then for him to ask, whose? Or to start remembering.

He said, "Where is Ewen's father now?"

252

When I didn't answer, he said, "I knew there was something odd about the whole question when Max told me that Ewen's father was supposed to have been killed in Indochina. I assumed that Dauntry Leigh was his father, but that for reasons best known to yourself you had decided not to let Ewen know. Then, when Leigh pulled that trick with Ewen and you said he was showing muscle, it seemed fairly obvious that it had something to do with Ewen and Dauntry's relationship to him. Only you made it so plain you did not wish to confide in me in any way, that I couldn't ask any further." His mouth twisted a little. "There've been moments, Antonia, notably one, when I could swear you liked me—a lot. Almost as much as I like you. But other times trying to reach you has been like trying to get through an electrified fence.

"I spent most of my life being a conceited oaf, as well as a drunken one. I've had a lot of that conceit knocked out of me. At no time have I been God's gift to women, as I thought I was. The only thing that can be said for me now, as opposed to then, is that I'm not drunk. But I know my face was messed up . . . That's a stupid thing to say. What I'm trying to get across is that if I turn you off now, I can well understand it, but the thing that baffles me is that there has been at least once when I know I didn't."

"Adam—" I said, quite bewildered to find myself in tears.

"Let me finish, Antonia, while I still have the courage. I didn't figure to fall in love again . . ."

My heart gave its absurd flipflop. "Were you in love with Sally?" I asked, before I could stop myself.

"As much as I was capable of it, yes. People thought I married Sally for her money. I didn't. At the time I married her, what with having been on the best-seller list for so long, plus the book clubs, plus the movie, I had plenty of money of my own. But I did fall in love with what she represented—all that her money and standing had brought her. It was fatally

253

attractive to anyone with my orphan asylum background. And she was like a lot of young girls of her class who marry outside to spite their parents . . ."

My mind was on an erratic course and I was only half listening. "Adam, doesn't it bother you that . . . Ewen is somebody else's son, I mean, somebody other than my husband's?"

He frowned. "Why should it bother me?"

"I thought you might . . . well . . . disapprove."

He was silent. Then he smiled. "You really are out of the last century, aren't you, Antonia? I must say that appeals to the male chauvinist in me, pig that I am. But, in reality, no. How could I object, given the life that I led myself? Besides, from everything I've gathered about Leigh, it seems to me you had every reason to . . . er . . . look elsewhere. The only thing I can't understand is why you concocted that story about a war veteran."

"Neither can Ewen," I said. "Neither, for that matter, at this moment, can I. But when I told that tale it was a long time ago and I was still the daughter of a country preacher of a rigidly strict sect and in my own eyes adulterous women first got stamped with the red A and then were stoned to death."

"After all that's happened in the country? After the sixties and seventies and the sexual revolution and women's liberation? You still carried your chains?"

"No. I just didn't think about it. I knew that sooner or later I would have to tell Ewen the truth, but since my middle name's McOstrich, I simply put off the evil moment by not thinking about it."

Adam rose out of his chair and came across the room to me. He held out his hand. "Get up, Antonia." He pulled me up and put his arms around me. Then he kissed me.

"There's still something blocking us. What is it?"

By this time I knew I was going to tell him. But the words

wouldn't come. I stared at his white shirt. He was a lot taller than I, and my eyes were on a level with his collar.

"Do you still wear that chain around your neck?" I asked deliberately.

His hands loosened for a minute. "When did you . . ." he started. Then, after a minute, "That night of the party at the college. What happened? Did we leave together?"

"Yes. Don't you remember?"

"No. I was in a blackout. I didn't come out of it till the next day, and when I did I was walking across the campus and I saw you. I remember that you gave me a strange look, and I wondered why. Had I . . . had we . . . what happened?"

"We went back to the studio and you made love to me."

He was silent for a beat, then let his breath out. "That must have been one of the few times I did it successfully, then. I wasn't exactly a star performer as a lover. Drunks seldom are. Booze and sex don't mix too well. I had learned that from my wife and one or two other ladies."

"I wasn't exactly a connoisseur myself. In fact, Dauntry had impressed on me that it was my fault that he . . . couldn't. So, aside from having fallen in love with you, I was terribly relieved to discover it didn't inhibit you—whatever was wrong with me. That it wasn't fatal. Of course by the next morning, when I got sober myself, my conscience had set in, and I became the scarlet woman."

"But all these years in New York? Have you lived a nun's life? I remember you as a very pretty girl." He ran his hands down my body and touched my face. "You still are."

"Yes. I've lived a nun's life. Out of sheer cowardice, combined with the fact that it's not easy to have a successful social life when you're the sole support of a child. Baby-sitting fees can eat up everything you make. I had to have them during the day when Ewen was younger, which meant I stayed with him in the evening. I've always told myself that when he was older . . . But I think it was more than that. I was just afraid."

"Did . . . did you say you were in love with me, Antonia? Back then?"

"Yes." It was like taking the high jump, but I decided I could be a practicing coward no longer. "I did fall in love with you. I've never loved anyone else. But there is one more thing I have to tell you."

He had hold of my hands. "Can't it wait?"

"No. Adam—Ewen is your son. There never was anybody else."

He was still holding on to my hands. Then he started to squeeze them.

"Adam . . ." I said.

"Oh, my God, Antonia!" Then he put his hands and mine up to his face. "I thought . . . after I had killed that boy . . . that I would never have any children. Like some kind of punishment. Because I couldn't imagine that anything at all— love, marriage, children, a life—would happen to me again." He caught his breath and then pulled me into his arms and held me.

After a minute he said, "Does Ewen know?"

"Yes. And he seems as pleased as you are. He, also, told me I was very old-fashioned."

"You told him?"

"No. He guessed. I haven't told you why, Adam. He looks very like you."

Adam started to laugh. "That's what Max said when he met Ewen. He said after we went home, 'You know, that's a nice kid of Antonia's. Funny thing, he looks just the way I think you must have when you were a kid. He's got that color eye—' And then he stopped because he was afraid he was being tactless.

He reached out and found my cheek. "Do you think you could manage to fall in love with me again?"

I put my hand over his. I wanted to cry and put my arms around him, and I knew in a minute I would. But at the moment I felt shy, so I said, mock-serious, "Give me one good reason."

"Well"—he put his hands on my shoulders and pulled me to him—"I'm not as good-looking—"

"You're still conceited," I put in indignantly.

"But I have a lot more character."

"Who falls in love with character?"

"You, I hope, because at the moment there's not much else going."

"Yes, there is," I said, and put my mouth up to his.

Twenty minutes later we were sitting on the sofa in my living room, having decided that love, though blind, was not immune to damp, and his living room was pretty wet.

"You know," Adam started to say. And then he sat bolt upright. "Oh, my God! I've entirely forgotten that I was supposed to meet Ewen at the animal hospital at five. What time is it?" He took his arm from around me and flipped open the front of the watch he had on his wrist. "Ten to five. I might just make it—"

Just then there was a ring at the front door. I looked out the window. Drawn up at the curb was a truck from the telephone company and a police car. A young man with bunches of tools hanging from his belt and two cops were standing on the top step.

"Who is it?"

"We're about to receive both the telephone company and the police," I said.

At that moment a taxi joined the other cars and out

stepped Ewen with a wrapped up bundle in one arm and holding a small cage in the other. "And Ewen's arrived, in a taxi, no less. What *chutzpah!*"

Ewen didn't notice the visitors until he was almost on top of them. "Oh. Hi." I heard him say, as I opened the front door.

"Mom, can you pay for the taxi?"

"Suppose I say no?" I said, groping in my handbag, which happened to be on the hall table beside the door.

"You wouldn't do that. Not knowing that I took a cab because of Einstein."

"True. How much?"

By this time the cabbie had joined the growing throng on my steps. He told me, and I winced.

"I do hope," I said, taking out my wallet, "that Einstein is restored—permanently—to good health."

Adam, walking carefully, because he was not as used to my living room as to his own, and with his hand on Tania's collar, came up behind me.

"The taxi's on me," he said.

"No—"

"Yes. Please, Antonia."

I turned. He had his own billfold out. "Will this cover the fare and tip?" he asked the driver, handing him some bills.

The driver looked at him carefully, took the money and counted it. "Sure. Thanks a lot." He went back down the steps to his cab.

"Thanks," Ewen said. "That's cool."

I saw Adam reach out, a groping gesture that I found somehow poignant as I had not before. Finding Ewen's shoulder, he gripped it for a moment. Then he let go. "You're welcome," he said, and dropped his arm. "How's Einstein?"

"A lot better. The vet said to keep him warm and dry and

away from drafts and gave me some medicine to put in his food. I'm going to have to get him out of that draft." And he went past me into the living room.

The draft, I thought, and something in my mind clicked over.

All this had taken only a minute or two, and none of the other men had spoken so far. Then the telephone man said, "We were told your wire was cut. I'm here to fix it."

"That's fast. Come in. It's over there." And I pointed to the table under the staircase. He brushed past me and came inside.

I turned back to the two policemen. One of them said, "Can we speak to you a moment?"

"What is it about?" I asked, although I knew.

"About the intruder in the downstairs apartment. The man who knocked out . . . er"— he referred to his notebook— "Adam Kingsley. We rang the bell down there but there was no answer." He looked behind me to where Adam and Ewen were talking, or rather, I saw as I turned around, Ewen was talking, and from the way he held Einstein, now without his blanket, about his pet.

"Yes," I said to the policeman. "He's up here. Just a minute." I turned back. "Adam, these officers want to talk to you." Then I turned back to the policeman. "Come in."

"Now, sir, if you would tell us what happened?" The officer said when we were all inside.

Adam went through the whole thing again.

"You mean you got knocked on the head and had a fire?" Ewen, standing there, said. "You mean you nearly got killed?"

I went over and put my arm around him. "Yes, but we're all fine now, so we'd better let Adam talk to the policeman."

"And you didn't know the man?" the officer insisted.

"No," Adam said. "I didn't know him."

The other officer, a younger man, suddenly said, "We realize you couldn't have recognized him by sight. But was his voice at all familiar?"

Again Adam hesitated. "Yes," he said finally. "It was familiar. But I have no idea who it was. I can't put the voice and a person together."

Perhaps I made a sound or a movement, or drew in my breath. Whatever it was, Adam, who was standing beside me, put out his hand and touched my arm. Then he lowered his hand until it found mine and held it.

"But you have a notion who it might be," the policeman persisted.

"That's a little too vague to answer yes or no."

The officer turned to me. "Was there anyone in the house—other than Mr. Kingsley here—when you arrived?"

I stood there, frozen, aware of Ewen standing a little back of us. He knew everything now, why was I hesitating?

"I should tell you," the young officer went on, "that your neighbor across the street, and one down the block, both saw a man run out of the house just before the fire engine arrived."

"All right," I said. "There was somebody." And I described what happened.

The young officer looked at me. "He took a shot at you, knocked out Mr. Kingsley here, and probably set fire to the house with the idea of burning anyone in it, and yet you weren't going to tell us. Why?"

"I think I can answer that question," Adam said. He held out one hand. "Ewen, come here. This very much includes you." Ewen came forward and Adam once again put his hand on his shoulder. "This is my son," he said. "And Mrs. Moncrieff is his mother. But why this concerns what happened tonight goes back more than thirteen years." And he gave a precise, unemotional account of what happened that led to Ewen's birth and the more recent events.

As I listened, my anger drained away. The revelation I had most dreaded and had gone to such silly lengths to avoid had now happened. The earth didn't tremble. The trumpets for Judgment Day had not sounded. No angel had arrived to send me tumbling into the pits of the lost. All of which meant that Ewen did not recoil or look shattered with disillusionment. As a matter of fact, his attention was elsewhere altogether.

"Well, I think Dr. Leigh's got to be bonkers. I mean *nuts.*"

"Was it Dr. Leigh?" the officer asked Adam and me.

"I don't know," Adam answered. "To my knowledge I met him only once, and that was thirteen years ago."

"Didn't you recognize him?" the policeman asked me.

"No, he rushed out of the smoke which was pouring up the stairs and there was a cap of some kind on his head. I barely made out that it was a man, let alone who it was."

"Where is Dr. Leigh now?" the officer asked.

I told him the name of the hotel and with that the policeman had to be content. They went over the whole thing again once or twice, but when nothing else emerged, they left, with strict orders to let them know any further developments.

After they were gone we all three stood in the living room for a moment. "Well, I'm glad *that's* settled," Ewen said, and it was obvious what he was referring to. And then he added quickly, "I think I'll go up and feed the animals."

"Ewen shies away from emotion," I explained, in case Adam felt slighted.

"Yes, I know. I understand that very well. So do I. Come back to the sofa while I think."

"That sounds to me like a non sequitur," I said. But I went back quite happily.

Adam sat quite still for a while, his elbows on his knees. I suddenly remembered him as he was, back in the classroom, pacing back and forth, like a restless animal. And it occurred to me that keeping still might have been one of the hardest lessons he had had to learn. Pacing back and forth in a confined and relatively unfamiliar area would not be something a blind man would feel secure in doing. I put my hand on his back.

He reached over his shoulder and took it and brought it around front and held it. "What were you thinking about when you did that?" he asked.

I told him.

"Yes. That has been a problem. That's why, out in the country, I walk so much. For that matter, I have done it here, too. It keeps the nerves quiet, apart from exercising both Tania and me."

"Where is Tania?" I asked.

"Behind me, asleep. Taking five."

I glanced back. The picture of relaxation, Tania was lying sprawled behind the sofa.

"You know," Adam said, rubbing my hand between his, "you have been so preoccupied with your scarlet sins and your terror that Ewen would not understand, that it doesn't seem to have occurred to you that there is another element in all this."

"What do you mean?"

"I mean that Dauntry—if it is Dauntry, or whoever he's hired—has made three attempts to kill you or at least frighten you: the man on the Esplanade, the phony FBI man, the man who tried to shove you under the train. Whether he wanted to dispose of me or not, I don't know. I could just have been in the way when he wanted something else. But I find it hard to believe that all this was to make sure he'd get that job out on the coast."

It was at that moment that I saw again the two children in the snow, the child that was I, and the boy, Dauntry. All that had happened after I got to the house had driven it out of my head.

"Oh—" I said.

He half turned. "What?"

"I suddenly realized this afternoon that I must have been here as a child. It's been haunting me ever since I saw the house. Just a flash, and then it was gone. Well, maybe being nearly shoved under the train shook something loose. Whatever it was—when I was finally on the train coming here, it came clear. I came here with my mother when I must have been four or so. And Dauntry was here. I remember how much he hated me . . . but I can't remember why."

"Dauntry Leigh here, at this house, when you were both children?"

"Yes. I didn't tell you. Lance Metcalf, the lawyer, said he was a distant cousin of old Mrs. Standish. And after he'd told me that, and following on something Dauntry said the day we had lunch—something about his mother's coming from an old New York family—I remembered that I always thought it odd that Dauntry only talked about his mother's side of the family, although to my knowledge and memory he never mentioned the name Standish. But it was as though he only identified himself with that side: that those were the only relatives that were important to him."

"Then he's a cousin of yours?"

"No. We're not related. I inherited the house from my aunt, Alice Moncrieff. She was old Mrs. Standish's housekeeper, and it was to her that Mrs. Standish left the house, to spite all of her relations who had been so unsympathetic about her prolonged and expensive search for her grandson."

And I told Adam all about Susan Standish, who had married the German painter and had, with her son, been swallowed up after arriving in this country just before the war.

"Mrs. Standish hired investigators and inspectors and heaven knows what-all. She could never find either her daughter or her daughter's son. But she kept on trying, every time she had a new idea or somebody seemed to come up with a lead. And the rest of the family, who were nervous about the estate anyway, because it had diminished so much after the crash and the depression, were wild with frustration that she was bleeding it dry. Anyway, there was a big family bust-up and she disinherited them all, and made my Aunt Alice the heir."

"How old was Dauntry when this scene that you remember took place?"

"He's five years older than I am, so he must have been about nine."

"Old enough to know that he, along with all other relatives, had been disinherited, if, indeed, Mrs. Standish told them so."

"I suppose so."

"But you don't know?"

"No. All I remember are those scenes."

"Your mother never told you?"

"Mother died when I was seven. Aunt Alice had died a year earlier, leaving the estate first to my mother, then, after her death to my brother Ian, and, if he died, to me. But apparently the Standish family blocked the probation of the will, claiming that it was made under duress, that Aunt Alice had used her influence when Mrs. Standish was old and ill to induce her to leave the estate, including the house, away from the family. I only learned this recently from the lawyer. I'd never heard anything about it before."

"I find it odd your father wouldn't have told you. With your mother dead, after all, his son, Ian, and, failing Ian, you, stood to inherit a house and the remains of a fortune."

"It would seem odd if it were not my father. He was a

terribly strict and austere man. That makes him sound unloving, but he wasn't, in his way. But his way was neither warm nor demonstrative. And he had a deep suspicion of worldly goods. He believed that they led people astray, encouraged character weakness, that kind of thing. Now that I think of it, he and Mother used to have arguments about something after Ian and I had gone to bed; about what, I never knew. But I did know it concerned something she wanted us to have and he didn't. She died before I ever found out, and I would never in a million years have asked him. I'll never know now whether it was this house or not. But I think it must have been."

Adam sat for a while, then he said, "So Dauntry, the child, even then, wanted the house, probably as part of, and to back up, this total identification with his mother's blue-blooded family, the Standishes. They were the ones who were important. And he may have been led to believe by his mother that, failing the appearance of Mrs. Standish's grandson, the house would be his. Several years later he learns that the house has gone to Alice Moncrieff and her heirs. Then he meets you in college when you're a freshman and he's a graduate student. Do you suppose that's the long arm of coincidence? Or do you think that he planned that meeting—went out there—with marriage in mind, figuring that getting the house by any means was more important than his sexual preferences?"

He asked the question so casually. But it was as though a truck had hit me. "My God!" I said. "It never occurred to me . . ."

"You told me he changed radically after your marriage. What reason did he give for that?"

"That he might cure himself of his homosexuality. And when he . . . couldn't, it was my fault."

"And now, still pursuing the image of the compleat heterosexual, he makes three attempts on your life—or hires thugs to do so. All because in the enlightened seventies, he wants a job heading up some West Coast lab. I just don't buy that. There has to be a lot more."

"We don't *know* that Dauntry is behind all the attempts to kill me."

"Who else do you suggest? Let's get back to your marriage to him. Wouldn't it make more sense that he *knew* you were the heir to the Standish estate and deliberately went out there to that cow college to marry you. I mean, who would ever go there for any other reason?"

"Well, you went there to teach."

"Only because they offered me a flattering sum to take that chair."

"That's right. You weren't on the staff proper."

"No, it was the Harbach Chair of the Humanities. A yearly thing. Sometimes given to writers, sometimes painters and occasionally musicians."

"The *what* chair?"

"The Harbach Chair. Some rich easterner donated the trust in memory of a daughter or something."

"That's where I heard the name, only we called it Harbaitch. Adam—this is weird. Lance, the lawyer, told me that Mrs. Standish's daughter married a German painter named Egon von Harbach. It was their son, what was his name?—Johannes—that Mrs. Standish spent all her fortune trying to find."

Suddenly Adam stood up. "What did you say his name was?"

I stood too, a queer breathlessness in my throat. "Egon von Harbach. Why?"

"I told you I was brought up in an orphan asylum in Nova Scotia. Actually, I first lived with an elderly couple who found me after a car wreck. The woman I had been with, presumably my mother, was killed. I had been flung clear of the car. Well, the car was on fire and the woman had been partially burned. She had no identification on her, whatsoever. And if there was any in the car it went when the car exploded. Anyway, the only jewelry she had on was a wedding ring, which was given to me and which I wore on a chain around my neck."

He tugged at his tie and collar and pulled out the chain. At the end was the roughened circlet or ring I remembered. "The trouble was, when they looked inside the ring for initials, they had been partly effaced by the fire. Later, when I had sold my first book and came to New York, I took the ring to an expert to see if they could find any trace at all of what had been there. All he could tell me was that the last initial looks like a V, which had been partly burned, although I see now it could have been a small v. And there was a large H.

"It was for that reason that when the various offers to teach in colleges around the country came in, I took the one out there. Since the letter H was the one link I had with whoever I was, I always looked on it as a good luck symbol. That and the fact that the name Harbach was German. I was told at the asylum, where the couple had eventually placed me, that apparently I didn't speak at all for months after the accident, and that when I did, I spoke only in German. But—who knows?—maybe I remembered subconsciously that my name had been Harbach. Psychologists say that nothing is ever truly forgotten. Only buried."

"Adam, where did you get the name Adam Kingsley?"

"From the asylum. They just went through the alphabet with Christian and surnames. They had reached A in the first name and K in the second. So, having arrived at the initials, they went to the telephone book for the names . . . There's one other thing. The only other thing they found was a rolled up painting, a small one. It was found a few feet from me and they assumed I had been holding it."

"What was the painting of?"

"A girl."

"Was it signed?"

"I think it must have been. But the canvas had obviously been sliced off at the bottom. There was no signature left."

I went over everything Lance had told me. "Lance Metcalf said that all Harbach's paintings had been confiscated. He was considered an enemy of the German people. I think he was also half Jewish, as well as being all anti-Nazi. Maybe she couldn't have got it out if it had been signed. Where is it now?"

"Up at the farmhouse. Is the telephone working, do you suppose?"

"The man said he'd fix it."

Adam found his way to the telephone. "I'll get Mike, the farmer I work for, to put it in a mailing tube and send it to me."

"You know, I'm surprised that while you were going to jewelers about your ring, you didn't get some art dealer to look at that painting."

"I meant to. It seems insane that I didn't. But my knowledge of contemporary art is pretty rudimentary and I didn't think it was anything remarkable. To tell the truth, I thought it might have been a painting of my mother, and I hung on to it for sentimental reasons, not artistic ones."

"It might be—a picture of your mother, I mean. There must be photographs of Susan Standish von Harbach around. I could check it against one of those."

"Yes, you could."

"If it's a real von Harbach, then it's pretty valuable, according to Lance. Tell him to send it registered." And while Adam was talking to his friend, I thought about the fact that if it turned out that Adam's portrait and the photographs of Susan were of the same girl, then Adam would never see a photographic likeness of his mother. Or, for that matter, of his father. I wondered then if he had thought of that himself, while we were talking about it. I wouldn't ask him, so I would never know. But somehow I felt that he had—how could he not have?—and accepted again the fact of his blindness and gone on. I, too, would have to learn to accept it, and if I felt pity, to keep it private and to myself.

When the telephone call was completed, Adam came back to the middle of the room. "You know, Antonia, you never said why you went to that college. I know your father was a minister, and the school was church-oriented, but was that the only reason?"

"No," I said slowly. "My father told me that funds had been left by my aunt for Ian and me to go to college, and suggested we go there. Apparently she'd had some business correspondence with them. Probably, I realize now, something to do with the Harbach trust." I thought for a while. Then I said slowly, "So I went there for a reason, and you went there for a reason and Dauntry went there for a reason, and all the reasons come back to this house."

"Yes. I was just thinking that. Your brother is dead?"

"Yes. He and Father were killed in a car accident when Dauntry and I went there after we'd been married. It was terrible. Father and Ian, who was then fifteen, were going to some Bible school meeting along the coastal road. It was a small road on top of a cliff leading only to the church, and it wasn't either properly paved or fenced. Something went wrong with their brakes and they plunged over down to the rocks beneath."

"And Dauntry was there . . . Didn't you say that your aunt left the house first to Ian, and then to you?"

All of a sudden I sat down. I remembered the sheriff of the small community.

* * *

269

"I'd like to call the Portland police in on this, Mrs. Leigh."
"Why?"

"Well, it's just possible the brakes were tampered with, as much as I can tell from the wreck that's left."

"But that car was nine years old. Father never would buy a new car until the old one all but fell apart. He felt it was wasteful. And it must have been in the garage twenty times."

And when the garage people said they'd been telling Father for a year that the brakes wouldn't hold, the sheriff had abandoned any attempt to call in the police. As Dauntry kept pointing out to him, again and again, I'd been through enough, losing both my father and brother, without having to be put through some kind of senseless police hassling. . . . That was his phrase, brought from the more glamorous and politically sophisticated campuses he had attended, and it stuck in my mind, "senseless police hassling."

So Dauntry and I went back to school, and after that everything between us started falling apart.

"Oh, God!" I said now. "Ian!"

Adam, who had been walking slowly around the room, came back to the sofa and put his arms around me. "Tell me," he said.

So I did, all about Ian and the car and the accident and the sheriff and Dauntry's determination that I shouldn't be bothered.

"Yes," Adam said. "It looks as though he killed your father and your brother, although after all this time it can never be proved. But if he would go to such lengths to get possession of the house, why would he turn against you the way he did? And why the long silence until now?"

"I don't know," I said slowly, "but I could call Lance. I know it was in litigation for years and years. Maybe he thought I wouldn't inherit after all." I sat up. "Shall I call him?"

"Yes. There are a couple of things I'd like to ask him."

"There are? What—Adam! I just thought. If you really are that boy, then the house is yours."

"That's just what I was thinking," Adam said. "I'm curious about the litigation angle. Why don't you call your lawyer?"

"Good heavens!" Lance said when I got through telling him on the telephone what had happened. "Lost heir restored! It sounds like one of those gothics. But as far as I can make out it's only speculation."

For some reason his reaction irritated me. "Well, we can see when that painting arrives, can't we? I'm sure the experts could tell if that's a real Harbach."

"Of course. When are you expecting it?"

"Adam's friend said he'd send it registered airmail today. Maybe tomorrow. Maybe the day after."

"That'll be a nice thing for Ewen to have."

"What do you mean?"

"Nothing really . . . I just thought . . . well, if you must know, Dauntry's been on the telephone. He told me about the relationship."

"Oh?" A cool little wind seemed to go down my back. "I didn't know from what you said that you and he were such friends."

"He's a member of the family, Antonia. Remember?"

I was thinking about my father and brother hurtling over that cliff when I was suddenly aware of Adam beside me. Gently he took the receiver from my hand. "This is Adam Kingsley," he said pleasantly. "I gather Antonia told you our news."

I watched Adam's face, trying to read it. The lines around his mouth seemed to be deeper than I remembered them. There were times when all he had been through showed on his face. This was one of them.

"Okay," he said into the receiver. "As soon as it gets here I'll let you know." He put the receiver down.

"Why did you do that?" I asked.

"Because I wanted to hear his voice. I've been thinking who it might have been at the door. Now I know. It was Metcalf. When you picked up the phone I remembered I'd met him briefly the day you moved in. But I wanted to be sure. He was the one who knocked me out and took a pot shot at you and probably set fire to the place."

Chapter 12

"What on earth can we do?" I asked.

"At the moment, nothing. But I'm still confused. Although I can't see it, I have every reason to believe that this is a beautiful house. But I have a hard time believing that Dauntry and Laurence Metcalf would go to the lengths they have simply to get title to the house. There's something else. Is there anything you haven't told me, Antonia?"

"No, there's noth— My God!"

"You've remembered. What is it?"

"The Standish paintings. Lance said that if they were ever found, they'd be worth three quarters of a million."

"Then he must know that they're here. But if so, why didn't he get them sometime in the last decade when the house was being rented out?"

"I don't know . . . but there must be a reason."

We went back to the living room. Adam felt his way to the sofa, and I knelt down and lit the fire.

Adam didn't say anything but sat there, with that stillness that was so much a part of him.

"Antonia," he said slowly, "have you—recently—told Metcalf anything about the house? Anything at all? When, before just now, did you last talk to him?"

"It seems like four years ago, but it was just this morning."

"Can you go over the conversation in your mind? Who called whom?"

I sat back on my heels. "He called me."

"What about?"

"He said to see how things were going."

"That could mean anything. An excuse to find out what was happening, or something more specific, although I can't think what."

"If he and Dauntry are in cahoots, Dauntry could have put him up to it to see what we're doing."

"True. What did you talk about?"

"As far as I can remember, Einstein—his health, his trip to the hospital, his important role in the household. I can't help thinking that if he was after some vital information, a detailed report about Ewen's pet rat must have taxed him sorely."

"Anything else?"

"Oh—yes. He said the contractor he had put me onto was free and did I have any more work for him to do?"

"Hmm. That sounds like a poor excuse for a call."

"Not if you knew how hard it is to get contractors."

"It's still odd."

"Well, it could be. On the other hand, I'm forced to say it could just as easily be friendly concern."

"There must have been something else. Did he react to anything you said, show any interest?"

"Not that I can—He reacted strongly when I thought the name Harbach had a familiar ring."

"If it's the paintings he's after, I can see why. Anything else?"

"No ... Nothing that I can think of. Hello, Ewen," I said as Ewen came down the stairs in his usual manner, that is, like a falling sack of potatoes.

"Isn't it time for dinner?"

"Good heavens." I stood up. "Yes. And long past. My poor darling, are you starved?"

"I could eat," Ewen said carelessly.

"What would the two of you like?"

"What about it, Ewen?" Adam asked.

"Well, personally, I like hamburgers."

"Personally, so do I. How do you feel, Antonia?"

"It's very lucky that I like them too. Hamburgers rank either just below or just above Einstein with Ewen. By the way, how are the other animals?"

"Fine." Ewen and Adam followed me back to the kitchen. "I think Wilma is braving up," Ewen said, and stopped. "I haven't taken her out this evening. I'd better do that while you're doing the hamburgers."

He turned and bounded up the stairs.

Adam turned and made his way back to the living room and over to the table where he'd put Tania's harness. "Come along, Tania. Let's take a walk."

Tania, who had just waked up, leaped over, jumped up on him, licked his face and then stood still while he fitted her harness. I had come out of the kitchen. "Are you going with Ewen?"

"Yes."

"I see. Man to man. Father to son."

"Something like that."

I grinned and started to go back to the kitchen. Then I realized he couldn't see me smile. "That's a good idea," I said.

When Ewen came bounding downstairs preceded by Wilma, I waited to see the meeting between the two dogs. It could have been between the Queen of Sheba and the slave girl. Wilma, who was five years old and knew better, suddenly reverted to puppyhood, leaping back and forth, down on front paws, rear end in the air. Tania, whatever her inner emotions, stood with the patrician obliviousness of true royalty.

"I can't help thinking that Tania is speaking the canine version of 'We are not amused,' " I commented.

Adam grasped her harness. "That's just a cover-up for her own frustration. Come along, girl. You can play afterwards."

After they had gone, I got out the hamburgers, potatoes, and salad, started to set the table in the kitchen, and then decided that we might as well celebrate by using the dining room. Leaving the salad waiting to be tossed with dressing, the potatoes cut up and ready for frying and the burgers under a very low flame, I went into the dining room to lay the table. As a matter of fact, I thought, turning on the lights and drawing the long curtains, a pleasant dinner with the three of us might take the hex off the room for me. For some reason I had never liked it. Perhaps it was the dark paneling, now scratched and dull and in sore need of attention, with its heavy carving along the shoulder-high molding and down the vertical joins of the panels. Whatever it was, a sense of depression descended on me whenever I had been in the room before. And then, as I opened the drawer of the sideboard to get out the silver, my memory shutter flickered open again and I saw a child who I knew was myself, finger bleeding, crying and being scolded by a young woman with red hair, my mother, and beside her a woman with white hair, Mrs. Standish . . .

Mrs. Standish, I thought now, standing still with amazement. But why should I be amazed? If I were about four, she would still have been alive . . .

And then it was gone. But my sense of depression was there strongly. A little shaken, I took more silver out of the drawer.

Like my room and Ewen's, the dining room faced the garden and had the same odd shape, as though someone had taken a bite out of one corner. I had set two of the places and was starting on a third when it suddenly struck me how quiet the house was. I paused, fork in hand, puzzled as to why the quiet should bother me. And then I understood. It was not only quiet. It was cold. The room was terribly cold, as though a cold draft . . .

A cold draft. . .

Automatically I glanced towards the windows. They had not, to my knowledge, been open since we'd moved in. Yet the cold was steadily growing, and it was coming from behind me, from the curious angle where that wall jutted into the room. I laid down my fork and went over to it. Then I put my hand on the molding level, where the heavy carving extended from the edge of the mantelpiece. Curious, I thought, that the heavy carving should run vertically down the sides of the paneling where they met at the join of the angle.

And suddenly the shutter opened again, and I saw myself in this room, the dining room, bored with the grown-up conversation going on next door, running my hand over the ornate, beautifully polished carving, a bunch of grapes here, an apple, some cherries, what was that? a sheep, a dog, and then pricking my finger against something sharp and metallic and watching the red blood flow onto the fine gold carpet, and crying because I knew I would be punished . . .

My heart thudding, I ran my finger under the carving

again, a bunch of grapes, an apple, some cherries, a sheep, a dog . . . There it was. Gently I fingered it. Then I pulled it with the edge of my nail. Under my hand the panel moved and then stopped. I put my nail under the little metal tongue again. There was another shift in the panel.

A little breathless, my heart pounding, I gave it a third flick. One panel creaked, groaned and started to slide back against the wall. When it was finally back I saw it was a square space with a narrow rugged ladder going up the opposite wall with just enough space for a person, a fairly thin person, to go up and down.

"So that's how it works," a man's voice said behind me. I whirled around. There was Dauntry, standing just inside the dining room door, a pistol in his hand aimed at me.

He strolled in.

"How secretive of old Mrs. Standish not to tell anyone about that. It's obviously at one end or the other of that ladder that she's stashed the paintings. It would have saved everyone so much. Your life, for instance."

"How did you get in?"

He pulled some keys out of his pocket. "Lance always had an extra set. All I had to do was to wait until you were alone."

"But why do you have to kill me?"

"Don't be stupid, Antonia. How else can Ewen inherit?" He gave a distorted version of what I had once thought of as his winsome smile. "And I am, after all, Ewen's father. Legally."

As he came towards me I started to back away from the opening. "So it was the paintings you wanted, all along."

"Of course. All along. Houses are a dime a dozen. Wives even cheaper. But seven paintings, all of them collectors' items—they're worth a lot of sacrifice." He grinned at me.

"Such as a bad marriage—or, for that matter, any marriage. After you."

By this time I was well along the paneled wall. I turned to make a dash for it.

"Oh, no you don't, Antonia. You're going into that panel with me. This is obviously the end of Great-aunt Elizabeth's underground railway. Not the priest's hole, as in the English country houses, but the ex-slave's hole. I knew there was passage in this house. I knew it, but the old witch wouldn't tell me. Come along," and he took hold of my shoulders and pulled savagely.

Dauntry is a slender man, but wiry and very strong. One hand started to slide over my mouth. I took a deep breath and screamed as loud and long as I could, which wasn't long, because I received a blow on the mouth, then Dauntry's hand came down over it.

"You deserve for me to kill you for that. But I'll let you off easy. I'll just leave you in the hole. You can have a good time seeing if there's any way of opening the panel from the inside. Come along."

I fought with everything I had, and managed to give Dauntry's hand an enthusiastic bite. He swore and for a moment released my mouth. I was prepared for this and gave out another scream that would have done justice to an air-raid siren.

But I paid for it. I got a savage blow on the head, and after that everything became blurred. I had enough sense left to resist him as he dragged me back towards the opening. I caught the curtain and brought down the rod, I took hold of the table and clung to it until he pried my fingers off.

"My dear," he said, panting, "who would have thought you had such powers?"

I kicked his shins, and tried to bite him again, but I was

slowly and inexorably being dragged towards the narrow companionway. I knew that if I ever got in, I would never come out alive. Surely Adam and Ewen should be back soon. But I didn't know how much a blind man and a boy could do against the monster that was dragging me inch by inch to death.

Then I heard a sound and gave a convulsive shove.

"Not so fast, my dear. Did you think it was your son and ex-lover? Sorry to disappoint you, but I think Lance will take care of them quite well. That may be Lance now."

He relaxed his hand on my mouth for a few seconds. I yanked my head free and then one arm. Before Dauntry knew what had happened, I had wrenched myself free and was halfway across the room. But it still wasn't enough. Dauntry's hand drove itself into my shoulder. "No," I yelled. I knew that if he got hold of me this time, I would be gone. "No," I cried and tried to scream again. But I was almost spent and I knew it, and I felt myself dragged back and back, one arm across my chest, the other hand clamped so tight over my mouth that my lips were bleeding.

I heard then Adam's voice, amazingly, almost irritatingly calm. "Let her go, Leigh."

Dauntry turned, and I could see Adam standing there.

"Adam, he's got a gun," I yelled.

Dauntry said tauntingly, "And you're going to make me let her go, I suppose?"

"Yes," Adam said. "I am." Then he called quickly, "Ewen."

And on cue there came into the dining room, not my son, but a white rat whom I recognized instantly as Einstein. Tame and friendly, he trotted across the carpet towards Dauntry and me. I felt a shudder go through Dauntry and was taken by an insane desire to laugh. Of course! I had told Ewen about Dauntry's aversion to laboratory rats!

On came Einstein. Dauntry's leg shot out. If it had connected, Einstein would have been no more. But in trying to kick, Dauntry had loosened his hold on me. I gave one final wrench and was free, deflecting his foot. I saw Ewen's anxious face in the doorway and realized in that second what it had cost him to risk his pet.

"I've got Einstein," I called and scooped him up and tucked him in the curve of my arm.

"Ewen. Now!" Adam called, and Ewen's head disappeared. A few seconds later the house went black. There was a muttered sound from Dauntry. I plunged across the room and under the dining room table.

"All right, Leigh," said Adam's calm voice. "The fuse has been switched off. We'll have our battle in the dark, which will equalize things. I'm used to not seeing. You're not. Antonia, I heard the pistol drop. Get it and try to stay out of the way."

I, too, had heard the gun drop and was groping around the floor with my free hand. Then I found it. "I've got it," I said. But in the dark there was nothing useful I could do with it, so Einstein and I stayed where we were, under the dining room table. I heard one of the men moving and knew it was Dauntry. I also realized that Adam, with his acute hearing must know it, and that the best way I could help him was to stay as still as possible so that the only moving sound he would hear would be Dauntry.

It seemed a long time, hearing those steps, cautious, quick. Then there was the sound of a blow. Then another and a grunt. Then there were running footsteps and a thud. From the street there was the sound of a car and a police siren. Then there were more footsteps and I knew that others were in the house, falling over things, cursing. Then there were more sounds of hitting and then Dauntry's voice, almost hysterical, "You goddamn—" and a thud.

Then I heard Adam's voice, out of breath. "I'm out of training. All right, Ewen. You can put the fuse on again." He added drily, "To quote an unimpeachable source, 'Let there be light!' "

All the lights went on. The house seemed filled with people and animals. There were two policemen, Laurence Metcalf in handcuffs with a bloody bandage on one arm, Ewen, Wilma, Adam, who was sitting on top of Dauntry, and Tania, still with her harness on, crouched by the front door.

"Confusing yourself with the Almighty, Mr. Kingsley?" the younger of the two officers asked.

"No." Adam stood up, and Dauntry, looking considerably the worse for wear, got slowly to his feet. As he did, the older officer clapped cuffs on him, too. "But," Adam went on, in a voice that betrayed great satisfaction, "you've no idea how good it feels after all these years to know that under moderately equal circumstances, I can still give a good account of myself."

"Yeah, I guess," the officer said. He looked over at me. "Is that a rat you're holding?"

"Yes, indeed. And he was a great help. Meet Einstein. Ewen, I think it was *brilliant* of you to remember what I told you about Dauntry hating rats."

"It just occurred to me," Ewen said, trying to sound modest and failing.

"Would you like to take Einstein now? I think he'd be more comfortable with you."

"You mean you'd rather not hold him."

"No, I don't mean that. I'm extremely grateful to him. But he's wiggling."

Ewen grinned, took his rat and cuddled him.

"Okay," the younger officer, who, I saw, was a sergeant, addressed the older. "Read 'em their rights."

As the elder officer complied in a sturdy monotone, I noticed that Laurence Metcalf's arm was bleeding all over the parquet. "Did you get shot?" I asked without much regret.

"No, that murderous hound of yours is responsible."
Even disheveled, bleeding and under arrest he managed to
sound urbane.

"Mom," Ewen put in excitedly, "you should have seen
it. It was just like the movies . . ."

". . . and you have the right to counsel," intoned the
older officer without missing a beat.

"This car drove up at about sixty miles an hour and Mr.
Metcalf leaned out and was trying to pull me in—"

"Tania," I said, overwrought with emotion. "You wonderful, brave dog."

"It was *not* Tania," Ewen said indignantly. "It was *Wilma*. When he got hold of me she went for him and he had to let
me go. She deserves a medal. The police saw it. They were
just coming along, weren't you?" He turned to the younger
officer.

"That's right. Would've chewed his arm off. That's a
good dog, that black Lab."

"You see? You've never appreciated Wilma *or*
Einstein."

"*Mea culpa.* I certainly do now. Steak for both tomorrow
night." I turned to Lance. It seemed incredible that this
polished young lawyer, scion of a family distinguished in law
for several generations, should be standing there handcuffed.
"Why?" I asked. "What on earth did you have to gain? Did
the paintings mean that much?"

"They did to my father."

"Your father?" I remembered the photograph in his
office of the elderly man who looked as though he would be at
home on the bench of the Supreme Court.

"Yes. My father. A gambler. The money Mrs. Standish
handed over to him to hire detective agencies and investigators went to gambling. It was a disease with him."

"You mean he never looked?"

"Oh, sure. And found the boy. Up in a farmhouse in Nova Scotia. Not able to talk. Shock or something. But he never told her—or the farm people. Instead he said longer and wider searches were needed. And he had the power of attorney."

"He must have known it would all come out."

"But it didn't. Not for forty years. He had the perfect excuse for the collapse of the fortune. We—he, and later, I—kept the estate tied up in litigation hoping to find those paintings. We knew they were in the house. I wish I knew how many times we'd tapped that paneling. My God! It's ironic. The tenants complained constantly about the cold draft. We just thought they were trying to get a reduction in the rent or an increase in the heat, so we ignored them."

"But when you finally decided to hand the house on, why didn't you get in touch with Adam? You knew he was the heir."

"And let him root around in the estate and discover what happened? Don't be silly. There was far less risk in pronouncing you the heir. Besides all that, you were marriageable. And Dauntry had a claim on you."

"But what did you hope to get out of it, Lance? Your father may have been a gambler, but you're not, are you? What could the house and the paintings give you that you don't have?"

"Money, Antonia. Money. It makes the world go round. My father gambled us out of our firm. Why do you think I'm living in that crummy hole on the West Side? I wanted all the things—the clubs, the right people, the whole package—that rich people had. The kids I went to school with had it. But I didn't. And I wanted it. If you had been willing to remarry Dauntry. If you had . . . died . . . And Ewen had been taken over by Dauntry as his son, we would have split the money. If, if, if . . . What does the reason matter now? It was a gamble and we lost."

"But your office I met you in?" I asked, remembering its luxury.

"A good address and handsome office are essential if you want to impress the right people."

"Okay. Let's go," the policeman said.

"How did you happen to come along?" I asked the younger officer.

The policeman nodded towards Dauntry. "We decided to keep an eye on that ex-husband of yours and we thought he might be here. On our way we saw the guy, Laurence Metcalf, try to haul the boy into his car and get bitten by the Lab. He got back in his car when he saw us and took off. So we chased around looking for him for a while until we found him." He turned to Dauntry and Lance. "Okay, you two. Let's move it." Dauntry went to the door without a backward look. But Lance turned.

"It must be the lawyer in me," he said. "Unbowed though bloody. Plus my fondness for life's little ironies. There's something you should know. It was part of the reason Mrs. Standish left the house to your aunt. It wasn't just an accident that Alice Moncrieff went to work for her. I allowed you to think that when I first told you about it. But Mrs. Standish went looking for her after she discovered that the founder of the Standish clan had been the illegitimate son of a Squire Standish of Westmoreland, in northern England, and a Scottish servant girl named Alice Moncrieff. I can't tell you how much pleasure Mrs. Standish got out of digging that dirt up. When he got over here, the first Alton Standish called himself after his father's family—quite without the legal right to do so, but who over here was to know? Anyway, when Mrs. Standish's in-laws proved so unsympathetic about her search for her German grandson and the money they thought she was spending, Mrs. Standish wrote to Scotland, traced that servant girl's family, and came up with your aunt. Then she wrote, suggesting she—your aunt—come over and work for her, Mrs.

Standish. Which she did, incidentally bringing her younger sister, your mother." Lance gave a malicious grin. "This house has always been known as The Standish Place. Remember those prints and lithographs?"

I nodded.

"Mrs. Standish got quite childish as she got older. Small things upset her. One of them was that even the most distant relatives would frequently use the old engraving, *The Standish Place,* as a Christmas card. In view of their indifference to her *idée fixe,* she found this particularly annoying. So she once asked my father if she could forbid them by law. He told her, of course not. But she wouldn't be stopped. She decided that by will and bequest the house should be known as *The Moncrieff Place,* and was having a brass plate made to that effect, to put on the door, plus leaflets to give to the local library and historical society about the real name of the Standish family, when she died. Well, she got her wish. It's not the Standish Place anymore."

"You said you knew there was a hiding place here?" I asked.

"I knew what I told you that day in my office. That Great-aunt Elizabeth, an ardent abolitionist, had allied herself with the underground railway for runaway and escaped slaves."

"That's curious. That neighbor, Mrs. Cunningham, said something about the real history of the family as being discreditable. Surely she couldn't have meant that! I think that's highly to the family's credit."

"No. She undoubtedly meant that some of the Standishes, not being too enthusiastic about losing the Southern market during the Civil War, were rumored to have helped the Confederacy by supplying ships to run the Union blockade in Southern ports. Great-aunt Elizabeth, who had been to school in Boston and knew the Alcotts and Mrs. Stowe and others, was all the more fanatic because of what she considered the family disgrace. But to go back to the slave's hole, as it was called, Mrs. Standish told my father that that hole had been closed in her father's time. I half believed her, fool that I was . . ."

"But how could she have expected me to find the lever? To remember?"

"She told me once, airily, that you had learned the house's secret. I didn't really know what she was talking about. As I said, she'd grown childish. But that was why, when everything else failed, I got in touch with you."

I looked at the policeman standing near the front of the door, his hand around Lance's arm. "There are some questions I'd like to ask."

"Be our guest. There are a lot of things we'd like to know, too."

I looked back at Lance and Dauntry. "One thing—which of you two hired those thugs: the one on the Esplanade and the phony federal agent who tried to shove me under a train?"

Dauntry's mouth turned down. "Oh, Lance has the brains."

"How true," Lance murmured, his self-composure still intact.

"But it was you, Dauntry, with the dark glasses and the dog that that boy, Bonzo, saw. Why? Why did you want me to think it was Adam?"

"Because I wanted to see the house without being spotted by a nosy neighborhood. With dark glasses and a dog they'd think it was Adam. Just a precaution."

"And who called me on the telephone this afternoon and then hung up?" I persisted.

"Oh that was I," Lance said. "It was a gamble, of course. Like everything else I do. But it worked. You started worrying, just as I thought you would, and finally left to go home to see who was doing what—again as I thought you would. My thug, as you call him, was waiting at the entrance to your

building. He followed you to the subway. Unfortunately, the
man your boy friend hired to keep an eye on you pulled you
back to the platform."

"Adam, did you hire someone?"

"Since I couldn't watch you myself, yes."

I looked back at Lance. "And that couple, models, who
came to buy the house. Suppose I'd said I'd sell it to them?"

"They would have called up later to back out. I wanted to
see how serious you were. What I couldn't allow to happen
was to have you rent the house out to somebody else where it
couldn't be . . . er . . . got at."

"By you."

"Precisely."

"And what would you have done if I had changed my
mind later and put it up for rent?"

Dauntry spoke bitterly. "Oh, he would have thought of
something. He's a great contingency boy. I'd given up on you
years ago, Antonia. He was the bright boy who called me back
to see if I could reestablish myself with you, or, failing that, to
be ready to step in and take over the care of our grieving
son—if something should happen to you."

"Yuch!" Ewen said.

Dauntry flushed angrily, which was interesting, because
nothing I had said had touched him emotionally.

"Well put, Ewen," Adam commented. "But, Metcalf,
there's one thing that baffles me. Why wait till now? Antonia's
been here in New York for ten years."

"Because until then I thought the old girl really had sold
the paintings. I knew people who would have bought them
secretly. But when the Harbach collection came over, every
would-be fan, buyer and owner came out of the woodwork.
The paintings soared up in value. After careful investigation it
became obvious that the Standish paintings had not been sold.
Nobody had them. So I knew then that the old lady, who'd

grown secretive and childish, and who, in her last years, never left the house, had hidden them here somewhere. If I could have torn down the place, I would have. But I didn't own it. All I'd been able to do was to tie up the title in court. Then I had to wait to get the tenants out. Which is why when you, Antonia, were dawdling around trying to decide whether or not you were going to move in, I applied some pressure by way of a fake robbery and break-in."

"So it was your doing?"

"It was. And it worked. You could hardly wait to move in."

I stared at him. "You're certainly imaginative."

He gave a mocking, and remarkably graceful, bow.

"But what about the Standish relatives?" I asked. "Didn't they inquire about the paintings?"

"Constantly. Making their leisurely way from their place in Maine to their other place in Palm Beach, they would drop by the office to see if anything had turned up. But I think most of them, too, thought the old lady had sold them and spent the cash looking for her wretched grandson."

"But why did you think I'd unlock the mystery?"

"Because I thought you already knew it, and knew that you knew it and had simply been taking your time till the house was declared yours. After all, I told you old Mrs. Standish said you knew the secret of the house. That's what I meant when I said I wanted to send the buyers to find out if you were serious. But then I decided that maybe you knew, but didn't know you knew. That's why I sent you that trunk full of papers. I'd been through them dozens of times. But I thought they might mean something to you that they didn't to me. That's why I kept bugging you to look at them. But until you talked about the draft I thought she'd put the paintings somewhere else outside the house. Boy, those drafts—how the tenants complained! I should have listened."

"Serve you right for being a stinking landlord," Ewen said.

Lance laughed. "I suppose you're right, morally speaking. But then the moral view of anything has never had much appeal for me."

"You can say that again," the older policeman muttered.

"It's a pity," Adam said drily, "that you couldn't have put all that effort and devious intelligence into something more . . . er . . . rewarding. Even profitable."

Lance shrugged. "What's more profitable than three quarters of a million bucks? That's as big a brass ring as you'll find anywhere."

"Yeah, but you missed," the younger policeman said. He looked at me. "You all through with the questions?"

I nodded.

"Okay," he said. "Let's go."

When they left, Lance gave me an insouciant wave. But Dauntry never even turned around.

"Dauntry," I said, although I didn't know why. He had never meant anything but ill to me. He'd tried to kill me. I was quite sure now that he'd killed my father and brother. Yet in some strange way, remembering the handsome young man who had crossed the dance floor towards me, remembering everything Lance had told me about his background, I felt sorry for him.

"I'm sorry," I said.

He just stared at me. And I knew it meant nothing to him.

"So it's our house for sure," Ewen said when the front door closed.

"It's your father's."

"Yeah, that's right. It's Dad's."

He said it casually. As though he had used the term all his life. But his cheeks were a little pink.

"Ours," Adam said. "And now that it looks like I might become a man of property, Antonia, will you marry me for my real estate?"

"No. Not for your real estate. But I'll marry you."

"Well, I think you ought to tell him why you're marrying him," Ewen protested.

"All right, Ewen. You're not too young to learn the hard facts of life. In the publishing business we'll do *anything* to hang on to a successful and profitable author."

"You two," Ewen said disgustedly. "Cop-outs!"

Adam reached out, found me and put his arm around me. "What do you want, Ewen? An X-rated movie? I tell you what, you can be best man."

"Cool! When?"

"As soon as the law and the license bureau allow."

"Can I bring Einstein?"

I saw the corners of Adam's rather austere mouth twitch. "As far as I am concerned, of course. How could I have forgotten to invite him?"

Ewen frowned. "Are you laughing at me?"

"A little. Do you mind? If you do, I apologize." When Ewen did not reply, Adam put his other hand out and touched Ewen's shoulder. "You can laugh at me if you want. I think it's part of being . . . friends."

Ewen's hackles almost visibly went down. He smiled. "Okay. It's a deal."

"Speaking of Einstein," I said as we turned towards the kitchen, "where is he?"

"I took him upstairs to bed."

I said to Adam, "Did you think there was going to be trouble when you went out with Ewen?"

"Yes, I didn't realize Dauntry would make for the house. I was fairly sure that the police would be watching him. But I was afraid that Ewen alone would be in danger."

"I had Wilma," Ewen said firmly.

"Yes, but she's been hiding her light under a bushel, from everything I've heard."

Ewen frowned. "If the opening to the secret stair is in the dining room, how come we felt the draft in our rooms?"

"Because I suppose the joins go all the way up and down. Remember how many layers of wallpaper I made the paperhanger take off?"

Adam said, "Describe the hole to me."

Ewen did. "Where do you suppose the paintings are?" he asked.

"Wherever the top or the bottom of the ladder ends, I guess."

Ewen went over to the opening and put a leg on to the ladder. "I'm going up to see."

"Ewen—" I said.

"It's safe, Mom. Really."

"We don't know, Ewen, please—" But he had gone.

Feeling his way, Adam went over, put his hand out and grasped the ladder. "It seems fairly safe. By the way, what's that smell I've been aware of for some time, as though something were burning?"

"Ye gods—" I tore out to the kitchen. Smoke was pouring from the broiler. Cautiously I opened it. Flames leaped out. I closed the door, filled the nearest saucepan with water, opened the stove again and threw the water in.

There was a powerful hissing.

"Shall I call the fire department again?" Adam asked. "Now that they know the way. What's burned, by the way."

"Our dinner. Isn't it lucky I always buy extra hamburger."

Ewen's voice came faintly from the attic. "Hey, come up. See what I have."

He had the canvases still in their frames lined up against the attic wall. What I had taken to be an angle in the wall turned out to be thin wood covered with plaster.

"I just poked from the inside and it opened," Ewen said. "These were stacked inside."

Adam said, "Tell me about the paintings."

So Ewen and I did our best.

Then Ewen said, "Something else. There's a hole where the wood joins the wall. The plaster broke or something and the wood's been gnawed or splintered. Rats, I guess."

I shuddered and then looked at him. "No offense to our hero, Einstein, but I think we'll have the exterminator to make sure they're not still with us. They may have got up somehow from the cellar."

He grinned. "No. I know. But the hole looks pretty old, like it's been there a long time. Years. Much longer than we've been here. And you know what the house was like when we first came to look at it. Who'd care about rats? But I bet that's where Cleo got into the passage that night she turned up in the basement. Only I've been trying to figure how she got out down there."

"By the hole that's behind the stove—or so the fire captain told us. The kitchen was obviously cut out of the back room—it's right under the dining room."

"Good heavens," I said. "Of course. But how would she get up and down—by the ladder?"

"Yes," Ewen said, "or the wooden lathes in the wall which are uncovered there by plaster. It wouldn't be too hard. But what a climb! She must have been terrified! I'll stuff some paper in the hole up here and the one in the basement."

"Do," I said with great feeling. "I don't want Cleo, or any other animal, known or unknown, using that as some private staircase. I'll get the plasterer in tomorrow."

293

We left the paintings finally and came downstairs. Wilma, Nemesis and Cleo were waiting for us at the bottom, and all three, when they saw us coming down, made for the kitchen. Tania, in her harness, was still where Adam had left her.

"What are you going to do about the paintings?" Ewen asked.

"First I have to prove who I am. Until then they, like the house, are your mother's. What would you do with them, Antonia?"

"Give them to the museum."

"That's what I would do."

I looked at Adam. "Are you going to change your name to what it really is, von Harbach?"

"No. I've lived my life under this name. I think I'll keep it."

Ewen said, "Are you sorry? I mean, sorry that everything happened the way it did? You'd be rich now, sort of, or at least you'd have grown up in this house and probably gone to prep school and everything. Maybe you wouldn't have gone to prison, even. Would you change if you could?"

Adam went slowly across the floor to where Tania sat. Bending, he took off her harness. "That's a good girl." She jumped up and licked his cheek. He patted her and caressed her. Then he came back towards Ewen and me and took an arm of each in his hands.

"I'd be a liar if I didn't say I'd give a lot not to be blind, and not to have killed that boy. But for the rest, astonishingly, no, I wouldn't change. Did you say we were having hamburgers? Can I count on it this time?"

Acknowledgments

I would like to express my thanks to Evelyn and Everett Ortner of Park Slope, Brooklyn, for their information and help when I was trying to decide where to place *Moncrieff*; to Carole Silver of Brooklyn Heights for her hospitality and for allowing me to walk up and down the floors of her attractive home in the Heights and for the history and lore she imparted; to Carolyn Anthony of David McKay and Weybright and Talley for her original suggestion of Brooklyn Heights as a site for the novel and her guided tour of the Brooklyn Heights area;

To the American Foundation for the Blind for its help and the use of its library, especially to Morton Kleinman, who steered me into the areas that interested me, and to Edward Ruch, who first talked to me about the working relationship between a blind person and his guide dog, and introduced me to Rena, his black Labrador guide;

To Morris Frank, co-author of *The First Lady of the*

Seeing Eye (Henry Holt & Co., 1957) and the first blind person to bring a guide dog to the United States, with whom I spent half a day learning more about a blind man and his dog; and to the later Hector Chevigny, whose marvelous book *My Eyes Have a Cold Nose* (Yale University Press, 1946) not only describes the sensitive and rewarding relationship between a blind man and his guide dog but also reveals what it was like for a vigorous and intelligent man to become blind in mid-life. Somebody should bring that book back into print!

I.C.H.